Alessia Malatini

LUX IN ARCANA

Novel

Translated by Samuela Scarponi

To those who believe that there is no absolute Truth.

INDEX

Few men are able to prove the position of the research institute of the Schutzstaffel: the SS Ahnenerbe.

I am Alexander Wagner, one of them.

Recalling each day I still remember, I am determined to recount, with meticulous accuracy, all the events that really took place from August 1937 until today, 20th October 1938.

I am now sitting in the sleazy carriage of a train that's taking me to Washington. How I ended up in the States is just the epilogue of a number of circumstances that rewrote my existence and my name, too.

When I look up, I meet the fleeting glimpse of a silent and bald-headed man in his forties, who promptly diverts his attention to avoid conversation.

I follow the slow flow of the farmland, losing myself in the vision of a totally different world than my own. The lulling pace of the train and the twilight made me drift off, but when I close my eyes memories feed old resentments, strong enough to smother even reason. Then I feel the sins from my service in the German aviation, the Luftwaffe, flaring in me. I suppose the expression on my face reveals my emotions and maybe that's the reason why my fellow traveller refrains from talking.

Germany – Berlin, August 24, 1937

I was walking along the streets of Berlin gripped by a soft melancholy. A few blocks from the Potsdamer Platz, upper-class buildings, with masonry balconies and newly painted wrought iron fences, gave place to a variety of shops. I could already distinguish the tower, with the four quadrants of its clock in the centre of the square, and the frenzied traffic swirling around it. Not much had changed since the last time I was there, not even the big billboard of Chlorodont, that every Berliner could no longer do without for their own oral hygiene.

I was crossing the street while a tram was going past me with its load of impatient but resigned-looking passengers. The dull grey sky foreshadowed an upcoming downpour, impelling the pedestrians to crowd into every means of public transportation in the capital city. A middle-aged woman, just out of the pharmacy at the corner, hastened to get onto the first bus, but the long and enveloping skirt, hindering her solemn gait, turned even her flawless model of feminine grace into the grotesque.

Soon I felt some raindrops hitting the visor of my cap; instinctively, I looked up and, with a child-like wonder, followed the westward migration of a scant flock of mallards. I recalled when, as a boy, I used to hunt wild boars with my father. I lost him right after my adolescence.

3

That day I realised that the only way not to give in to distress was to grow up quickly. Today, I regret neither that choice, nor the years of youthful unconsciousness I couldn't enjoy. I'm just saying I underwent a precocious adulthood I'd have imagined to be more pleasant if shared with a father.

I don't know how, but when I came back to the present, I found myself staring at the empty shop window of Adam Pfeffer, a Jew I have known all my life. The policemen had posted a sign on the door to discourage Germans from shopping there, thus forcing the tailor to move elsewhere and permanently give up his business. I wondered what path his daughter Myriam had taken. I remembered well her sharp intelligence, her desire to transgress her father's rules and her pathological thinness.

The Berlin from my past had been replaced by the Führer's city. Everything belonged to him, even the inhabitants and their souls. I couldn't recognise Berlin, all covered in anti-Semitic propaganda bills. I had significantly changed of late, too, just like the city; for the better in some ways, for the worse in many others.

I tried to judge my image mirrored by the Pfeffers' shop window with a critical sensibility. I recognised that Luftwaffe officer as a tall young man, with green eyes and jet-black hair, whose Mediterranean features didn't suit the regime standards. Honestly, I hadn't fought to make the Führer proud, but rather for the sake of economic self-sufficiency and to prevent my name from falling into the hotchpotch of mediocrity. I must confess I have always opposed servility, but in a time foreboding a war, an academic degree and a lecturing post licence weren't worth anything. Although I would have preferred debates on historical matters rather than the Reich manoeuvres, I chose to join the armed forces, much to my regret. Despite my superiors considered me a skilled aviator, my unconcealed intolerance to protocol had already damaged my curriculum irreparably, thus legitimising my assignation to the Condor Legion, the German unit supporting Francisco Franco's revolution. I had recently returned to Germany and still didn't know when and if I would go back to Spain; that conflict had already left me with a permanent scar, though. Awaiting new orders, I was testing state-of-the-art airplanes, so, I had been travelling back and forth between Berlin and Wiesbaden for several days. That afternoon I was going to be a guest of a long-standing friend of my family, who lived a short step from Potsdamer Station.

Receptions at Karl Kopf's house were always interesting, but sometimes went off the rails, not so much for the host's lack of sobriety, as to the excesses of his guests, usually high-ranking Berliners.

A Jewish woman, I had known for years, announced my arrival with the reverence befitting a flawless maid. Her black dress, covered by a white apron, was pressed and perfect except for one little irredeemable thread sticking out of her sleeve. She became uneasy as soon as she realised I had noticed it. With a quick and abrupt gesture, she tore it off, then she fixed herself up and, with an uptight smile, encouraged me to make myself at home.

Two taut Reich flags stood out against the opposite walls of that plainly furnished hall. Their bright colours looked more vivid than usual in the closed and gloomy room. Each object was meticulously, almost obsessively, displayed. Karl had always been a man of deep-rooted convictions and old age had sharpened his obsessions.

That was yet another proof there are only three impossible undertakings in life: silencing a woman, containing a child's exuberance and changing an old man's mind. One of Karl's favourite quips, I recall, was the comparison between his servants and his furniture: both excellent, both unobtrusive. He would say that kind of analogy was better than a compliment; to me, it was only yet another expression of that cynicism - legitimate in a sense - which was permeating the whole of Germany.

After the customary Hitlergruss and the appropriate introductions, I had a word with Karl, whom I hadn't seen since my recruitment. I didn't recognise the usual cheerful friend in him, rather, I saw a man marked by a deep loneliness. That could be clearly gathered from his words, his house and his recurring receptions. He never married because he always refused emotional bonds, except for the marriage with his beloved KK Chemische Fabrik AG. A few years earlier he had obtained substantial tax benefits, as the result of an important covenant he boasted he had signed in the presence of the Führer himself. His chemical laboratories had never been as productive as they were then and his name was inextricably linked to fumigants and pesticides. After a misstep in 1917, that had forced him to discontinue the production of gun-cleaning solvents, he had built himself a new entrepreneurial identity. Sign of his rising reputation, celebrities kept arriving one after the other for longer than an hour. The architect Hermann von Keitel, in his current mistress's company, and Friedrich Poelzig, manager of the renowned I.G. paint industry, were among the best-known names.

By half past five I and the other guests sat at the tables. The waitress served tea and coffee, with a few biscuits and a slab of butter.

The married couple to my right was from Vestfalia, but had been living in Berlin for over a year. He was the bureaucrat Rutger Blancke, a man in his fifties, shy and clumsy. His wife, on the other hand, was a regular guest at the social gatherings of the wealthy Berlin, though she was of poor culture and as weighty as her build. At his lady's side, Rutger Blancke, slender as a stick, disappeared and, since he had a very bad relationship with dialectic, his presence was entirely obscured by his wife's chit-chat. So he would try to put himself in the spotlight at the first opportunity, giving vent to the most unbearable talkativeness.

The other guest, sitting in front of me, was the SS Obersturmbannführer Franz Haase, a man as cold as steel in both manners and appearance. His flat face and pronounced jaw reminded me of a wary mastiff. I realised I was right about him when he vented all his indignation for the presence, that evening, of a local businessman, whose name I frankly don't remember. It seemed that, after the Olympics, the man had gained some fame, thanks to the multiple victories achieved by the American athlete he equipped with his innovative running shoes.

Blancke indulged Haase like a faithful dog; on the contrary, I preferred to remain silent, looking forward to a more constructive debate. Sensing the guests' general lack of interest in the topic at hand, the Obersturmbannführer thought well to regain his audience solemnly announcing what sounded more like a threat: «It's rumored that the Führer will visit us in a few months.»

«In that case, let us hope for a favourable weather» Karl added as he sipped his coffee.

«It amazes me that such a remark comes right out of your mouth. I would have expected it from him» Haase replied, pointing at me like I was a snotty kid, «not from a man like you, who knows well our Führer's charisma!»

I was unable to ignore that comment, so I rebutted annoyed: «I didn't know the Führer's authority extended even to the weather phenomena. That means I'll beg him to give me a sunny day next time I take off.»

«The weather is always favourable during celebrations of the like, Hauptmann Wagner. The people call it "Hitler's weather".»

From the very beginning it had been clear to me how deplorable humour appeared in Haase's eyes, especially when quips concerned the Führer.

Like the impudent man I've always been, I piled it on: «Germany is reviving, that's true, but I don't believe it's appropriate to divinise a man for that.»

«I remind you, Hauptmann Wagner, that you're wearing a uniform and you're referring to the one who works to ensure a glorious future for you and our nation. I'll see to it that your direct superior is informed.»

Mrs. Blancke clapped her hands with childish enthusiasm and improvised as moderator.

«Come on, you two! What a dumb conversation is yours; let's imagine what building renovations and cultural events we might expect from his visit to the city, instead!»

Karl, who knew his starched guest well, shot me a withering look and, after a cough, he ordered the servants to bring more cookies. Rutger Blancke sighed indolently and stepped away with a glass of brandy in his hand, leaving his wife to swallow tea and pastries.

That soiree was saved by the providence or, to be more precise, by the visit of Fräulein Angelika Anne Blumen. When she showed up, the freshness of her figure seemed to bring spring in that hall smelling of old antiques.

I watched her carefully as she took off her wide-brimmed hat with the charm of a gifted actress. I confess I was deeply bewitched by her, and so were Blancke and Haase, although already accustomed to her presence. Karl welcomed her informally, as he considered Angelika like a daughter, then he kissed her on the forehead and introduced us. It was impossible not to desire her, radiant and statuesque as she was. In the presence of her, Mrs. Blancke was a cumbersome and pesky lifeless object. As the beautiful guest approached me with an expression of veiled disbelief, her long hair, draped over her shoulders, softly followed the movements of her body. Mesmerized, I couldn't help but contemplate so much femininity: the ideal stereotype of the Aryan race.

Karl cleared his voice. «Angelika, let me introduce…»

«It's not necessary» she interrupted him with grace, «the reputation of the brilliant Hauptmann Wagner precedes him, although I prefer his insights as a medievalist to his feats as a pilot.»

I was struck by those unexpected words and, visibly proud, I kissed the hand of one of the most seductive women in Berlin. «Thank you, Fräulein Blumen, but it seems that the Reich finds my military skills more interesting.»

«Let me contradict you, Professor.»

«Angelika works at the Neues Museum; she manages the Egyptian collection» Karl clarified and, at that point, I understood the reason of the little feather-shaped pendant swaying from her bracelet.

«Do you always let yourself be guided by the *Maât*, Fräulein?» I asked her, yearning for a discussion on that matter.

She didn't answer, but by the smile she gave me, I

convinced myself I hit the mark.

«Good heavens!» Haase spoke out of turn, «I thought we would have talked about his reputation as a libertine, but we're ending the evening discussing tribal doodles instead!»

«Franz, don't belittle the *Maât,* if you don't know its meaning!» scolded Angelika, then directing her attention elsewhere: it would have been pointless discoursing about the Egyptian precepts of truth, justice and righteousness with Haase. She sipped her tea chatting with the other guests about social events, and after that, she made small talk with Blancke, too, but her empty and resigned expression, showed her regret for even talking to him.

Karl had to withdraw with Haase and Poelzig for business reasons and I thought to entertain the beautiful guest with the gentleman's elegance and insolence that earned me my fame as a seducer.

«I imagined a very different professor Wagner» she confessed after she had inspected me from head to toe. «I hope you are not offended by the way I'm addressing you. I can call you Hauptmann, if you prefer it.»

«You don't offend me at all. I don't despise my role as a pilot, or else I wouldn't wear this uniform, but...»

«But it was not your dream.»

«Karl must have told you a lot about me. Too much. I don't know whether to be happy or worried about that.»

She laughed as her clear eyes shamelessly lingered on the features of my face for a long time. I could tell she was a resolute woman from the way she held my stare.

«How about hanging up your pretty uniform? I'm offering you the chance to fulfill a dream, go back to your beloved books, and not for pleasure, but as a profession.»

A little later, the study door opened abruptly. While

Poelzig and Karl were calm, Haase was visibly irritated. Before going away, he coldly took leave of the other guests and threw a spiteful look in my direction. He closed the front door behind him vigorously, without waiting for the maid, and disappeared like a ghost through the streets of the city. Soon in the house we could breathe a healthier air, so oxygenated that I could even tolerate the smell of cigarettes now permeating the hall. After all, the anti-tobacco campaign had only affected public places and, whenever at a private party, you could see smokers in withdrawal satiate their need.

«Did you ask him yet, Angelika?» Karl demanded seriously, beckoning to me.

«Yes and I'm waiting for his answer.»

From her expression, the woman in front of me looked like she wouldn't accept a refusal, but I was still wondering what they were really talking about.

«Define the matter in detail, Fräulein. As far as I know the Reich prefers burning books rather than reading them. I'm not interested in adding my name to the list of unemployed people» I objected. «I was in the Opernplatz when they burned thousands of books they considered unbecoming by our regime propaganda. After four years I still feel it on my face, the warmth of that huge bonfire, which was nothing short of an outrage to knowledge. I won't hide that from then, the cultural vision of the Reich, I deluded myself into partaking, has been deteriorating. And now you are asking me to believe again in the authors of that crime.»

«I share your disappointment.»

«"Disappointment" is a euphemism.»

«You're right, but the people I'm working with are scientists and philologists, so you don't have to fear for

11

your disquisitions. There will be no more fires» she reassured me and sat down in the armchair sensually crossing her legs. «I asked Karl to let us meet after I heard you were friends. Among five hundred dissertation papers and various publications, your theory on the origin of the medieval Sator seemed to me the most interesting. All the more so in the light of the new developments in historical and archeological fields. Would you be willing to supplement your study?»

I still couldn't understand it clearly; actually, I was really groping in the dark. «I just can't imagine who might be interested in my analysis on the Templar square and anyway, I can't picture myself locked up within the walls of a museum» I responded.

Angelika glanced at Karl who was snickering at what I myself would have called later an innocent supposition. She pierced me with her eyes and then, masking a certain arrogance, asked if I had ever heard of the SS Ahnenerbe. I confess that I stiffened when I heard that name. The Ahnenerbe foundation: the SS research institute at Heinrich Himmler's command had found my study interesting! For a moment I thought it was a joke, but then I changed my mind, and felt urged to point out that it was just a theory about the Templar Sator origin.

«Exactly. It's time to find the validation for your assumptions. If I were you, I wouldn't think twice about it. Also, the economic benefit would be considerable.»

«Assuming that I accepted, I couldn't get out of the Luftwaffe overnight, in any case. I'm an officer and I have obligations.»

«Ah, you don't have to worry about that» Karl barged in patting me on the back, «you accept, and we'll take care of everything else. Hey» he whispered to my ear, elbowing me like a little boy, «the uniform could still help you with women, you never know… it's better to keep all options open.»

The SS Ahnenerbe was a separate chapter from that Nazi world I no longer fully agreed with. The voices about Himmler's elite were many and confused, even disquieting sometimes, but its studies of ancient texts and its expeditions all over the world were legendary. It was an extraordinary chance. The sheer idea to be able to even touch part of their knowledge made me smile, and I found my good mood again. I answered my friend: «No. I can do without, I have alternative weapons of seduction» and I caught Angelika Blumen's satisfied look. «Why don't we talk about it at dinner tonight, Fräulein?» I proposed, foretasting our tête-à-tête, spiced up by a pinch of history that would have taken us back to the Golden Age.

«Not tonight, maybe on the weekend» she answered me with a stealthy smile.

When Angelika and the other guests left the scene, Karl sank into an armchair. Our talkativeness died out abruptly, so I asked the maid for my cap and set out to go home.

«Don't you ever do that again» he warned me out of the blue.

«What, can't I invite a beautiful woman to dinner?»

«Never use that tone with an SS officer again, or there won't be a second time.»

«Haase is a slimy butcher. You know that, everybody knows. I don't understand why you grant him your friendship.»

Karl, unexpectedly, sprang to his feet and shouted at me, enraged: «You'll end up lying in the street with a bullet in your forehead. You've been irresponsible! That is not courage. Your resolve is the outcome of your recklessness, not to say madness! Bloody hell, Alexander» he suddenly calmed down and stared at me in the face, «you have your mother's green eyes and your father's temperament. Don't defy Haase. And don't mislead yourself into thinking you're going to impress Angelika with that aristocratic composure you show off with the others, either. She's a special woman and should you hurt her for any reason, I swear I'll kill you.»

«I'm a gentleman. I'm going to take her to a club where they play some good and transgressive jazz. Music by Armstrong and Miller is ideal for a candlelight dinner» I replied, well aware that Joseph Goebbels had labelled that musical genre as heathen and Decadent. Karl was silent, but appealed to his most criminal gaze to make me get the message unequivocally.

When I got home, I felt like I was at a crossroads in my life, where only the names of the two roads to follow were signed, but not their destination. The confusion was just a momentary interlude, though: I had a very seductive and charismatic guide who knew what path to advise me. Despite the frictions between the men in that long afternoon, the reception at Karl's house had been the best in the recent years: what with Angelika's presence and the dream that she knew how to masterfully shape before my eyes.

It looked like she knew all too well my predilections, or maybe she was skillful enough as to detect them and then use them to indulge me. The fact is, that talking to Angelika was as satisfying as looking at her.

To this day, no more remains in my memory than I have already retraced, but the insight into that dream of knowledge, that was the exclusive prerogative of the

Ahnenerbe, and that I tacitly decided to pursue, is still vivid.

Germany – Wiesbaden, August 27, 1937

Three days after meeting Angelika Blumen, I still thought about her so often that I disapproved of myself. I had not confirmed my eagerness to her, yet, although she certainly never had any doubts about my final response. I had decided not to be hasty, many were the dark sides of that proposal for which, in all honesty, I could hardly contain my enthusiasm. Life had taught me to repress impulsiveness and detest allusions. As a matter of fact I had learned, at my own expense, that in between gaps and omissions the worst perils always budded.

That morning, however, something else came to my mind. I was in the open country, a few kilometers from the city of Wiesbaden, where a thin strip of land served as a runway dedicated to testing new planes. The sun was rising when I left the meeting room, displeased with the unreasonable demands of some of my superiors. I strode towards the hangar number three to look for the chief mechanic, who I spotted under a Messerschmitt prototype.

I called out to him rudely.

«Get a move on, Feldwebel Ritter» I shouted at him from a distance, «I have to take off at once. That idiot Schulz has promised a detailed report to the upper echelons by tomorrow.»

I was furious because there was no reason to let that

aircraft take off and because sudden changes of schedule never led to anything good.

Ritter stopped tinkering and stuck his head out.

«You have to give me one more hour, Hauptmann, otherwise you won't be lifted an inch off the ground. I'm fixing up these pipes and…»

«You've got twenty minutes» I punctuated the words loudly, still annoyed from the previous discussion.

«Well, it means that I'll have to do without some pieces!» I heard him mumbling.

I knew that man well enough to understand that he never worked thoughtlessly; so, in order not to compromise our relationship, I promised him a cup of coffee, if he made it.

«If you want me to finish the job in half an hour, you'll need to add some sweets, too, sir.»

Though the day had begun badly, his impudence managed to get a smile out of me. «Deal. Cookies, too, but I remind you I said twenty minutes» I answered while walking to the edge of the airstrip.

After the agreed time, a tray of cookies and a coffee were delivered to him. When I showed up in the hangar, I saw Ritter coming out from under the Messerschmitt looking serious. «I did my part, did you?» I asked him.

«Your toy is ready to fly» he answered indolently, while he was nervously wiping his hands with a worn and greasy rag.

I supposed he had been ordered to hasten the maintenance operations by my superior officers as well and that they had not used better manners than mine. His tense face proved it. I thanked him with a nod and boarded the plane. I looked for the greyhound from habit, the one I had painted on the fuselage of my single-seater

Bf109B. When I was in flight, in fact, I was known by the name of Windhund, but on prototypes there was no reference to the officer, because they were assigned to several test pilots before being dispatched to active duty. I was a bit upset about that. Not that I deemed it to be a bad omen, but the greeting to the greyhound had become an essential ritual to me.

The first two attempts to start the engine failed, then, finally, the new Messerschmitt model started up. A dark smoke, coming out from the exhaust nozzles, vanished as usual, as the temperature rose. Among those metal sheets, I felt happily isolated from the rest of the world: the plane was my refuge, my hermitage. I opened the throttle and headed towards the runway threshold. The terrain was so uneven that the aircraft was kicking like a foal. Then, I directed it towards the compacted strip of ground, pushed the engine to maximum revolutions per minute and, after a sigh of satisfaction, I released the brakes.

Take-off had always had a galvanising effect on me, especially the moment when the wheels would rise off the ground and I would head towards the sky. I loved pushing my Bf engine at top rate: hearing the roar of the most powerful thruster in the world gave me a feeling of omnipotence. At that time I already had about seven hundred flight hours under my belt, but every time it was a new emotion. Up there, I felt an integral part of the plane and its every vibration, creak or oil spurt was familiar to me.

I had established a very good bond with that new Messerschmitt as well. It was promising. That plane was powerful and handy, so I decided to put it to the test by performing some extreme manoeuvres. I climbed until it stalled and afterwards, in the nosedive toward the ground,

I tried to gain a speed not far from the structural failure; finally I brushed the runway so close as to see my comrades in the face. It's really exciting to feel alive and that machine was amazing me with its speed and acceleration, both so much better than those of its forerunners. Its structure was dedicated to aerodynamics and by no means to armament. It was really a magnificent airplane, but it was no good for the Reich.

Then I decided to verify the precision of the flight instruments, so I flew far from the base and enjoyed a quieter flight. A few minutes passed before I reached the Mosel valley, when a slight loss of trim led me to do some testing. Nothing I couldn't handle. I pulled up and the engine underwent several losses of thrust as if the fuel had failed to power it. For that test flight a supplementary three-hundred-liter tank was installed, in addition to the standard four-hundred-liter. I couldn't be short of fuel nor have a leak from both tanks. I reversed course, but before completing the turn, the engine sputtered again. I kept my presence of mind until the engine was about to stall again. Unfortunately, the situation soon became unrecoverable. The unmistakable squeaking of the propeller slowing down gave me the chills. No more fuel flowed into the pistons, and yet there had to be! There had to be enough fuel for at least another two hundred and fifty miles, unless the tank dip tube had been damaged. I couldn't work out any other alternatives to sabotage. Many wanted me dead, but I immediately figured Haase was the first of that list. I looked for a clearing to attempt an emergency landing and decreased the altitude to limit the violence of the ground impact. After a few moments the altimeter hand began spinning as if it had gone mad. I was relentlessly losing altitude, but I stubbornly persisted in operating the plane and hoped that a miracle would keep me from hitting the forest. I have never believed in miracles. When I heard the racket of the first branches lashing the fuselage, I cursed like I had never done before. There was no better trajectory than the one I had followed, even so, when the additional tank, placed under the fuselage, hit the trees, it poured a rain of fuel on the vegetation and caught fire. The wings of the Messerschmitt, two sturdy spars, bent, slowing down its race while I was by then a prisoner of a fiery dart, which was tearing apart at the impact with the ground. The ripped sheets of metal were enveloping me, and a shred cut into my calf. I felt my flesh slashing like worn out tissue and an irrepressible pain clouded my mind. In a matter of seconds, what little was left of the plane stopped in the undergrowth. I had to get out of the cockpit quickly, but my leg was anchored to the fuselage. I hesitated, but only for a moment, then, with a resolute tug, I pulled the metal sheet out of my flesh and saw my blood flowing relentlessly. I cried out like a savage and doubling over in pain, hoped that the canopy had not got stuck because of the impact. Covered in fragments of various kinds scratching my neck and face like sharp claws, I tried to open the canopy but, just as I suspected, it didn't unlatch. I braced myself and hit at the lock with my shoulder. Finally, it gave way folding back to the side.

Sure that in a few seconds the fire would reach the cockpit too, I dragged myself out. The heat was as unbearable as the pain in my calf, which marked my descent from the aircraft leaving a blood trail behind. I realised, however, that the worst wound was the one suffered by my pride: I had always returned to base, even that time the enemy artillery had hit my hydraulic oil tank.

I watched the Messerschmitt burning for a while. I

knew that it was not a failure of the injection system. It was just a prototype, but such a plane, designed to have a constant flow of fuel, such as to facilitate the most different manoeuvres of combat pilots, would not react like that. It had been a sabotage.

At that point, I only knew I was between Wiesbaden and Cochem, but I was ignorant of my exact position. I sat on the ground to treat the wound and stop the bleeding before going on. I couldn't expect help. It often happened that many missing aircrafts reappeared a few days after an emergency landing, due to unfavourable weather conditions or loss of bearings. In my case, the Luftwaffe would certainly conduct searches to recover the Messerschmitt and determine the causes of the failure, because it was a prototype and such an incident was likely to jeopardise the possible delivery of the aircrafts. Unfortunately, the rescue team would have never arrived before my death, so I started walking through the undergrowth with my calf burning as if set on fire.

After two hours' walk, a clearing opened in front of me. Some cows were grazing and ruminating apathetically and the tinkle of their bells, after so much racket, sounded even melodious to me. I tried not to disturb them, but they were following me with their large, vacant eyes wondering, perhaps, why I was trampling on their meal. In the distance, I saw a beautiful vineyard surrounding an old timber-framed house and I quickened my stride careless of my aches. I crossed the vineyard and, worn out by fatigue and pain, collapsed onto the ground to rest in the shade of green rows full of vine leaves and grapes clusters close to ripening. My vision was beginning to blur because of the heat, but mostly because of the blood I was losing. I tried to medicate myself, but I couldn't even bring my leg into focus anymore. Suddenly a noise of footsteps behind me compelled me to turn abruptly worsening the laceration.

«That's a bad wound! Come to my house, Hauptmann, my wife will take a look at it» a deep but friendly voice ordered me.

My eyes took a while before I could clearly make out the figure who had spoken to me. It belonged to an affable man in his sixties with thick and yellowed mustache. A true-born German, wearing a checkered shirt that barely contained his belly. «I'm a soldier, too» he said to me, «discharged, it's true, but once a soldier always a soldier. Leutnant Thomas Krüger from the old Keiserliche Marine. I fought in 1915, I was one of thirty-five men aboard the U-20 under Schwieger» he emphasised with a pride that made me smile.

I breathed a sigh of relief and, although close to the point of exhaustion, I answered: «It couldn't have been easy living in a submarine! You have my admiration, sir. Alexander Wagner» I introduced myself, shaking his hand without rising from the ground. «I've had a breakdown and crashed several miles from here, in the forest. I don't know where I am.»

«Ha ha! Do you usually fly without knowing where to? It won't be easy to win a war!» he laughed nicely. «We are near Sauerthal on the Rhine…»

Those were the last words I remember. I guess I passed out right after. I just know that when I came to, I was lying on a bed. There was a tray on the ground with a syringe and a bottle of Prontosil on it to prevent infections. Thomas Krüger's wife, Agathe, had been taking care of me for all that time and had bandaged my calf with the skill of a nurse.

I lost the sense of time in that house. I was firmly

convinced that I had only slept for a few hours, but the weak light of the morning sun persuaded me that a whole day had already gone by. I heard knocking on the door. It was Agathe who was bringing me a steaming, fragrant broth. She smiled at me shyly, pointing at the clean clothes placed on the dresser. I supposed that she felt embarassed in my presence and that she was not used to having guests in her house, definitely not in my condition. I showed her all my gratitude with a very prosaic "thank you". It wasn't like me, but I couldn't find any other words to tell her how much I owed her and her husband.

After laying the hot soup plate on a small rustic cabinet, Agathe, with a look, asked for permission to lift my leg, as if she feared my reaction to her act of kindness. She didn't say a word, but, from her attitude, I sensed she was grateful for my consent. Then I realised, that much deference showed she was afraid of me. I was very sorry about it, not only because I inspired that feeling, but also because I recognised my wicked self mirrored in her meek eyes. She took her leave with the same tenderness as before and left me to think about my present, as well as about what would await me outside that haven of peace.

I recovered in a couple of days, despite having lost so much blood as to faint three times in twenty-four hours. I guess the credit for my recovery had to go, not so much to Agathe's medications, as to the aura of serenity that you could breathe at Krügers' house, and to the harmony they had been able to foster in their household. The wound was healing up, and although I still limped like a battered old man, I could get up and down the stairs without compelling the dear Agathe to serve me meals in bed.

As I sat on the wooden steps facing the courtyard, the crimson sun was fading behind the trees of that wood, which had swallowed me and my plane both. I felt a strong and reassuring hand resting on my shoulder: it was Thomas's, who sat at my side handing me his best wine.

«Drink up! This is going to get you back on your feet. How are you feeling today, Alexander?»

«Better, much better» I answered after a sip of wine. I turned to look him in the eye. «If it weren't for you and your wife, sir, I would certainly be dead.»

«Friends don't need so much formality and help each other out in time of need» he stated with rare calmness and simplicity. Even now, the memory of that dialogue moves me: it was the first moment of unconditional humanity I had experienced for years.

«Your wife's amazing. If she had not taken care of me, I would have lost my leg and maybe even my life» I told him with heartfelt gratitude. «I suppose she's a skilled nurse.»

«Indeed she isn't! Luckily she had some of that modern medicine left, the one we use for the cows!» he answered laughing and I humoured him. «I'm kidding. Agathe used it on me when I got this...» and lowered his trousers showing me a scar on his left buttock. «Nice, isn't it? That damn mare bit me for no reason at all!» he exclaimed and, as if the euphoria had suddenly vanished leaving the place to bitterness, he tried to clear his throat. It took him a while to find the right words to tell me what had happened the day of my arrival. He admitted he went to the site of the disaster that night, when I was still unconscious and closely guarded by his dog. As he spoke, I sensed his reluctance to go into detail, so I thought I'd better make it easier for him.

«I'm used to be prepared for the worse, Thomas, so relax and speak freely.»

«Around your plane there was a crowd of soldiers and a couple of officers. They were pretty upset that you didn't broil in there.»

«Yes, I assumed that much» I confessed smiling in the face of adversity.

Thomas tried to play it down, but I realised he was as concerned as I was.

«Well, I heard them talking about you like a hard-skinned pain in the arse. You know boy, you should try a little harder to earn the respect of your superiors!» he exclaimed and then laughed at his own joke. «There's something more and I don't think you'll like it.»

«It wasn't a rescue expedition but a firing squad. Right?» I anticipated his words to relieve his burden. So he told me how, while I was unconscious, he moved me into the tool shed and covered my body with straw to hide me from the sight of my persecutors. It seems, only after a dozen glasses of wine, he managed to convince them that he absolutely wasn't involved in the incident.

«I'm sorry to tell you, Alexander, but you're in trouble», he concluded sympathetically.

I felt hatred and disappointment growing in me. And a thirst for revenge that could hardly be quenched except with its fulfillment. It was as if hell had refused me and I found a reason for that: those who had planned my murder, had to go before me. I decided I would see to it personally.

Thomas was smoothing his moustache and stared at the horizon as I was struggling to put back together the mosaic of my life. He didn't ask a thing, he just looked at me with his good-natured and sincere air. And precisely that discretion encouraged me to confide in him as if he were my father. He had saved me and his action was the result of a selflessness which was long lost in people like me; his nobility of mind was not artificial and I knew I could trust him.

I told him every detail about the events I had been protagonist of in the days before the accident. Thomas listened very carefully to the whole story and finally sniggered when I mentioned Haase.

« Bloody hell, you've really picked a pretty good target to snipe at! I know people like him: frustrated by their loneliness, they rage against others. Such men are never a fount of wisdom! They show off because of their influential friendships, but they're just cocksure brainless fools who end up using aggressiveness just to compensate for the failure of their lives. Sabotaging an aircraft would be too much of an undertaking even for someone like Haase. No, I have doubts about him. Destroying a prototype, with all the consequences connected to the responsibility for the accident... and all of that to pay you back·for disgracing him? No, boy, there's someone more powerful behind it; someone you've wronged more.»

«So who do you think it is that wants me dead?» I asked him hoping for a clue.

«How am I supposed to know? I really can't imagine, but I can tell you something: you will always find a safe haven here.»

«You don't even know me, Thomas. How can you trust a man who escaped an attack? How can you be sure that I don't deserve to die?» I asked him still unable to understand the reasons that had kept him and his wife from handing me over.

«I like you» he replied in such a childish way that I was surprised. «I have been keeping an eye on you these past days and I know that you are a determined man, a daredevil, but with brains. And wit is a rare gift these days.»

«Don't overestimate me. If I were as smart as you say, I should have hung up my uniform long ago. But perhaps I'll do that and maybe I'll accept Ahnenerbe's proposal.»

«Like I said, once a soldier always a soldier, even on leave or in a coffin. And by the way, I know who you are. After all, even a blind man would understand that something weighs on your conscience. But that doesn't mean that you are a fool, let alone a murderer. You must toss your memories behind or else regrets will undermine your future choices and prevent you from redesigning the present as you wish. Take it from me: I am older than you, and made many more mistakes.»

«But maybe you've never had experiences like mine» I replied even then shaken by memories. «I'm not yet thirty and I have already killed hundreds of people, mostly innocent. I joined Franco's army. I fought for a cause I didn't even believe in, and yet I carried out orders without hesitation, as cold as a sniper.»

«Why, do you think there are ideal wars, conflicts to believe in? If there was good diplomacy to begin with, there would be no wars and we would be just a vinegrower and a professor. Someone higher than you must take on the responsibility for all those victims. Do you think I've never seen innocent people die?»

I was sure that Thomas couldn't really understand how I felt, so I gave vent to my emotions and described in detail the horrors of that day in Guernica. I expected him to be horrified any time, he stood still, instead.

«We opened fire on a market day! More than seventy planes of ours and as many Italian ones wreaked destruction. I heard my comrades boasting they had machine-gunned a street full of people on the run. They were pranking with each other and comparing the city to a trampled anthill. And so it was indeed! No human trace was left on that ground after our intervention. Three hours and twenty minutes of uninterrupted bombing on the railway station, on the square, in the countryside. My God, Thomas, there's no redemption for what I did! My superiors had ordered me to show them how skilled I was and if I was really as quick as everyone said. They wanted to see the Windhund, they wanted the "Greyhound" to spring into action and I couldn't wait to astonish them. The other pilots and I tested a new attack technique by razing to the ground a town of poor innocent peasants. It was just a terrorist action, nothing short of that. "The best way to ensure success" the commander had said to us, "is to scare the enemy to death before the real conflict begins. Preliminaries count, you bet!" To me, it was just vile cowardice.»

«Hmm, and do you think you're the only one who feels that way? A three-hour carpet bombing of a small town, a torpedo destroying an ocean liner in a few minutes... what's the difference? I saw more than a thousand passengers of the Lusitania die. The ship sank just off the Irish coast, thirty miles from Cape Clear. The torpedo was supposed to flounder the British liner slowly, allowing passengers to abandon the ship, but it didn't. The Lusitania listed to starboard side, they couldn't throw the lifeboats which fell on each other. The bow sank, the propellers surfaced, and when the stern also began to dive, it dragged with it those who had jumped overboard. Do you still think I'm more innocent than you are? »

«But you didn't...»

«I fired! I myself did it!» emphasised Thomas, his eyes

brimming with tears. «I carried out an order and killed innocent people, just like you did. Twenty-two years have passed and, God knows, a day goes by without the memory of that day haunting me. Don't be too hard on yourself» he told me and got up to go in. «Perhaps it's a trivial coincidence, or maybe it's the will of God who still hopes for my redemption. I'm happy I helped you out and I think that, sometimes, digging up the painful past with someone who's able to understand you, can really relieve the burden weighing on our conscience.»

I glimpsed a different gleam in his eyes; then I nodded, reassured by an unexpected empathy and a friendship that had meant more to me than I dared to hope. Before he went, I told him I was going to leave the next day. In fact, I seriously feared I had upset their perfect harmony with my presence. If I had, I would have never forgiven myself.

«I have to go back to base, happen what may» I reluctantly told him. According to my ordinary ways, I would visit the maintenance chief to bestow upon him a nice bullet in the forehead, but this time I'll curb my impulsiveness. In the report, I'm going to write that I had an engine failure and I'll see what happens before doing anything.»

«Well done, boy, so you can study your enemy's moves clearheadedly, but be careful, because suspect is often ascribed to the innocent, whereas the culprit is usually absolved.»

The next day, early in the morning, I picked up my belongings and prepared to leave the farm. The Krügers were waiting for me downstairs.

«I would have died without your help. I will never forget what you've done for me. I'll find a way to pay you back, I swear on my honour.»

«No» Agathe immediately butted in, hugging me with tears in her eyes, «we didn't do that to receive a reward. It was a pleasure to help you. Our door will always be open for you.»

«Come back whenever you want, but avoid crashing into my vineyard, please!» Thomas told me, disguising his emotion.

«I'll do my best. Actually, I hope I didn't get you into trouble.»

He burst out laughing in a strange way, then took me aside and whispered: «You have to die of something sooner or later. And then, I've been pissing blood for some time now and I'm swollen like a bagpipe! At least I'll die with a clear conscience.»

Suddenly, I felt a pang in the heart, as if my breath had been knocked out of me, just like when I had learned about my father's death. I asked for an explanation, but he knew very little about that strange disease he had been hiding from his wife for months. He cut me short and hugged me with his usual joviality. I, on the other hand, was left speechless.

I sadly remember Agathe's farewell, too, sealed by her worn-out look and the grieved face of a woman seeing her son go to the front. I wondered who would take care of her, if Thomas died. When I realised I was powerless in the face of her suffering, I felt a pain more excruciating than the physical one, and I left that house willing to go back at the first opportunity.

Germany – Leipzig, September 2, 1937

In the days that followed the plane crash, an insatiable desire for vengeance got the better of me, clouding even that last trace of rationality I had left in me. After getting Ritter's address, I reached Leipzig without thinking twice and I immediately went to the mechanic's house in the suburbs of the city. The Ahnenerbe issue had moved to the background and I understood that other obligations had priority in my life.

Ritter's abode was humble, but with an original two-tone roof that gave it a touch of modernity. I imagined that the bedrooms would be on the first floor and that no one would notice me if I kept away from the street.

I decided to move under the cover of darkness. I clenched my teeth and, despite the stabbing pains in my leg, climbed the wooden fence near the balcony. The beautiful wrought iron railing, chiselled into floral motifs, would give me a firm grip to reach the upper floor, so with a strong leap, I jumped from the fence to the terrace.

While massaging my sore calf, I heard a terrible noise coming from one of the rooms. I had confirmation that I was on the balcony of Ritter's bedroom. My word, I had never heard a man snore so thunderously!

The window was open because of the heat, so I took advantage of that and pushed it enough to sneak inside undetected. I inspected the room until, groping, I touched an armchair at the foot of the bed and a small round table beside it. On top of that, there was a lamp I nearly dropped to the ground. I couldn't say if it was the hatred for that man to enhance my boldness that evening, or rather the irrepressible desire to shed light on my attack.

I lit the wick with a match and a faint light brightened the room; then I sat comfortably in the armchair and put my feet on the table. I waited for my victim's sleep to subside and the dim light in the room to rouse him from his torpor.

«Good morning, Feldwebel Ritter» I greeted him.

He and his wife jumped and sat bolt upright in their bed. They were dumbfounded to find me there, especially the woman, who stared at me, her eyes nearly popping out. Ritter, however, looked like he was seeing a ghost and a mask of dismay appeared on his face.

«Oh, my goodness, Albert, who is this?» the woman stammered shaking her husband, who suddenly yanked the drawer of the bedside cabinet open and furiously rummaged inside.

«Are you looking for this?» I asked him showing his old revolver. You haven't been able to get rid of me by sabotaging my plane and now you want to kill me in your house. Why don't you confess to your beautiful lady that you're a murderer, a mercenary?» I insisted when I saw him wavering.

Ritter, panic-stricken, stuttered something I didn't understand, then he put his hands on his face and let them slide down to the neck before turning to me.

«Hauptmann Wagner, I'm innocent. Your aircraft had a breakdown: the technicians who inspected it afterwards, proved that, too.»

Those words made my blood boil and I didn't give in to the temptation to fire just because his wife was by his side. I laughed at that meager explanation.

«Right, and you were among them, an expert on Messerschmitts» I replied, mad, hitting the table with a punch, «in fact, you knew well enough how to sabotage it and cover up the evidence. And I'm also sure you didn't act alone. Who paid you to kill me?» I saw him look down and I knew for certain I hit the mark. « Be a good guy and tell me who paid you, maybe I won't waste a bullet on you.»

I had gone to Leipzig consumed by a blind fury I supposed would drive me to the most heinous deeds, but then, all the hatred I felt for Ritter wore out in a few moments. I loaded his revolver just to urge him to reply, but I would have never killed him, and even the initial idea of murdering that man was beginning to disgust me. It was like I was playing a role and that room was the stage of the theatre of my life.

«Believe me, Hauptmann, I have nothing against you. I had to do it, they forced me!» he confessed right after, crying like a child.

«Albert, what are you saying?» cried his wife with the air of someone who can no longer tell family from strangers.

«You can kill me, but I'll take that man's name to the grave.»

I didn't see fear in his eyes, so he wasn't lying.

«Why are you protecting him? Don't you care for your life, you idiot?»

I care more about my wife and daughters', sir. I can only tell you that the man is a Sicherheitsdienst's officer. He told me he's part of Section B of the SD.»

I couldn't hold back the surprise for that disclosure and

couldn't imagine what the SS Intelligence wanted of me either.

«I had no choice» Ritter kept justifying himself, seeking with his look his spouse's approval. «I don't know who he is. He only told me that you are accused of belonging to a group of Italian dissidents, people who try to derail the agreements between our Führer and Mussolini.»

«And tell me, how much did they pay you to believe that nonsense and fulfil the task? How much is my life worth to the SD?»

«Not even a fucking mark, Hauptmann. They said that my wife and my little twins would be the first guests of the Ettersberg internment camp, and that Colonel Koch would be very happy to use them for his medical tests» he confessed with tears in his eyes before kissing his wife and coming towards me. He said he wouldn't resist but begged me to settle things outside that house. His wife burst out in tears and made to grab hold of him, but the man silenced her with a gesture of his hand. I appreciated Ritter's boldness and was convinced he wasn't faking it. Suddenly two perfectly identical four-year-old girls burst into the room. Their chubby little faces were very sweet though astonished to find a stranger in their home. With cat-like swiftness, they climbed onto the bed to comfort their mother, who drew her daughters close and held them tightly. I hid the gun before they could see it. I watched that family and it came naturally to me to wonder what I would have done in Ritter's place. I couldn't kill him. His reasons forbade me to do that. The little girls asked their father to get on the bed, but he was still standing in front of me waiting for his execution.

«You have a nice family, Albert» I told him with a hint of envy for the human warmth he could enjoy every day, «and you also had a good friend. Enjoy what is left to you and, should we ever meet again, take my advice, change direction, because you will no longer get gifts from me» I concluded and then turned towards the door.

I started off in the night towards the centre of Leipzig accompanied by a pressing bitterness only. I wobbled while walking because the pain in my leg would pierce me with cramps and throbs at every step. I reached the big market square in just half an hour. I knew well the Altes Rathaus, whose grandeur and beauty I admired, but that night the old town hall didn't affect me at all. I had a swarm of thoughts in my head that would have driven me crazy if I didn't disentangle them. I breathed in, then blew the air out as if to remove the confusion. Unless I had gone completely mad that night, I was well aware the role of the Sicherheitsdienst would only be limited to the identification of Nazism's potential enemies, while their arrest would be Gestapo's duty. So why would an SD man go beyond his duty? Could it be a private revenge? The hypothesis that Haase could be the instigator came back pounding in my head. But why would those organizations all belonging to the same man, Himmler, have to act in such an erratic and uncoordinated way? The SS Ahnenerbe wanted me and the Sicherheitsdienst was ready to kill me bypassing the Gestapo.

Riddles had always seduced me, that's why I had devoted three years to study the Templar square, nevertheless medieval puzzles seemed far too obvious to me compared to what kept my life in check.

Heinz Hilgenfeld, my philosophy teacher in Marburg, once told me: "Weapons are never the tools of rationality, but the confirmation of its failure." At that time I replied,

35

boasting an erudition as immature as it was insolent, that Alexander the Great had not civilised the known world by spreading words and collecting approvals.

That night, in Leipzig, our debate became more relevant than ever. Until that moment I was sure that revenge was the sole bargaining chip for any injustice suffered. I was wrong. The satisfaction I felt when I pardoned Ritter made my conscience lighter and, finally, I understood what Professor Hilgenfeld really meant: there is no dishonour in choosing an alternative to violence.

Germany – Berlin, September 4, 1937

That Saturday, September 4th, I was supposed to meet Angelika Blumen at the museum by 10 o'clock, and I was awfully late.

Several years had passed since I last discussed the Sator question, and yet it still managed to grip me, with that sequence of seemingly meaningless words: *Sator, Arepo, Tenet, Opera, Rotas.*

S	A	T	O	R
A	R	E	P	O
T	E	N	E	T
O	P	E	R	A
R	O	T	A	S

My exegesis of the magic square was the outcome of "Sitz im Leben": the method according to which every document should be analyzed considering its original, historical and cultural context. I had reached the belief that my predecessors' interpretations of the Sator were meaningless, since they stemmed from a prejudice on its origin. In my opinion, that magic square was at least five thousand years old and someone, finally, appeared to endorse my theory.

My briefcase, purchased after I attained my qualified teacher status, still gave off a strong smell of leather, which reminded me of the sternness of culture and the huge effort to achieve it.

The bus had left me downtown and I had walked the last stretch to the neoclassical building of the Neues Museum. I crossed the doorstep hastily and the impetuosity, forced by my delay, drew the attention of one of the guards. The strutting young man stopped when he heard Angelika Blumen greeting me from the bottom of the corridor. Her figure was still in the shade, yet I could already make out her elegant silhouette. I made an effort not to limp, but I wasn't capable enough to hide my impediment.

The office was large, bright and extraordinarily refined. When I entered, a Brunswick Panatrope was playing a piece of classical music. Above the high chest of drawers, with brass knobs that looked like they had just been polished, some vinyl records of local composers were neatly arranged, albeit their sleeves, still in perfect condition, revealed a sporadic use. That office exuded good taste.

«This is not my study, but the curator allows me to use it in his absence» explained Angelika, seeing I was stunned. A moment later she stared at me and asked what had befallen me. «I can see you limping and I didn't remember those scratches on your face. What happened to you?»

«A work-related accident that prevented me from returning to Berlin. In this regard, I'll reconfirm my invitation to dinner, if you are willing to forgive me» I said, sitting in the armchair, while the beautiful Panatrope was playing a piece by Strauss.

She laughed elegantly. «No worries, professor, you can make up for it today, at the end of this meeting. Now... I'd rather be listening about the background of your theory.»

«Well, for starters, I'd rather avoid so much formality» I proposed, in order to abridge the distances.

«You're right, Alexander, but please tell me now, what led you to your deductions on the Sator and the *Maât*? Forgive me, but I'd prefer getting to the point than indulge in idle chatter.»

At those words my masculine ego leaped, as I imagined myself reaching a more intimate mutual connection in a short time. On that occasion, though, I pretended I wanted to discuss exquisitely intellectual matters with her.

«Well, although the Sator is known by most as a Templar code, Egyptian harmony is the *incipit* of my idea» I explained to her. «I didn't go into much detail because the purpose of my dissertation was different: to demonstrate that the concept of Egyptian *Maât* survived until the late Middle Ages, conveyed over the millennia by the Sator, in fact, and by the work of Bernard de Clairvaux.»

«I love puzzles and mysteries, as well» she specified «but I remind you that pragmatism is always the winning card.»

Immodesty has always been my capital sin, however, on that occasion, the ease I sported with that woman was only the result of the trust in my research. «You know better than me, Angelika, that much of the Christian heritage is an Egyptian legacy. The textual resemblance between Psalm 104 and Akhenaten's Hymn to the Aten is now more than ascertained... therefore the Sator might well be a Medieval reworking of a primordial text, a code to pass the harmonic rules of the *Maât,* or the Egyptian theogony, on to posterity.»

«I like the idea, you know, but we're talking about very distant ages. Try to be more convincing» she replied as she glided on the sofa, stretching her long legs.

Her every movement was a provocation to me and I ended up observing her for a long time in that Venus Victrix pose. I lost the thread of conversation for just a second when she lifted her legs to lie down more comfortably. I was not sure that her attitude reflected a clear invitation to me, rather, I thought she wanted to probe the extent of my ability to stay focused. One thing I was sure of: before giving herself up to passion, Angelika wished to be intellectually seduced. I promised myself I would do my best to satisfy her.

«A Sator was found at Pompeii prior to the eruption in 79 AD and one was also discovered in Egypt, ergo it anticipates Gnosticism» I continued with determination. «Its words are divided into five rows by five columns, *Tenet* is in the middle of the square and acts as a keystone. It's a palindrome, therefore, if you read it from left to right or vice versa, either way you always get the same text: *Sator, Arepo, Tenet, Opera, Rotas.* Is there anything more balanced and dualistic than a five-by-five palindrome square? The Sator doesn't have its origin in the Middle Ages, the Sator embodies the Egyptian perfection and harmony, hence the *Maât.* Its geometry and numerology have made it a mirror of divine harmony whether for a Christian or a Jew or a Muslim.»

«You're a dreamer» she labelled me, amused. She remained silent, watching me from the couch and, from time to time, she adjusted the strap of her dress which kept sliding down the shoulder. Suddenly, she pulled her legs back, put on her shoes and went to the window. She left a pleasant lotus fragrance behind. She sighed and said: «If you want to find the Egyptian *Maât*, Alexander, you must first search for it in yourself. Only then you will understand the meaning of harmony, truth, justice and righteousness; those are the precepts that must guide you to the end of life and through the true meaning of the Sator. Here we're transcending both divination and the mere sense of geometric balance. If the Sator were an Egyptian cultural heritage, as you're claiming, then it should lead you to the hereafter and show you the Way of Horus. The Way of Horus is the straight and narrow path and the feather of the goddess *Maât* is the allegorical device showing you the way. It means that only the man with a heart as light as a feather will be able to access the Afterlife, only the one who understands the sacred precepts...»

«Yes, I know the forty-two rules of the *Maât*» I interrupted her.

«Knowing them doesn't mean respecting them.»

«Why, are you telling me that you do follow them all? I, for my part, take good care not to do that!» I replied before loosing myself in the vision of her body silhouetted against the light.

«And who does, Alexander? Who abides by all the rules? I don't care about the morals you base your life on, I just want to know what it is that you really see in the Sator. And leave the theories of your predecessors, or the clichés like the *Pater Noster* alone! No, so much secrecy wouldn't make any sense, it must take much more than a Lord's Prayer to solve the riddle. What is that magic square hiding?» she asked, coming closer to me like a cat luring its prey. She always seemed ready for combat. I wondered why, what led Angelika to always keep her guard up; I had never forced her to behave like that, at least not on purpose.

«So, admitting a dating of the Sator back in time of thousands of years, I imagine that this notorious magic square might have been a prayer or a litany from the Old Kingdom, translated only later into Gnostic language to allow it to get through to the new millennium. Maybe it was Imhotep himself, the Egyptian high priest, to devise its structure; maybe it conceals the name of God, of *Râ*, or maybe it's just the umpteenth amazing doing of the Shemsu Hors...» I ventured, letting the phrase float in the air.

Angelika looked staggered. «Shemsu Hor? You mean the elusive priests? I admit I adore your recklessness, Alexander, but boldness should be used in moderation, as well.»

I wasn't afraid of her disapproval, quite the contrary, her scepticism spurred me to show her my study material, including at least a hundred reworkings of the Sator in alphabetical and numerical form. We discussed at length each of the combinations before we got to the one confirming the Templar square as an Egyptian workmanship. Angelika assailed me with questions, challenging part of my beliefs at first, and eventually legitimising them when my explanation drew to an end.

The topic was unquestionably very broad and the documents to debate on countless, so I proposed resuming after lunch. I already had in mind where to take her: "Zur letzten Instanz" on the Waisenstrasse would have been the ideal place for that occasion.

The restaurant was not particularly crowded that day and I was glad, because I didn't love the commotion, especially when I was in the company of a beautiful woman.

«Herr Wagner, welcome!» called a voice from the back of the room as soon as I crossed the threshold.

«Rudolf, how are you?» I asked the hall director, who came to greet Angelika with an impeccable hand kiss.

«Herr Wagner, it's a pleasure to see you again. Would you like me to take you to the usual table, or do you prefer one in the Biergarten?»

I loved that restaurant for its history and for its cosy nooks. Since it was a business meeting, I preferred the first floor dining room to the tables in the Biergarten which, on the contrary, I favoured in other circumstances because of its medieval and particularly romantic setting.

We climbed the baroque spiral staircase to access the large lounge with its warm and inviting tones. That restaurant was a fixture in the city, contemporary and historical celebrities, such as Napoleon, had been regular visitors. At least so they said. I felt particularly good. In some ways I was reassured by that building, set like a gem in the historic centre of Berlin and I was confident that it would instill the same calmness into Angelika too.

We resumed our debate a little before the last course. Angelika was tenacious but I was more.

«I also read your work on the solar cult; I find your hypothesis on its evolution very interesting, but I absolutely don't agree about the connection with the Mother Earth and the alignment that you claim the cathedrals of Chartres and Loreto have with the Giza Plateau. It's utter nonsense» she went on looking around to make sure that no customer was sitting at the tables next to ours.

«You're beautiful and cultured, Angelika, but you don't see beyond that "shell" of scholarly knowledge encasing you» I dared, without thinking twice. She stiffened but I didn't relent. «You won't admit that the Black Virgins of Chartres and Loreto represent the evolution of Isis, just as you won't admit that the Templar Sator is basically the work of the ancient Priests of Horus. We are all unknowing devotees of the same goddess, who preserves her primordial features while changing her name.» I sank my eyes into hers, clear and cold as ice; they were disdainful like a frontline volunteer's.

«Yes, it's very exciting, but it will be no easy undertaking to convince academic conservatives. I don't want to appear sceptical, but you know the uncertainties of the job» she said with a little hesitation. «I'm about to tell you something that's not in my best interests to say. I'd like you to think carefully before you divulge your inferences and accept the job I'm offering you. I believe in your abilities, but you must be sure of yourself when you stand in front of my superiors. Sometimes trusting our intuitions is not enough to succeed.»

«I want to find my truth and I know I can do it with the right means.»

«Almost two thousand years ago a man tried to change the world and was crucified.»

And then I could no longer grasp the meaning of her criticism. That digressive speech was really starting to annoy me. «He fought for what he believed in» I replied.

«Every man wants to gain glory, but most of them end up being worn-out by unsuccessful quests. You don't have to be too impulsive, always question yourself and find the faults in your theory before others can point them out to you.»

«You don't make any progress, unless you have the guts to take the risk and I don't want my insights about the Sator to just look like the echo of a reverie. I will find the evidence, rest assured» I retorted.

«Hmm, good, that's exactly what I wanted to hear.»

Just then I realised I had passed an admission test. We were facing each other. She kept silent and studied me for several minutes, gently massaging her cheekbones. Then she looked towards an indefinite point in the room and explained: «Two years ago Heinrich Himmler founded a society which became, at a later stage, the erudite foundation of the SS: the Ahnenerbe.»

«Yes, I already knew that, a kind of cultural association in agreement with the Führerprinzip» I emphasised. «A community dedicated to the study of our protohistory, as rumors have it.»

«Kind of. That community is now in need of new nourishment. Himmler's becoming increasingly demanding and his passion for the occult is more alive and obsessive than ever. Some members within the association hinder your recruitment: they consider you potentially dangerous, as they have found your writings anti-Germanic, to some extent.»

That sentence made my blood boil. «That's ridiculous! I love my country. I spilled my own blood...»

«Shush, lower your voice, Alexander. Calm down. I've reassured them. They'll let you try, but first you have to persuade me that we can get a lot out of your conjectures or I will reject your admittance myself.»

«Come on, Angelika! I'm a Luftwaffe pilot, and you know all too well that some people only approve of those wearing an SS uniform» I answered her back resentfully.

«Friedrich Hielscher is a great scholar and one of Reichsführer Himmler's favorites, yet he's not part of the Schutzstaffel, so your beliefs must be revised. You don't even have to enrol in the Party to join. Be convincing and you will work for the Ahnenerbe Institute as a scholar, as a professor and not as a soldier. You'll get hands-on experience of the most secret past events, the history that your teachers don't even imagine could exist. Never lie, they would find out. Remove the skeletons from your closet and set the record straight from the beginning. If they let you in, the satisfaction will be great and history will remember you.»

I sighed loudly and found my calmness back. «Well, you want me to expose myself» I joked to defuse the tension and embarrass her, but she hardly got even uncomfortable.

«The foundation doesn't want a naked man; it carries out scientific research to retrieve Germanic traditions, it seeks sacred objects as well as the immortality in the union between man and sun. You are on the right track. You just need to emphasise, or minimise some historical events according to the circumstances, and then you'll be the perfect man for the Ahnenerbe.»

«We'll see. But I have a question for you now» I told her, approaching my face to hers. «Let's say the Sator was a message based on the *Maât* precepts to grasp the meaning of the Divine. Couldn't it be possible, in your opinion, that it underwent a sort of *damnatio memoriae* during a period of political instability and chaos brought by foreign invaders in the land of Egypt? I'm referring to the invasion of the Hyksos, the Semitic shepherds.»

She lifted her chin and rubbed her neck with the hand. Later, I would come to understand that she performed that ritual only when someone was able to tease her acuity.

«Are you telling me that the ancient ministers intentionally concealed their knowledge in the Sator, in order not to pass the Egyptian heritage on to the invaders, to the Hyksos?»

«It seemed plausible to me. The Egyptians were a very tolerant people in the beginning, you know that better than I do. Maybe that was exactly their mistake.»

She smiled maliciously. «Maybe you can make it, professor, maybe you can convince me.»

«Hypocrite, I've already convinced you» I replied offering her a drink.

«I find it hard to believe, yet we're talking about the genesis of anti-Semitism, the exclusion of the Jews from the knowledge necessary to create the Egyptian Sun-Man. My God, Dietrich should hear you out!» she exclaimed excitedly.

At that time, I didn't know who Dietrich Schrödinger was, but it wasn't hard to imagine.

«I'm not talking about a total exclusion, I think the ministers did select only an elite among Egyptians, Hyksos, Libyans and others deserving of that knowledge» I specified.

«Don't go too far. This part should be reconsidered before submitting your thesis to the twelve of the Ahnenerbe. If the Sator were really an anti-Semitic code, everything would be easier. Don't you think?»

«I didn't study the Templar Sator and its social and religious implications to fight a war against the Jews. I seek the absolute truth and I won't forge it for any reason, be it the banner of racial hygiene or that of the Jewish community. You, of all, should know that the scientists pursue their studies to prove the theories, thorny or anti-

47

ethical as they may be, so don't ask me to lie.»

I immediately read a hint of disapproval on her face. «There are rules you must comply with, too.»

«You don't need Alexander Wagner to have a fake reality. If that's what you want, get a puppet, but if you believe in my studies, then you will have to accept their outcome. Whichever it might be.»

«If we keep on living with subhumans who contaminate our economy, we will never be great», she openly declared.

«Well, neither will we be if we build the greatness of Germany on lies! The Führer has offered me the illusion of a homeland worth fighting for and dying for, and now he's revealing to me that, despite the bonfire in Berlin, there's still a part of the Reich eager for knowledge. Forgive me, but I can't imagine why they would involve scholars to forge a discovery; they might as well tell a fairy tale to feed the public opinion without wasting time and money on scientific expeditions!»

Angelika cooled down. «I think you misunderstood me. I just wanted you to suggest a possible anti-Semitic implication to the leaders of the Ahnenerbe and then, at the end of the research, we'll know if it can be confirmed» she replied softened, inviting me to toast with her. Her words didn't convince me, though, nor did they cause me to reconsider my position.

Germany – Berlin, September 6, 1937

After my visit to Angelika Blumen, I assiduously attempted to find a way to approach her and I had the brilliant idea of asking a high school mate of mine for some prints. I knew well what to look for, but if it weren't for him, I would be still wandering among bookstores and antique dealers searching for the illustration depicting the bas-reliefs dedicated to Isis and Horus in the Philae gallery.

That picture was one of the tables contained in the "Description de l'Egypte": the collection of prints illustrating the monuments of the Land of the Pharaohs at the time of Napoleonic expedition. I knew well, since Angelika had confessed it to me, that she appreciated that kind of art, so I played it safe by sending her my present. I imagined seeing her smiling in the contemplation of that splendid portrayal. Isis was breastfeeding her son: the most human scene that had ever been represented in a monument. For the Egyptians the value of that moment of the Goddess' life trascended the simple gesture. It was related to the notion of rebirth and might. The details of the headdress with the vulture, symbol of the mother, were precise and the pose of the Goddess, encouraging the little Horus to suck, was so natural. The great Isis: Goddess with ten thousand names and tender mother. Isis, *Virgo lactans* and ultimately Mary: millennia of godly maternal love transposed into timeless and spaceless art. I soon realised that I loved that deity for her strength, her wisdom and, at the same time, for the femininity that she exuded.

The following Monday I went home around eight p.m. When I reached the door, I saw an envelope sticking out of the mailbox. I immediately recognised Angelika's handwriting and read greedily: "If you seek the Truth, now you can find it. Saint Bernard wrote that the search for the Truth about God is the purpose of existence and that Harmony, the divine *ratio*, is every man's breath of life. Come to mine tomorrow in the morning and, perhaps, you will find the proof of your assumptions. I am sure that the Virgin will help you understand the innermost meaning of existence."

I smiled, enjoying the good smell emanating from the paper sheet and imagining the woman who, in those days, was monopolising my mind.

I entered my house elated and climbed the stairs two steps at a time, after throwing my hat onto the ottoman on the landing. I felt optimistic and I trusted I could involve Angelika to such an extent as to make her my ally. I went to take a bath not taking in the state of absolute chaos the house was in, then, when I left the room, a glass scrap cut into my foot. I had not yet given up the habit of walking barefoot and that was surely the punishment for not listening to my mother's recommendations. The green shard seemed to belong to the desk lampshade. I threw the door of the study open and was welcomed by sheer disaster: the library had been completely ransacked. There were sheets and books everywhere and while I was furiously picking up the pieces of my life, someone rang the doorbell. Unconcerned about who it might be, I went to open the door, still wet and covered only by a towel around my hips. It was Karl.

«Hmm, how elegant! Were you by any chance expecting a woman?» he asked mockingly, but I killed all his cheerfulness when I explained what had happened. He was surprised. «But who could do that?»

«I wish I knew. What do you think?»

«That you have been the target of the anger of some old flame of yours. I heard that you've been seeing Angelika...» he said to me with a note of blame I disliked.

«Well, to be honest, it was exactly your mutual friends I was thinking about.»

«No, it wouldn't make sense. You're about to sign an agreement with the Ahnenerbe. Why should they turn your house upside down when you yourself are going to provide them with all the information they need?»

First my plane had crashed, now my house had been broken into. I wondered what else I had to expect and from whom. I still had no answers, no one had, not even Karl, who knew that milieu better than I did. In all honesty, I made a thousand and more speculations, but not even one of the many seemed plausible to me. That intrusion was seemingly pointless, since nothing I owned had been stolen.

Germany – Berlin, September 7, 1937

Angelika Blumen's apartment was on the second floor of a stately building near Auguste Viktoria Platz. It was soberly furnished and devoid of any unnecessary objects, except for the magnificent fish tank. I moved closer, intrigued by an innovative oil-burning heater and a lamp dedicated to lighting the large tank; inside, a pair of bluish fish were intent on building the nest for their eggs.

«I·love those fish» Angelika said, offering me a cup of coffee, «because they have a strange way of wooing. They seem to be dancing... it's very romantic.»

I replied with an affected smile.

«What's wrong, Alexander?» she asked me, foreseeing some impediment to her plans.

«Nothing» I replied approaching the window that overlooked the courtyard of the building.

«You're not good at lying» she said gently seeing me pensive.

It was probably because of her ways, or because of my desire to share my unfortunate incident with her, that I told Angelika about the break-in at my house. She paled at the idea that maybe confidential information had leaked and that I was being targeted by the Ahnenerbe opponents.

«Please help me understand what's going on around me» I asked her amicably.

She remained silent and went to the desk shaking her head in disbelief. «I think they were looking for this» she admitted showing me a display case. «They knew that I would give it to you. Apparently, they were convinced I did already.»

The blood went to my head. «You know who they are, you know what they want and yet you didn't warn me?»

«I would have, today! Gosh, I couldn't imagine there was a spy among our collaborators. I must immediately tell Dietrich of the mishap and take the necessary measures or our deal is likely to fall apart.»

At that point, I freaked out. I pressed her hand on the receiver to prevent her from making the call, then I grabbed Angelika by the shoulders and pushed her against the wall. «You have to explain everything to me now! Come on, I have every right to know.»

«Try to understand me: I'm in a thorny position.»

«I am, not you!» I snapped furiously. I felt like a pawn in the hands of the Ahnenerbe. «In battle, at least, I know the enemy and I can decide how to act, but in this case my foes know everything about me and I know nothing about them. It's not you who's in a thorny position, I assure you» and I let go of her.

«But I am indeed! You've not been recruited, yet, and I am already staking everything because I think you're the right person to change things. I would have never dreamt of putting you in danger, I swear» she replied staring at me with a pleading voice, but I pushed her aside, irritated.

«I can defend myself well, don't fear, but you must tell me who they are» I said, examining the object contained in the glass case with more attention.

Although it was a typically Christian portrayal, the divine light dominating the scene was typical of the Aten: the solar disc idolized by the heretic pharaoh Akhenaten. That image enlightened me and, in an instant, I lost sight of every other concern to devote myself exclusively to the characters represented in it.

It was an antique painted linen: gorgeous. A work best appreciated dissociating yourself from the mere exoteric vision, where the Virgin Mary, Jesus and the Lamb were undisputed protagonists. Like the nonconformist I have always been, I tried to perceive a more archaic spiritual world, dangerously occult and bewitching. The beautiful Madonna wore a black veil on a dress, so revealing it bordered on sinfulness, although it was a holy picture amongst the most beautiful and pure that I had ever seen. The little Jesus sat on his mother's lap, while, on the right, the divine light was over a crouching ram.

I thought it was a depiction from the Late Middle Ages, where the ram prefigured the crucifixion of Christ and the word *Amen* reaffirmed its compliance with the prophecies. The face of the Virgin, smiling before her son, was exquisite. The purity of that expression and the brightness of the two figures imbued the soul with serenity and harmony. It was a Christian work in line with the Egyptian concept of *Maât*, just like the Sator.

«I have been allowed to show you the cloth and ensure that you examine it, supported by the right means. It's a one-of-a-kind piece» Angelika explained while sliding her hand down my arm. «Now, do you understand why I chose you? Your gift from a few days ago was the umpteenth confirmation that I wasn't wrong. The Virgin, Isis and Horus… you're the right one, Alexander.»

«A unique work of art and quite compromising for the

Holy Mother Church, too. The truth hidden beneath these figures is not exactly dogmatic...» I commented, with a hint of a smile.

«We believe it can reveal a lot. At first glance, you recognised already the Amarnian heresy: the Aten. If you deem it appropriate, I can help you with the ancient Egyptian. That aside, it's up to you to decide whether and how to move forward. This cloth reached Italy thanks to the Desert Fathers in the fifth century and it was studied by none other than Bernard de Clairvaux» she waited to see what expression I would show after that name. «The men of the Ahnenerbe took it from a monastery on the Monte Amiata. It was kept in what once was the most amazing medicine and pharmacology laboratory in Central Italy. Although its origins are much older, this linen was named "Il telo di Bernardo", because of the attention it received from the saint during his stay in the Val d'Orcia. About a century after this episode, the Vatican decreed the conversion of the monastery complex from Benedictine to Cistercian, in honor of the saint who so loved that house of worship. We believe that this relic and the Sator are two pieces of the same mosaic. That's why I wanted you, and no-one else, to study it. The Vatican knows of its existence but, for obvious reasons, has never considered it worthy of veneration and has been careful not to even catalogue it.»

At her words I smiled, resigned. «Ha, so I eventually get to know who destroyed my home!» and I finished my coffee, cold by then.

«The "old Lord of Rome" is not necessarily involved in this affair.»

«Pius XI might not be directly concerned, but his Curia could be. Correct me if I'm wrong, but you didn't buy the cloth from the junk dealer's on Tiergartenstrasse, did you?»

Only long after would I find out that the theft of that linen had cost the life of two innocent monks. In spite of everything, in that moment, I decided to neglect the issue: I was so excited by the historical aspect of the matter and animated by my own ego, so eager to accept that challenge.

«Have you already dated it? Who saw it before us?»

«So, are we still in business, Professor Wagner?» she asked me winking.

I left her hanging for a while. «Do I look like a man who backs down at the first difficulty?»

«Absolutely not. And what are you looking at now, with so much interest?»

I was so enraptured by that sacred image that she went on speaking, convinced that I was listening to her, while my ears translated all her words into an annoying buzz.

«There's a caption at the bottom of the canvas, did you know already?» I asked her after a few minutes.

She personally checked, snatching the case from my hands. «No.»

«It's concealed beneath an unusual color craquelé, but it's an *Ichthýs*» I lectured.

Something, however, was anomalous in the lettering of ΙΧΘΥΣ, the Greek acronym of "Jesus Christ, Son of God, Saviour": the unusual addition of two triangles and a partial erasure of some letters. I stared at them for a while, then went back to observe the Virgin. It was incredible, but every time my gaze landed on that figure, it seemed more beautiful and brighter. It was probably my enraptured expression that prompted Angelika to comment with a trace of disappointment: «You seem to be in love with her.»

«And you seem to be jealous» I promptly answered

back unblinking. She turned and showed me the shoulders, left uncovered by her silky dress, supple and sinuous. I had embarrassed her and seized the opportunity to move closer to her. I girded her with my arms and plunged my face into her warm neck, without wasting any more time. I kissed her right up below the ear, where her lotus scent was more intense, so as to encourage me to persist. As soon as she wrapped me in her arms, spurring me to go further, I realized that the shyness from a few moments before had just been for show. We were both loosing ourselves in that sensual dimension, where everything that was foreign to our bodies became worthless, when we heard the front door slamming violently. Our effusions suddenly froze. Angelika moved away from me and regained her composure, although her gaze clearly betrayed her regret for that inconvenience.

«Good morning, Fräulein Blumen» was the greeting from the cook, who burst into the house with the grace of a steelworker.

«Good morning, Uta» said Angelika after clearing her throat.

When the woman noticed my presence, she stepped back contrite and greeted me with a gesture of the head. «Is your guest staying for lunch, Fräulein?»

Angelika looked at me fleetingly and it was clear to me that I had to let time run its course, even though my certainty that she would yield soon was now strengthened. «I was just about to leave» I replied walking toward the door.

«Forgive me for encouraging you» Angelika whispered to me when we were alone again. She kept her eyes down as she spoke and became strangely thoughtful, as if the cook had reminded her of something unpleasant. I wanted her at any cost; it was a challenge that I couldn't lose, but suddenly I saw fear in her eyes. «You're dangerous, Alexander Wagner. Your emerald eyes and seductive smile make you awfully attractive but, now more than ever, we can't give way to distractions. The issues at stake are too important. Take Saint Bernard's linen, study its every corner and take good care of it» she recommended before opening the door to get rid of me quickly. «Take care. I'll call you as soon as I get new instructions.»

I hinted at an obliging smile and, after kissing her hand, I left without turning. On the way back, I thought about her attitudes, about my suspicion that she feared something, or someone. I knew that, sooner or later, "someone" would step up to claim his property, but I had no intention of giving up winning her over.

Germany – Büren, September 10, 1937

It was now undeniable that my days were going at the same pace as the needs of the Ahnenerbe, so much so that even the flow of time seemed to me so quickened that I struggled to keep up. They gave me three days to analyze the linen to the best of my ability, then I should have conferred with the high ranks.

That morning I was travelling in a sinuous and brand-new BMW, which had reached Büren after leaving behind the beautiful Paderborn, decorated for a village festival. I was accompanied by Angelika who, after our last meeting, was very careful not to provoke me.

I saw a huge manor on the hill: Himmler's castle, cold and majestic.

«And so I am granted the privilege of visiting the school for the SS highest ranks» I began.

Angelika nodded and brushed aside a strand of hair escaped from her clip. The driver, on the other hand, had not even bothered to greet us. He was a nondescript being, but he watched over us and would report our every move back to his superiors.

«Does this visit worry you?» she asked me after a quick touch-up to her lipstick. «They say there are tens of thousands of scientific texts in Himmler's library. Did you know?»

«Yes, I did» I replied trying not to sound overenthusiastic, since its residents weren't waiting for us to go for a tour of the castle, «but I guess they're not too expansive in there. However, I concur with the geographical choice of the Reichsführer: this area of Westphalia is...»

«Enchanting, isn't it? It's so green around here and Wewelsburg Castle reminds me of some stories from my childhood.»

«Ah, girls! You're not going to tell me you still dream of Prince Charming, are you?» I exclaimed, amazed by her childish tone.

«Better deal with a graduate pilot, then?»

«Why not? It would be a less ridiculous and certainly more exciting alternative.»

The BMW parked in front of the entrance of the manor dominating the thriving Alme valley. The castle had been almost entirely rebuilt by Heinrich Himmler, who had bought it for a few marks. Each stone of that place had its geomantic connotation and it was a sort of a contradiction that it stood on that little spot of Catholic Germany.

We crossed the bridge and reached a wooden door that still released the annoying smell of fresh paint. A man in uniform escorted us, after logging our data and paying homage to Angelika with a broad smile, thus showing a collection of teeth as large and square as the insignia on his collar.

When we entered the first room, a soldier, who looked haughty but had a vacant stare, was standing in front of a massive desk. I saw he hesitated in placing the black helmet on the walnut top and I noticed that, although the scratches had irreparably marked it, the sig runes of Victory still stood out on the white badge, as if the soldier had neglected everything else but the emblem of the SS. I stared at the two aligned lightning bolts, the *Siege*, as we call them in German. I had seen them so many times! I wondered if, behind so much study of symbolism, there was also a higher knowledge of mankind's history or if, instead, it was just a pathetic emulation of the greats of the past.

«Heil, Hitler!» shouted a man behind me. «Welcome, I have been waiting for you.»

I answered the greeting before I even knew who was in front of me. I found myself face to face with an elderly man with eyes as gray and wrinkled as his hands, and yet, although bowed by age, his proud bearing still commanded respect.

«Dietrich» said Angelika, willingly accepting his hand-kiss.

He looked at her with complicity, showing a smile of almost paternal satisfaction. «And so, my dear, you convinced our Hauptmann Wagner to yield to the will of the Ahnenerbe. I'm pleased with your success» he declared hoarsely, examining me from head to foot and handing some of my photos to Angelika. «These are no longer needed» he said gently.

I was not surprised that they had investigated my life: I wasn't allowed to have secrets and that further convinced me they were not involved in my plane crash. They had attempted to kill me two weeks before and then tried to recruit me? It was a contradiction I hoped Dietrich could help me comprehend. I let the elderly man talk for a long time to understand who he was, with his elegant style and quick gaze.

«A campaign medal would suit that uniform well, a recognition award for your contribution to Franco's war. Our Führer greatly appreciated the offensive of last April. I've heard that you actively participated in it. Windhund, that's how they call you in your circle.» I nodded without comment: I had little to boast about. That man spoke as if he didn't know I was being targeted by the Sicherheitsdienst. «Your skills as a pilot have been praised among the high ranks of the Wehrmacht. Did you know? You never back down, so they say. So far, everything suggests we should welcome you with open arms, your aptitude for insubordination aside» he blamed me, even if it looked like he had already granted me the grace. «Despite this, you served well under Generalmajor Sperrle and you are a man who believes in patriotism; which is wholesome from my point of view. For our part, we must mainly evaluate your knowledge and not your military skills. In this regard, I know that you have also been focusing your research on the issue of the *Invitto* and that you have been trying for years to stumble into that thin Ariadne's thread handed down by Gothic architecture. You're a man devoted to religious universalism and to the rehabilitation of the Sun worship...» and he fell silent. «I infer that you don't like talking about yourself or even about your feats in Spain, Hauptmann.»

I smiled bitterly. «Those who talk too much about themselves end up listening too little to others, and then I don't recognise any feat. You know our status well: the Reich's official stance is still that of non-intervention. I flew for over a year like a ghost in the skies of Spain. The war is not over, yet and no one can ever grant us an honour for what we did with the Condor Legion, although I'm bearing the weight of an Iron Cross on my soul already. I did it because I'm German and I'm a soldier. I only carried out orders.»

«So our intercession is saving you from perdition» the elderly man laughed bitterly as he dragged his age-worn legs along the pavement. «Well, what do you think of our gift, of Saint Bernard's linen?» he asked me, ordering a soldier to open the door before us.

«I wouldn't exactly call it a gift, since it's not for my pleasure, but for your interest, that you sent it to me, nevertheless I thank you for granting me this opportunity» I added, promising myself to weigh every word I would utter thenceforth.

«Our charming Fräulein Blumen has drawn up an interesting and somewhat detailed account of your assumptions, but I would prefer you to express your opinion of the relic in person.»

The ardour of that man inspired me with the respect due to a great scholar, albeit with prudence. I had spent hours, days, before decrypting the message of that image, so I replied without too many considerations: «Everything seems quite clear to me today, although I firmly believe that the relic hides much more. Râ, Aten, Amun, Isis and Horus have been concealed by medieval censorship. The linen mirrors the engraving of the Philae gallery» I explained, also earning Angelika's approval. «Bernard de Clairvaux may have seen the cloth in the Desert Fathers' original version, perhaps he himself was the one who required the concealment of its "less orthodox" features. This work of art embodies the entire history of sun worship. It's a thousand-year-old code. My whole theory is based on the demonstration that Aten, Amun and Râ are the sources of early Christianity and that, handed down since the Old Kingdom, there is an initiatory knowledge which reached us thanks to the geometry of European cathedrals and the magic square. The large basilicas or the mighty masonry works, such as Castel del Monte in Italy, are akin to the ideal Egyptian buildings, whose backbone was the strict geometric rules and the representation of God in the shape of numbers. Saint Bernard himself conferred vital importance upon geometry for the study of the Divine. The Sator is the result of the Egyptian *Maât* in the form of a code, since it is a square, which is the symbol for Earth; its size is five-by-five, Horus's sacred number and, weren't that enough, it's a palindrome, too, therefore perfectly balanced and harmonious. I postulated that the Sator conceals the teachings of the legendary Shemsu Hor, the Predynastic high priests» I went on after gaining Dietrich's undivided attention. «Their name is also confirmed by the King List preserved in the Cairo museum. I'm talking about a semi-divine breed that disappeared around three thousand BC, men of great physical and intellectual stature, people able to dominate nature and shape it according to their needs, supermen who worshipped the sun. I also conjectured that invading peoples, who longed for the sacred knowledge of the Shemsu Hor, for the secret of the reincarnation of souls, ergo for the eternal life, could have threatened that ancestral legacy» I underlined those last two words, directly connected to the Ahnenerbe, noticing the satisfaction that, for obvious ideological reasons, painted on Dietrich's face. «The invading people I'm referring to are the Hyksos: the Semitic shepherds persecuted by Merenptah, the pharaoh who had reached Canaan to eradicate them so that they could no longer have descendants because they were worshippers of Seth, God of Chaos.»

«A great man that Merenptah» Dietrich commented

cynically. «Please, go on.»

«The point is, the Hyksos ended up dominating Egypt and subjugating the people who, until then, had welcomed them generously into their own land. The Semitic shepherds may have played a role in the history of the linen and that of the Sator... if only I knew the dating of the first. I believe that the Egyptian nationalist sentiment was born right under the Hyksos domination, and that the ingratitude of the guests and their opportunism gave rise to social conflict in a country that had always welcomed outsiders with open arms. The apostasy of the foreigners in favor of the new deities was of no avail, because who didn't understand the value of the *Maât*, couldn't aim for the eternal life, nor deserve to draw from the secrets of Isis. Knowledge was not achievable by force, nor would a blameworthy spirit of emulation be enough to gain it. So, the Egyptian priests, faithful to the ancient tradition of the Shemsu Hor, translated the original formulas for the journey to the afterlife into a sort of an encrypted message. The message may be hidden in the cloth, but mainly in the Sator» and I went on, assertively. «The number five symbolizes the cyclic nature of life, the union between male and female. The magic square recalls the labyrinth, meaning the search for the Divine. God and enlightenment are hidden in the *omphalos*. Whoever reveals the secrets of St. Bernard's linen and Sator discovers the essence of God, because they are an initiatory journey themselves. I need St. Bernard's linen to get out of the Sator labyrinth. I'm a pilgrim in search of enlightenment.»

«Magnificent, Professor Wagner, magnificent! Then, even the Sator may guard the secret of reincarnation of souls or the very place where it took place» the old man fantasized, looking like someone who's foretasting success.

«I don't know exactly what this investigation has in store for me, but I know I've already started my journey along the *Uat Hor*, the Way of Horus, which is the embodiment of the number five» I concluded, proud of my presentation.

Dietrich looked at me satisfied before exchanging a glance of mutual understanding with Angelika, who smiled back.

«Then I'll make sure to help you» said the man. «I have decided to offer you the opportunity to take advantage of our innovative analysis tools» he explained after sending a soldier to summon a certain Professor Kirche.

I felt I was grateful to him, but strangely I was not comfortable in that place and, in all honesty, I hoped to leave Wewelsburg as soon as possible. I handed the linen to the professor and wondered what he wanted to do with it. Then I understood. The spectroscopic examination of the linen was more difficult than expected and we had to wait for hours for the results. I doubted, then, that there might be a device capable of revealing the invisible. I had to change my mind. Dietrich granted me the honour of being the first to view the results of the analysis.

«Ha, I knew it!» I said, slapping the sheet. «Welcome to the Second Millennium, Isis!»

Dietrich smiled. «A nice surprise, isn't it?»

I looked at him trying to appear not too euphoric. «A confirmation, I'd rather say. I read that traces of pumice have also been found on the cloth.»

«What do you mean?» Angelika asked amazed.

«You should know it: Nile delta. I refer to its alleged origin. Some scholars claim that when the volcano erupted at Thera in Greece, the remnants of the explosion reached the Egyptian coast and that occurred around 1600 BC.

The pumice may indicate that historical period as the genesis of the linen and, as coincidence would have it, that happened during the Hyksos domination. Their mythical capital city, Avaris, was located right on the delta. That doesn't necessarily mean that it was painted in the same period it was weaved, but it's clear that the work dates back thousands of years and was, perhaps, decorated at a later time under the reign of Akhenaten» I commented flashing a smile at Angelika, who smiled back looking vaguely concupiscent.

«You were right about the acronym of Christ written at the bottom, too» she pointed out the symbols.

«Blimey! It's almost as old as I am!» Dietrich exclaimed amused, showing an unexpected sense of humour.

«Forgive me, Dietrich, but I'm still wondering why you didn't do the test before showing me the cloth. You didn't need me. You can rely on very renowned scholars. I don't understand…»

«This is not just a dull meeting between scholars, Professor Wagner» he interrupted me letting a marked Bavarian accent slip out of his mouth, «but a real entry test. We have good scientists, it is true, but you are fascinated by esotericism and this is what we are looking for. You didn't conform to your colleagues, you didn't submit to history, but endeavored to rewrite it. You challenge academic culture, and that fascinates me. The test was necessary anyway. Clearly, I didn't doubt Fräulein Blumen's words but, as you can imagine, I, on my part, have superiors to answer to in order to finance your studies. You understand that the Ahnenerbe is a rather closed community, so confidentiality and absolute trust in its scholars are the foundation of our actions. Besides, your Italian forefathers, Catholics no less, didn't make my task any easier» he confessed pretending to be sorry. «I had the privilege of meeting your father once. A man of great culture and an admirable soldier. You inherited his stature, his demeanor and, apparently, also his ascendancy over the fairer sex, whereas your mother's parents were originally from Central Italy, correct me if I'm wrong…»

«Genetics prevents me from boasting pure German origins. My grandparents moved here in 1888; my grandfather was a construction worker. I'm not an Ahnenerbe stereotype, I know that, but my mother was born in Germany. She was a fervent Catholic, it's true, but I know that Commander Himmler's mother is, too.»

«*Touché*, professor. I didn't mean to offend you, I'm trying, in my own way, to anticipate some obstacles you might find while working closely with Ahnenerbe operators. Around here the "origins of blood and soil" rule is in force. But at this point, it doesn't matter who or why some of our collaborators opposed your recruitment. You have the task of looking for the roots of our race. Now, more than ever, I'm sure you'll find the source of our mysticism and the sacred writings, those which are the exclusive prerogative of the superman, of the Sun-Man» he emphasized the word as though it were a password. «Sonnenmensch. The day will come when we will go through mystical death and then rise again. To achieve that sublimation, we must repress any impurity as the Egyptians did with the people of Israel. The aim is to create the true and only Arius, the one who's born twice. I trust that you will be able to recover the sacred text and give us eternal life. Make us proud of you, Herr Professor.»

That's when I got lost. I watched Angelika exchange glances with the old man. But what was Dietrich talking about? I thought he was crazy, or maybe I was!

«The linen is a depiction and the Sator is an alleged litany. We never talked about holy scriptures» I said. «What sacred text do you mean?»

Angelika held my wrist and anticipated the old man's words. «We believe that, thanks to the interpretation of linen, we can discover the location of one of the twelve texts of the Sonnenmensch, some call them the Twelve Gates.»

«I infer that we're not talking about a collection of breviaries» I said ironically but slightly resented for her omission.

«We had mainly followed the Templar line but, in light of your conjectures, we were forced to review many of our queries» Dietrich confessed, wrinkling his blade-thin lips.

I stared at the imposing wooden spiral staircase that dominated that cold room. I leaned on the handrail and thought aloud. «The linen and the Sator: two codes that reveal how the pagan Egyptian cult had laid the foundations of the great monotheistic religions and what mystery had been precluded to the infidels.»

«I would listen endlessly to your discourses on the subject» Dietrich confessed to me. «Professor, enlighten us with your knowledge and you will have the glory that belongs to the great men. I admit, however, that the part I like the most is the ousting of Israel people from sacred knowledge. Exactly the kind of revelations that we consider "valuable" here. You hypothesized the participation of the Shemsu Hor priests in the writing of the Sator» he squinted and sighed. Then he resumed calling up the sacred texts: the Twelve Gates. «Zwölf Türen, Sator... who says they cannot have the same parents?»

«Um, it looks like number twelve occurs quite often in Ahnenerbe's initiatives» I observed, hoping to learn more information than those I already knew about that institute.

«Who told you about the organization in such detail?» he asked giving Angelika an accusatory glance.

«Rumors about the Reichsführer's passion for the occult and the divination of numbers proliferate among the soldiers at the front. Didn't you know?»

«Twelve are the SS generals sitting at Commander Himmler's table, as you already know, apparently» he replied, moving with difficulty and leaving behind that metal chair which rattled like an old locomotive.

I smiled. «Number twelve symbolizes initiation through sacrifice, but I don't think the commander took into account the fact that, in addition to perfection, it also represents the tribes of Israel and the gates of Heavenly Jerusalem, otherwise he would have certainly reconsidered the number of members of his inner circle!» I commented, amused by my own impudence.

«So, Hauptmann, I am not quite sure which Jew you would like to associate me with» an imperious voice from the upper floor thundered.

I moved abruptly away from the staircase and looked up in search of the man who had spoken to me. A senior SS officer came down the steps with a heavy pace; he stared at me as he proudly exhibited the lozenge displayed on the hierarch uniform. Two thick black eyebrows arched over sunken eyes and a large nose towered on the tense face of the General Director who came forth.

«Heil, Hitler!» we shouted in unison.

Angelika's face blanched, while Dietrich was anxiously waiting for my reply.

Unperturbed, I looked him in the eyes before

answering. «It was not a provocation, Standartenführer, but a way to underline how any number boasts countless interpretative facets, more or less consistent with the intended aim. It is the assignment of the scholar to go beyond the exoteric aspect of numbers and symbols to fully understand their true meaning, without spoiling their exquisitely historical value in doing so.»

A few moments of reverent silence passed, then the General Director approached me. He scanned me for a long time, perhaps to spot in my eyes some sign of disquiet that, contrary to his expectations, I didn't feel at all.

«Be careful not to draw certain comparisons next time, Hauptmann…» and he examined my Luftwaffe uniform as he waited to hear my last name.

«Hauptmann Wagner» I answered, all the more convinced that the only livery which would achieve respect in that place was the SS uniform.

«Dietrich, follow me» ordered the Director. I saw the elderly man walking away with him to a corner of the room. They spoke in hushed tones, then the hierarch came back to me and, showing a certain distrust, he addressed me again. «We are already working in Italy, in Val Camonica, and here in Germany we are undertaking various excavations. Then there is Tibet, too… Given the relevance of the topic, I would certainly be able to obtain new resources of men and means for your expedition, however I do not intend to do it before next summer. For certain matters, we need to activate the bureaucratic apparatus. Moreover, I wouldn't be able to follow the group as the manager of the expedition, since I need to face other urgencies» he explained, leaving some crumpled sheets that displayed my life on the table: identity documents of my parents, my certificates, the copy of my thesis, several photos of my childhood, the mission in Spain, and much more.

In that moment I felt a strong feeling of anger I barely held back. In fact, only a few minutiae of my life could be described as confidential, everything else had always been an open secret: from the list of my lovers to that of my friends, as well as my favorite clubs and restaurants. Before that officer, who was turning myself into a piece of worthless paper too, I replied, trying not to spill the hatred that was consuming me. «I fully understand, Standartenführer. As a matter of fact, I believe that economic resources can be reduced to a minimum, but also that, despite everything, it's important to go ahead with the work already undertaken. I would like to bring to your attention, though, the possibility not to involve your professionals; it's hardly worth it.» The officer eyed me up, annoyed that I had spoken to him and gone so far as to suggest him how to act. «I don't even expect for you, sir, to grant for my own safety. I will be able to juggle well among those savages. I have travelled a lot, I'm a pilot and know how to handle weapons well. I don't need an escort, but only equipment and a contact person on the spot.»

«Um, Shemsu Hor» he replied as if nothing about my presentation had surprised him, and even less that sacerdotal caste of which, perhaps, he pretended to have already heard. «Professor Wagner, Hauptmann, you are overly self-confident and too impudent. Do you realise that disciples of that doctrines you accuse of mendacity, might be right after you? Neither my men nor I will be there to take up your defense, should you ever find the evidence we seek.»

«I can take care of myself.»

«Always ready to do your duty for the Reich...» he left the sentence hanging with its load of allusions, which he then hastened to make explicit, «as in Spain, when you didn't have any qualms about dropping bombs on women and children.»

«In a battle, sir, we carry out orders without thinking: killing the enemy means allowing one of our compatriots to live... only later do we deal with our conscience. You see, Standartenführer» I looked him in the eye without any deference «just as a blind man develops the other senses to make up for the missing one, a man whose sins will never be forgiven, strengthens his recklessness because he has nothing more to lose, like me... or like you.»

The Director approached me with the impetus of a bird of prey ready to claw its target. «Sometimes you have to take deplorable actions for a greater good. We seek proof of the existence of an ancient Aryan-Germanic people, the Nordics; we don't hire scholars to reveal that we are all sons of a foul African priestly caste. We're bordering on blasphemy with this kind of research that opposes our precepts and you should learn how to quell your exuberance, Hauptmann, if you know what I mean.»

«Yes, sir, you've made yourself clear. However... would it make any difference if I reminded you that the Shemsu Hor belonged to a higher race?» Then I had confirmation that his knowledge of the Egyptian priests was just a bluff. «It is assumed that they came from a continent completely different from Africa, that they were more akin to people belonging to the Caucasian family and, above all, that they were the superhumans we're looking for, sir» I remarked defiantly. By then, I was making it a matter of principle: it was a duel between us. He would have had to shoot me to break me.

«If the enthusiasm you pour into the study of the past equalled that for the Reich...»

«It does, sir, or else I wouldn't have blindly executed the orders of my superiors» I interrupted him.

«If you have been allowed to enter Wewelsburg, you owe it exclusively to Dietrich. Put that dull uniform away, Wagner; from now on you become part of the Ahnenerbe, but make even one mistake and I will be personally proud to reserve you the treatment fit for presumptuous men» and, after that, he turned to the old man. «Inform him of our connections among the Egyptian nationalists. He is your idea and you will be held responsible for his actions.»

Dietrich was going to be responsible for my actions? After all, I felt sorry for him. The senior officer whispered in my ear a "Viel Erfolg" before leaving. At first I was taken aback, but then I realised that our altercation was, basically, just another entry test and that the Director was right to wish me good luck, because I would need it to untangle that yarn.

When we left the room, a breeze refreshed us. I put the cap on my head and watched our shadows stretching out toward the walls as if to separate themselves from the body which, reclaiming what little light was left, summoned them back, like a father with a disobedient son. I looked around again and saw, within the walls of that grey castle, men in uniform wandering like threatening nameless ghosts in search of the catharsis they would achieve through their ideals and their yearning for knowledge.

Dietrich explained that the gathering would have taken place in the great hall at sunset. He waited for the soldiers to leave and wiped his forehead with a handkerchief, on which the symbol of the SS Ahnenerbe had been embroidered: an oval containing the runes. «You put my heart to the test, Professor, but now we have to worry about something else. Since I will be responsible for your work in Egypt, I demand that Angelika accompany you and inform me of your every move. Go straight back to Berlin and arrange the expedition. You both have a week to let me know the planned route. And you, Professor, don't lose sight of the fact that the ultimate aim of your work, and your whole life, must henceforth be to pursue the anti-Semitic trail in Pharaonic Egypt and recover the sacred texts of the Sun-Man: Sonnenmensch!» he repeated to me over and over, and once again when we got into the car.

I turned to look at the old man as the BMW took the main road and I saw him, motionless under the dim light of a lamp post. He was intent on following us with the confident look of someone who is close to make his dreams come true. I was not sorry at all to be accompanied by Angelika: the journey would have been more interesting and her presence essential for the linguistic matter, since few Egyptians are able to interpret hieroglyphics. I stared at her and had the impression that she felt my gaze upon her, but she didn't turn around. She opened her purse and pulled out again the mirror and the ivory-colored pencil she had used shortly before to refresh her eye makeup. After that, with the utmost indifference, she wrote on the surface of the mirror and turned it in my direction: "My office - Thursday 8 a.m. You are crazy!"

How to blame her if she judged me deranged, but her appointment made me understand how much she liked my mad streak. I smiled careful, lest the driver would notice, and wondered why Angelika was being so secretive, it was a work meeting, after all.

Germany – Berlin, September 13, 1937

The Monday after my visit to the SS lair, I spent the entire afternoon in the library, supported by Gottfried Schmied, an old acquaintance of mine who had been working there for years and who had allowed me to stay even after hours. Actually, it was not just because of our friendship that he stayed there for such a long time, but rather for his interest in an auburn haired foreign woman who, to tell the truth, seemed to have taken up residence there.

On my way home I was trying to imagine how the Cistercian architecture and the doctrines of Bernard de Clairvaux could help me with the geometry of the linen and the Sator, but after nearly six hours of study I gave up reasoning, aware that I wouldn't find any answers, tired as I was.

Not even a lamp glowed along the way and the cool air invited me to lift the collar of my jacket. I stared at the ground, heedless of those who came from the opposite direction, and I lowered my hat over my eyes. At that late hour, I knew that few would walk along those streets, and yet, as if to shatter my convictions, a car pulled over. Suddenly, I felt myself being dragged into the car. I got punched in the face by a man whose massive body ended up crushing me against the car window and prevented me from even breathing. My chest was compressed in that grip and, right after, I felt a twinge in the ribs. If I didn't react at once, they would fracture. With the back of my head I hit him in the face, then I managed to give him a blow at eye level with my elbow.

I finally caught my breath and gained a few moments to look at my attacker: he was a man of indefinable age, whose size was about twice mine. He moved clumsily in the back of the car and I knew I had a huge advantage over him. The driver, instead, was a poorly dressed beanpole. He stopped the car in an isolated spot and quickly got off to help his pal who, in the meantime, I had started beating on the back.

He opened the car door and threw me on the street with a tug. He hurled himself at me trying to immobilize me while the beastly giant pulled out my Walther PPK from the holster I kept under my jacket. I cannot remember how, but I wriggled away from the driver and threw a punch at the genitals of the other man, who dropped the gun before falling down. The weapon skidded at a distance, but the taller man snatched it before I could and pointed it against me. I wasn't scared, I was rather angry with myself because I failed to forsee its trajectory.

«You must return the linen, we are its legitimate owners» he said to me in a good German, which nevertheless revealed his foreign origin. «You're not one of the chosen» he said authoritatively.

«You got the wrong man» I growled at him, rubbing my chest. Standing in front of me, there was a man more than two meters tall and slender, whose somatic traits were concealed by the gloom and his dark headdress.

«No, you're the right person. Where are you hiding the

cloth?» he insisted and I replied as I did before. He asked me the same question four or five more times and I got annoyed by his doggedness, which I tolerated just to buy myself time. «To you, it's just an image like many others» he added, «to us, it's the token of the thousand year-old Nūr šamši Alliance. We have been committed for years to quell the crazy exuberance of your Ahnenerbe and of societies like the Vril, which draw upon your knowledge, along with that of other scholars, to reach a semi-divine stage. Have you ever heard of eugenic purification, Professor Wagner?»

When he mentioned my name, he finally managed to freeze my blood. I was the target of too many people. I didn't want to hide from them, but I couldn't fight on equal terms and, at that point, I no longer had any doubts they were involved in the intrusion into my house.

I .saw the man soften his grip on the gun before resuming his complex speech. «They want an Aryan-blooded Germany. Herr Professor, do you really believe that once the research is completed, you'll have the privilege of belonging to the restricted circle of German supermen? They are using you, the linen and the Sator to bring chaos into the world. The Ahnenerbe foundation doesn't support your studies to achieve universal brotherhood. The true God fraternises with man, he doesn't discriminate, as they would like. Although it may seem impossible to you, we are the good guys here.»

«Good guys don't hold people hostage» I said and, with a quick reaction, I snatched the gun from his hand.

You could tell he wasn't used to handling a firearm. He was taken aback and I took the opportunity to hit him with a punch in the stomach and a second in the chin, while, with the butt of the PPK, I definitively broke the nasal septum of the stout guy who looked like he was coming to.

«The next time you decide to threaten someone, make sure the gun is ready to fire» I told the tall man, staring mercilessly at him. I took off the safety lock staring at both of them, after which I pulled the slide and loaded the gun. The bullet was ready in the firing chamber. The two strangers drew back but, just a split second before pulling the trigger, the taller one started talking to me. I don't know what reason pushed me to wait for that speech, but as of today I don't regret having listened to him.

It was late night by then, but I could see in his eyes a deep humanity and there was something else, something spiritually noble about him that I didn't understand and that, in some way, I feared. I could no longer afford any other misjudgements; I promised myself I would never use a weapon against the wrong person again, so I gave him another minute before shooting.

«You are aiding the enemy, Professor Wagner» he said with unwavering voice, as if he didn't have a gun pointed at his chest. «You must follow your conscience, not your ambitions, to be on the side of righteousness and truth. That cloth must be protected and spiritually understood. Your funders, who drink blood in their initiation ceremonies and are guilty of abominations, don't understand the inner meaning of the *Maât* and will never be able to access archaic knowledge. But you can still redeem yourself. Don't let their materialism smother your desire for inner search, because sooner or later their exuberance will lead even you to an intellectual regression and then nothing of what you have learned will be able to guide you towards Harmony.»

I had a moment of uncertainty. The destabilising

presence of that man, his words, his manners did nothing but further alter my vision of the Sator and of that far-fetched story of which I was protagonist and antagonist at the same time. I hid my doubts behind my usual mask of cynicism and replied firmly: «I've already sold my soul to the devil, you're late. Leave before I decide to kill you both. Look for your cloth elsewhere, not in my house» and I shot at their feet to prompt them to run off, then I lowered the weapon and put it back in safety once they were gone. The two men had disappeared, but the memory of our meeting would not vanish as quickly.

I picked up my hat and got into their car, not knowing what to do and where to go. After a few miles I left the car in a remote area and thought to go to one of the people closest to me: Rosemarie Meyer, Romy to her friends.

Caught up in the thousand thoughts that crowded my mind, I didn't worry about the time and I rang the doorbell, waking up the neighborhood, too.

The light from inside lit up and a silhouette beyond the stained-glass door approached and opened. Romy stood impassively for a few moments, looking at me: I was reappearing in her life after two years of absence with no explanations of sorts. She hadn't changed much since the last time we met, but she looked more womanly, or perhaps it was the dressing gown that underlined her femininity. I know for sure that she didn't wait one more second to slam the door in my face. So I was left to stare at the polychrome pieces of glass that separated us, like a beggar. I stood there for several minutes before she decided to give me a second chance and let me in.

When she turned on the lamp in the hall, she realised that I had been beaten up. «Who did this to you?» she asked, worried.

«I'd prefer not to tell you.»

«As usual» she replied with two brimming eyes that made me feel like lowlife. I only managed to tell her that I was sorry, so she thought well to show me all her indulgence by giving me a fat slap. «You are sorry, uh? You disappeared overnight with no word about your enlistment and now you are sorry! I only found out thanks to your friend Kopf, who apparently knew more than I did. Couldn't you tell me? I thought our friendship mattered!»

«If I had told you, you wouldn't have let me go and I couldn't allow myself to change my mind at that time» I justified myself.

My God, I would never explain my actions to anyone, not even to my superiors, who demanded that I did, instead, but with her, everything took on a different tone and, although I hated to admit it, she knew how to manipulate me into showing myself to her as a totally different person. I had so many memories related to our friendship, many of which unforgettable. Romy had always been the embodiment of my best conscience, a sort of guardian angel, or perhaps just the colors missing from my life in gray and red. We had known each other since school and I would never hurt her for any reason. But I already did.

«You can swear I wouldn't let you go, I didn't want to see you dead!» she exclaimed furiously. «Damn it, you frightened me and now you come back to my door! I should throw you onto the street and call the police.»

So I thought I'd resort to my brazenness as a defense weapon. «But you won't, because you adore me.»

«You're such a brassy, impudent man! Maybe you just need another good smack» and she finished the sentence in a funny laugh that erased any grudges. She was just like that and I loved her for it.

With the light bathing her face, I saw that she was more beautiful than I remembered. Her golden brown hair, twisted in a soft braid, made her delightfully feminine, and her face, sweet and refined like that of a nineteenth-century lady, reminded me how pleasant it was to observe her features. She had always remained true to herself, immutable and admirable as a work of art.

Romy soaked a handkerchief in alcohol and placed it on my cheekbone. «Let me take a look at the wound. Uhm, why did you come here if you don't want to explain anything to me?»

«I have been working for the Ahnenerbe» I chilled her.

Romy stopped and immediately realised that something in me had broken. It was clear from her expression that she didn't share this last life choice of mine either. Her smile became unhappy and her eyes lost all their glow. «You! My God, I would never have imagined...»

«That the war had changed me so much?»

She threw the bloodied handkerchief to the ground and looked at me in disbelief. «You can put on the clothes of the man without scruples, but you know better than me that it doesn't suit you. There are many controversial stories about the Ahnenerbe. You'll end up contemplating only the dark side of an existence others decided for you!»

I had the impression of re-enacting the conversation I had had with Thomas Krüger. «No one decided for me. Nobody forced me to work for the foundation, just as nobody forced me to fly for a living!» I raised my voice and then regretted it. «Do you know what the truth is? The truth is that I am the only cause of my pain and, even in the case of an imposition, I could never feel at peace with my conscience by blaming somebody else.»

«I know what you're like, Alexander, and I know that it's not like you to struggle to repress the moral strength you have inside, so stop it, please, stop playing the conscienceless man to conform to your superiors. Does the Ahnenerbe have anything to do with your attempted execution? Because that's what it was, wasn't it?»

It's not easy to describe what I felt while I was talking to Romy about certain matters. She had to stay out of them, yet I hoped for her help, for the comfort that she could give me just being close.

«It was two foreigners who wanted some information» I told her, trying to minimize what happened. «I don't know who they were yet, but they spoke to each other in Arabic. I remember well only one word, nothing more.»

«Now everything's clear to me!» she exclaimed sarcastically.

Romy was then working as an interpreter for the authorities in Berlin and, although I had not planned to ask her for help with a translation, I thought I would take advantage of it. «Those two dudes talked about a certain Alliance of Nūr and then something I don't remember the pronunciation of and...»

«Nūr šamši?» she immediately responded.

«Yes!» I exulted impressed by her perspicacity. «But how the heck did you know, what does that mean?»

«Nūr šamši means "sunlight". The two terms often go hand in hand, I'm no Saint Malachy!» she replied and pulled her long dressing gown closer around her.

«The Sunlight Alliance» I repeated aloud.

«The past few days the delegates of the Grand Muftī of Jerusalem and other people of their retinue have been visiting the city» she explained. «If you can boast friendships among the SS, I don't understand why they would clash with you, since their leader, Al-Husaynī, is a great friend of the Führer.»

«Perhaps they work in another Islamic faction outside the Muftī. What else do you know about Al-Husaynī?» I asked her, more confused than ever.

«That it is confidential information» she replied pretending to be haughty, thus arousing my hilarity.

«What? Don't make me laugh, you never keep anything from me.»

«Far from it!» she took offense.

«Stop this charade, Romy. I've been beaten up… don't you want to help me unmask my attackers? Some friend you are! Maybe you hired those two criminals yourself, didn't you?»

«I thought about it, then gave up. Now, back to the diplomatic issue, it has been rumored, for some time now, that Hitler is inclined to finance the Arab movement for at least two reasons: anti-Semitism and the supply of Iraqi oil. I'm pretty positive that, Al-Husaynī is already on the Abwehr's payroll under a false name. However, I don't think they ever referred to their alliance with the term Nūr šamši. You have to look for another explanation. Also, your relationship with Himmler's foundation keeps you safe from Grand Muftī's extremist Islam.»

Romy's argument was flawless.

«From now on, I'd better watch my back: my enemies seem to be popping up like mushrooms» I told her as I got up from the chair to reach the door, still limping from the wound in my calf.

«What are you going to do now? Will you disappear again for a few years or will you show up from time to time?» she asked me with a streak of reproach.

«It's better that I stay away from you, believe me, it's for your sake. In the last two weeks they've already tried to kill me twice!»

«I have nothing to do with it. Just so you know.»

«I really hope so, you're the only one I can still trust!» and I embraced her amicably.

The heat emanating from her body had the power to warm me up, inside my very soul, and the scent of her dress made me recall happy memories. I brought my face close to hers to enjoy, probably for the last time, that moment of endless tenderness. I realised in a second that my inner turmoil would only ever be appeased in her arms. I looked at Romy to impress her face on my mind and make it indelible, then I left with the certainty that I could still count on her love.

Germany – Berlin, September 16, 1937

It was late. Angelika had been waiting for me in her office since eight o'clock, but a setback with Karl, who had seemed to me more intent on hindering our meeting than having a chat, delayed me. He had showed up at my house to tell me about his trip to Italy, his latest fling and how much he had appreciated I accepted Ahnenerbe's assignment. I managed to get rid of him, more or less politely, only an hour later. Outside, the storm would have drenched me from head to toe, but if I had waited for the next bus, Angelika would never have forgiven me. So I went on foot. The smell of the rain on the tarmac was pleasant, the same could not be said of its impetus. To my rescue, providence sent Gottfried: that raving lunatic invited me to get into his car. From the moment I closed the door till I got out of the vehicle, he didn't stop talking for an instant. I was so focused on that morning's meeting to plan the trip that I listened only to a tenth of his ramblings. I quickly thanked him and ran to the museum entrance, feeling relieved.

It was pouring down and the wood of the door was so damp that I had to pry it open to enter. I was soaking wet. I unloaded all the water puddled on my hat outside, but I couldn't prevent my shoes from leaving footprints on the shiny floor.

I repeatedly knocked on the office door, but no one answered, so I went in, while calling for permission. The curtains were still drawn; I pushed them aside a bit to let some light in and placed the bag on the desk top, waiting for Angelika. She appeared as a vision a few moments later. She was drying her bosom with a towel when she jumped at my sight. We were both stunned. I inferred that the rain had caught her unprepared, too. The white cotton dress, which adhered to her body like a second skin, didn't leave much to the imagination. I saw she was deeply embarrassed by my unannounced presence and she stammered something incomprehensible.

«Hello. It's really a beautiful, beautiful day» I said.

She folded the towel and laughed looking at the pitiful state in which we both were. «Sorry, I... you see, I know I'm not presentable, but...»

I smiled at her. «Even so, you're beautiful.»

I hurried to lock the office door to prevent us from being disturbed again by some "Uta" guarding the museum.

«I've already told you, Alexander, I can't allow this» she hurried to clarify as I moved closer, «not now and not with...» she tried to repeat, but her sentence faded as she melted like butter in my arms, ready to surrender herself to me without any restraint.

I felt her lips burn on contact with my skin and I returned that voluptuous pleasure she gave me with equal passion. When I spotted a different light in her gaze, I had the certainty I possessed her. Since I had never been able to temper the surges of my soul, I made love to her with ardour and stayed until late. We were still lying when, after caressing my shoulders, her hand trailed up to the nape of my neck uncovering my tattoo of the Templar cross pattée along my hairline. It was a tribute that I owed, in some way, to the Order. I still remember my mother's anger when she found out about it, as well as her "absolution" for that sin I had indulged in; after all, she knew well the reasons that had led me to make that gesture. Angelika, on the other hand, was amazed.

«You are...» she started, lying down beside me like a Greek goddess, covered only by a small flap of that dress, which was by then laying abandoned on the backrest of the couch.

«No, I'm not one of them, but I owe the Order a debt of gratitude» I replied while removing that annoying strip of cotton. «When I was ten, I gravely damaged a cervical vertebra. I don't even remember how long I was in the hospital. I knew that, at best, I would lose the use of my lower limbs. My parents were inconsolable. I remember seeing my father cry for the first and only time in my life.»

«I guess it's a bad memory you'd rather not dig up» she said, receiving all my tenderness like an ephemeral gift.

«Far from it. My mother was convinced that the healing was due to a holy card depicting the Madonna of Loreto next to five Templar crosses. That sacred image had been given to her by my grandfather and she prayed to it so much that I can still see the scene before my eyes: sat in front of the window with the holy card in her hands, she whispered and hissed while softly uttering the litany under her breath. That went on for a long time until the impossible happened: the damaged vertebra healed without any surgery. Overnight. Just like that. I think doctors, as of today, are still wondering how it could have happened, and mention me among the cases incomprehensible for science.»

«So that little cross pattée is your tribute to the Virgin?»

«No, I'm not a Catholic, but I wanted it to remind me to believe in miracles. Unlike believers, I cannot give any name to the Creator, although I firmly believe that there is an impartial one somewhere. In spite of everything, I still cannot explain why he wanted to save the life of a man who, years later, would sow death and destruction. Maybe it was an oversight.»

«If so, I'm happy with his mistake» she replied as she picked up the clothes we had scattered all over the room.

I was laying on the couch and watched her getting dressed. I confess that I caught every movement of her body and hands, mesmerized, as she was slipping the stockings back on, rolling them up her legs.

«If Karl knew...» I told her, amused at the idea of letting him stew in his own juice, but Angelika immediately changed her expression, as if I had touched a sore spot. «What's the matter with you? Do you think he doesn't imagine?»

She knelt beside me and kissed my hand. «I prefer that he doesn't know about us. Please deny everything should he confront you.»

«Who cares, Angelika! You're not a little girl and then, why should he oppose? I've known him since I was a kid!» I exclaimed, springing to my feet, annoyed by the request.

«Please, Alexander, Karl has become extremely protective of late. He considers me as a daughter, really, and I owe him. He took care of my education, he gave me a home, a maid and secured me a respectable profession. If he finds out that we are lovers, he'll get into a towering rage, I'm sure of it, and I don't want our intimacy to be limited to one day.»

«That means he'll kill me only when he discovers it, but it will be worth it» I replied trying to play it down.

«I wish I could plan the future to my liking, believe me, but for now I prefer living in the present as best as I can. *Carpe Diem*. Always remember that we are part of a higher plan... like the great Sinuhe said: "As if it were the design of a God".»

In all honesty, the idea of being part of a higher plan made me feel a puppet in the hands of the Ahnenerbe once again. Luckily, Angelika decided to entice me with her proposal to spend the night at hers and so I suddenly abandoned all my grey conjectures.

«Well, that way we can study the expedition route before dinner» she said happily, only to realise that the trip was the least of my thoughts. «We have to submit the program to Dietrich, have you forgotten?»

«Try to calm down» I reassured her, «we'll have all the time.»

«Don't say nonsense, we haven't studied anything yet!» she replied, pointing to a box full of maps and photographic images.

«What if I astonish you?» I asked her, sure of myself.

«Why, isn't that what you always do?»

«Then you have no reason to worry» and I showed her a collection of papers on which I had noted down, step by step, all the stages of our journey in search of the origins. «And tonight you'll be staying at my house. I don't want to wake up tomorrow morning and find Uta's ugly face instead of yours.»

Angelika laughed as she imagined the scene. «I don't mean to share you with other women, least of all my cook! Anyways, she'll be gone for a few days» she winked.

«Whew, shrewd and far-sighted, darling» I replied while I was buttoning up my shirt, which was dry already. «You should do me a favour. I need this material» and I handed her a list that she hesitated to accept. «I'd like to stop by at the monastery on Monte Amiata before leaving for Egypt. I have to figure out where the linen was kept and if the SS men underestimated some details. Please take care of the documents and everything else.»

Angelika looked at me, puzzled, before bursting into a loud laugh. «Oh, well, it's not at all flattering that my man, right after he has had me, wishes to go lock himself up in a monastery!»

I smiled at her, assuming that, if I had devoted myself to prayer after every woman I seduced, I would certainly have taken the place of the Holy Father. Since I couldn't possibly confess what my true thoughts were at that moment, I opted for something more elegant: «You're not a sin to be forgiven, Angelika, you're rather a reward to relish.»

She winked at me while fixing my tie's knot, after which she granted me her full cooperation, although she imagined Dietrich's disappointment at my unscheduled departure only a few days before the expedition.

In fact, I strongly doubted that I would have his full support, on the contrary, I was convinced that he would forbid me to leave Germany to go to Italy, since the Secret Service had already opened a dossier about me. I needed to clarify the story Ritter had told me, though. Therefore, if the SD had really considered me a threat to the agreement between the Duce and our Führer, surely the Ahnenerbe wouldn't have endorsed my unplanned trip, and the SS men would have stalked me for the whole time. I also tried my luck for an ulterior motive, too: I needed more material for my evaluation and where else would I find new details, other than in the place where St. Bernard's linen had been preserved?

Italy – Val D'Orcia, September 19, 1937

Somehow, Angelika managed to convince Dietrich to let me go to Tuscany, so I left, my fake identification document in one hand and a small suitcase in the other.

In the northernmost part of Monte Amiata lies the Val d'Orcia, with its rich history and endless rows of cypresses. Before me, a pastel landscape of green and golden hills, whose soft curves stood out on the horizon and filled my eyes.

I had been travelling in a shabby car for more than an hour, when the driver abandoned me in the middle of a cluster of houses in an unnamed village. From there on, I would continue by bicycle to the abbey, which was about four miles away.

Before reaching the monastery complex, I found a sheltered area where I could change my clothes. Although paradoxical, for the occasion I chose to wear the cloak of Don Vincenzo Valli, assistant to the Prefect of the Vatican Apostolic Library; I slipped on a pair of moleskin pants under the cassock and reached the entrance of the monastery. A Cistercian monk on his knees was uprooting weeds from between the stones of a low wall. I was behind him, but he didn't notice my presence until he saw my shadow stretching before his eyes. He then turned apathetically and, despite his venerable age, I could spot the signs of a lively intellect in his gaze. He was more stooped than a pastoral staff, but he still proudly wore the pale tunic and black scapular characteristic of his order.

When the old man asked me who I was and what I was looking for, I didn't hesitate to offer him my letter of introduction signed by cardinal Giulio Barberati. I explained, endeavoring to strip my Italian of the Teutonic accent, that the Prefect of the Vatican Library had decided to examine the cataloging, the restoration, as well as the copying process of the ancient manuscripts surviving the fire happened not a long while back. I had been sent there for an inspection with the intention of assessing the conditions of the documents.

The elderly man was very hard of hearing, it was then, that a young monk stepped in and introduced himself as brother Mariano. «I have to ask you to please wait at the gate and let me hand all your documents over to our father superior» he said obsequiously.

«Of course» I replied with equal politeness.

«Forgive our rigour, but following the recent tragic events, of which the Vatican is already aware, the abbot was forced to forbid access to the monastery to anyone not belonging to our congregation and, if I haven't his approval, I can't let anyone in. Not even you. I'm just a humble chorister» he justified himself before leaving me at the foot of a statue of the Virgin.

Time had apparently slowed down its flow or, maybe, nobody kept any track of it there. I had gone from one extreme to the other: from the impatience of the Ahnenerbe foundation, to the imperturbability of monastic life. The fact is that I waited for a solid forty minutes for someone to come back, trying to appease somehow my anxiety, that would only vanish before the face of that Madonna and her merciful gaze. I wondered what I was doing there, in a monastery and, what's more, wrapped in religious garments! It was like bathing the devil in holy water! I felt like a sinner more than ever, but I managed to find a reason for that absurd chain of events: I was on my way to find out who I really was. Romy and the good Thomas saw one man in me, Angelika and Dietrich saw another, diametrically opposed, and in that place, I realised I preferred the Alexander Wagner of the formers.

Suddenly, as if he had materialized among the greenery, brother Mariano appeared with a hesitant smile printed on his face. «I'm sorry I kept you waiting» he said, beckoning me to go in.

We walked slowly along the road lined by trees whose chiaroscuro effects encouraged mysticism. After passing an ancient fortified entrance, we finally entered a beautiful garden, set like a gem amongst the buildings of that enormous abbey complex. Despite the essentiality of its architecture, the towering church attracted the gaze towards its rose window, symbol of the Almighty, while some spindly palm trees cast their silhouettes onto its walls in a play of light and shadow. At the base of the building, the slender columns of the colonnade, which looked like they could barely hold the weight of the roof, alternately showed and concealed the monks walking by while raptly reading their breviaries. The beauty of Bernardine placidity and balance, and that of the rigor and logical order inherent to the *Civitas Dei*, cocooned everything in that place.

In the distance, I saw the ruins of the monastery wing that had been destroyed by the flames and I strongly resented the authors of that destruction. Only four blackened walls remained of the ancient pharmacy, along with the worn-out memories of what was once the most amazing laboratory in Central Italy.

The monk invited me to follow him and not linger in front of the rubble, since the father superior was already waiting for me. I headed towards a wooden door that brother Mariano pushed back with great effort and, before crossing the threshold, my attention was caught by some Cistercians who were washing their neck and face by three large stone tanks, into which water flowed from as many bent spouts. I was astonished to learn that, not only did they sleep in the same robes used for the day, but they didn't strip out of them for their morning washing either. Two of them, probably two postulants, considering the different color of their tunic, turned in my direction and looked at me with understandable distrust.

I entered without hesitation, but felt out of place. We climbed a large marble staircase before reaching the Abbot's office.

In that room, the shutters hadn't been opened that morning, yet and brother Mariano, instead of doing it himself, switched on the desk lamp and left quickly. I thought he didn't wish to confer again with his superior. I sat down and waited patiently.

When the Abbot appeared on the threshold, he greeted me very formally and went slouching to open the shutters wide, so that the daylight outlined his broad silhouette. After a first glance, once again he asked me to give him my documents, masterfully forged by Dietrich's men. I waited in silence for him to allow me to speak and was troubled by his equivocal look. Clearly I had started off on the wrong foot.

He opened a drawer of his desk and pulled out a small

yellowed piece of paper, little more than a scrap, on which he traced horizontally an elongated arch from left to right.

«May the Divine Master enlighten you» he said, turning the sheet one hundred and eighty degrees and offering me his pen: a splendid red ebonite Aurora.

A self-satisfied blankness appeared on the Abbot's plump face, while his round eyes peered at me demanding a response. I got the sheet closer to me and completed the drawing: countering his first arch with a second one, I started from the left apex and intersected it on the right side so as to outline a stylised fish. It was the symbol identifying the first Christians at the time of persecutions: the *Ichthýs*.

The Abbot smiled, easing the tension. «Welcome amongst us» and he held out his hand for me to kiss.

So I did but, even now, I still feel a certain disgust for that gesture of false submission. «Thanks, Father» I said.

He read my letter of introduction again and, tapping his fingers on the desk, asked me perplexedly: «Cardinal Barberati? I thought the Prefect of the Vatican Library was Cardinal Mercati!»

He caught me unprepared. It was unacceptable. What had become of the professionalism of the Schutzstaffel informers? Did the Secret Services prefer tailing an insignificant pilot like me, rather than high prelates? In order not to blow my cover, I tried to make up for that huge mistake by specifying that it was a recent designation, due to Cardinal Mercati's health problems. «Pity that he was forced to give up his office... he's a man of great culture» I improvised.

«You are absolutely right, of a very high culture. I hope he gets better soon. Well, I will have the brother you already met accompany you on your visit to the remains of the east wing. Are you going to stay with us for long ?»

«I need to take care of other duties back in Rome, so I'm confident that I'll be out of your way by tomorrow evening, or the day after that at the latest» I replied resentful.

«I didn't mean to be rude, on the contrary, it was my desire to arrange a suitable accommodation. If you wish, you can leave your luggage to...»

«I'm a clergyman, like you, Father, and I don't wish to put my brothers in a position of subservience. I'll see to take care of my luggage myself, thank you. Just give me a bed to sleep in for the night and your authorization to visit the monastery.»

I managed to calm down only when I was dismissed and entrusted to the care of the good Mariano, who motioned for me to follow him quickly.

I tried to elicit more specific information about the wing where the cloth was kept, but he seemed reluctant to talk and, before leading me into the crumbling structure, replied almost annoyed: «Unfortunately, we still don't know the causes that led to the fire. If you have specific questions, you should ask them directly to the Abbot, not to me. I'm authorized to show you the building, but please don't take anything away.»

«Yes, brother, I understand your position perfectly» I reassured him. «I don't go against abbot's orders if I take some pictures, I suppose. You won't deny me that too, I hope» I said playfully, trusting in his benevolence.

«I had no instructions on this regard, so I think you can photograph.»

I had already set up my beloved Zeiss Ikonta bellows camera for outdoor shots. The area where I decided to stop was sun-drenched and the pitch black camera body, was scalding hot. The coupled rangefinder system was one of the most advanced and the focusing accuracy of the device was unquestionable, but, to tell the truth, the pleasure of drawing freehand whatever fascinated me was greater than any photo. I realised that I paid more attention to detail when drawing and, in that circumstance, scrupulousness was paramount. I took my notebook out of my bag and, since I have a decent hand as a draughtsman, I sketched a first representation of the ruins of the building in the hope of getting rid of my wet-nurse as soon as possible. Unfortunately, the plan produced quite the opposite effect and Mariano, intrigued by my drawing, instead of getting bored and taking his leave, sat next to me like a faithful dog until I finished my work.

«The fire was unstoppable, powerful as the Devil. It lapped but then spared us» he began all of the sudden while he was following the charcoal traits with his eyes. «The whole structure seemed to crave its own end: it blazed from the inside with inexhaustible heat. It burned like a sinner in hell!» he urged as to invite my response.

«It must have been terrible» I commented, placing a hand on his shoulder to comfort and convince him of my good faith.

«You may not believe me, but it was as if those flames had a voice of their own. I heard the fire change its tone according to the victim, be it a wooden piece of furniture, a book, or...»

«Or one of your brothers» I concluded awaiting his reaction. I saw him paling, almost fainting, then I apologized. «I know about the two monks. Everyone in Rome knows. I feel sorry for them and for all the charred pages of knowledge. Brother, if you don't feel like assisting me on with this inspection, please tell me. I couldn't certainly blame you» and, hoping he would leave, I walked towards the ruins. Unfortunately he continued to tag along.

Inside, the show was mephistophelic. Before my eyes was a blackened wall, whose paneless windows were now like two empty eye sockets on a lifeless face. Next to my feet, a heap of burnt-out wood resembled a bench and nearby only a few melted remains of a candlestick were left. The walls were riddled with metal parts which had projected in every direction when the roof caved-in. I advanced carefully, checking the soundness of the floor at every step and looked up to make sure that the ceiling would hold too. Mariano beckoned me to reach the top of the stairs I could make out at the end of the corridor.

I climbed those two flights and was blinded by the sunlight coming in through a gash on the eastern facade. The pharmacy, or what was left of it, had been destroyed by the flames. The texts that survived the fire had been removed and placed elsewhere, so the library was now empty and unattractive. I scanned that ancient laboratory: it was a true gem, although the Cistercian pointed out that the adjacent room, where there was a substantial collection of precious texts, was indeed the greatest heritage of the monastery. He explained that some of those books were a gift from the Desert Fathers, the founders of the first monastic cluster.

I placed my suitcase and bag onto the ground and

wished I hadn't made that trip in vain. «Good, then once I have done inspecting this room, we will move to the other, which I hope is in better condition» I said.

«Yes, fortunately it is less damaged than the pharmacy. It was used as a medical school a few centuries ago and you will find some interesting and still well preserved material there.»

As the monk spoke, I reached the edge of the floor, just where the wall had collapsed and a gap had opened to the outside. Deaf to his repeated calls, I leaned out to look at the remains of the destroyed laboratory ten meters below.

A warm wind was blowing that day and, with every gust, thousands of shreds of paper and parchment I could spot in the debris were being scattered like seeds across the ploughed fields. My university studies resurfaced at that sight, reminding me that centuries ago those lands belonged to the grange of the Order. Tens of thousands of acres constituted the rural property of each monastery, whose organized management led to the success of the Cistercian agricultural economy.

«But how is it possible that none of you thought of recovering what was left of the texts from the rubble?» I grumbled to the monk who didn't know how to reply. Stupidity is an incurable disease.

The floor was unstable and each tile wobbled under my weight. I even broke a couple stepping on them, while the others came off because of Mariano, who would drag his sandals along the ground so as to wear out his very toenails. I scanned that God-forsaken place without having the slightest idea what to look for, then, suddenly, the revelation: my apathetic cicerone lined the wobbly tiles up against the wall to prevent anyone from stumbling on them and, unknowingly, enlightened me. I started lifting all the loose tiles. Mariano tried to stop me, convinced that I was bothering to make his job easier, but I silenced him in a fairly "unmonastic" way. Removing the dust from my cassock I looked, satisfied, at the religious scholars' arcane work, partially hidden under some more recent art. In the center of the room, on a tile still firmly attached to the ground, an "N" stood out. It had been lying for centuries at the foot of a majestic cypress table, that not even the fire had been able to burn down.

«It stays for North» Mariano explained to me.

I shook my head smiling, but kept my comments to myself. It didn't indicate the North, but the heart of a Sator. It was in fact the only letter deliberately repeated even on the most recent flooring: the central "N" of *Tenet*; all the other letters, which made up the Templar square, were on the oldest layer, which had remained buried under the new for hundreds of years.

Mariano sprang up to keep me from taking the camera. «I should inform the Abbot of this discovery, first...»

«And are you also going to inform him that you have pulled out the tiles on your own initiative?» He froze. «Let me take some photos and roughly sketch the interior of the pharmacy, then we'll find a way not to upset your Father Superior.»

The visible Sator letters of the lower layer were dark and stood out against the remaining brown marble floor. I approximately drew that laboratory, but my interest was more focused on the ground than on broken and blackened mattresses. I was wondering, almost maniacally, why the Sator was in that room and why it was facing South. I assumed that my theory of its Egyptian origin was not as preposterous as some had thought, and that the connection between the cloth and the square was more real than ever. Brother Mariano waited for my work to be finished before asking me about my intentions.

«I'm going to help you put everything back in its place.» I left him jaw-dropping. «Come on, shut that mouth or flies will get in. Help me place the tiles back, because I mean to inspect the medical school next door.»

«But it's almost eleven o'clock and we should go to the refectory.»

My life was so anomalous and devoid of any rule that my day was never marked by the same number of hours as the previous one, nor by the same pace, therefore their habits were infinitely bothersome to me. «Let's fix the flooring tiles back quickly then» I instructed.

We were returning to the monastery and Mariano was proceeding to the refectory at a brisk pace. The smell of soup reached to the east wing and was anything but tempting. My nose, recalling the cooking smells coming from the kitchens of my grandmother and my mother, both so proud of their great national tradition, refused to believe that we were actually in Italy.

At the end of the meals, the monks prepared for the umpteenth liturgical office, the Sext, which was considered one of the minor hours. I soon discovered that I could not go back to the pharmacy before four o'clock, since the Cistercians would rest for a couple of hours before the None. I certainly didn't have all that time to spare: for every extra minute I stayed in the monastery, the chances of being unmasked increased. So I went to the Abbot to clarify the matter. In front of his office I ran into his assistant, who forbade me to disturb him.

«Marshal Gianni Orsini, of the Papal Gendarmerie and a sort of supervisor, or something of the like, named

Lorenza Annunzi, have arrived at the abbey, without notice, for that matter. They have been sent from Rome» he explained gravely, annoyed by the woman's presence. «If you wish to wait here for the meeting to end, you're free to do so, otherwise you can go to the accommodation that has been assigned to you and get some rest.»

I immediately understood that I was in a thorny and somewhat dangerous situation.

The monk read the bewilderment on my face and urged: «I'm surprised that you didn't know.»

«Have you got a vague idea of how many authorities and institutions the Vatican is composed of?» I acidly responded. «I'll wait here, thank you» and I sat on the bench hoping he would leave as soon as possible. I couldn't, I had to avoid meeting those two people. Unfortunately, the secretary stopped for ages at the top of the stairs to talk with another monk and I had to wait a long time. If the guests had come out right then, I could have been at serious risk, but since their voices reached the threshold, as if no closed door protected their confidentiality, I would have known when to slip away. I sat there and took advantage of the situation, trying to understand the reasons for their visit. It didn't take long to get to the point: the theft of the linen. The Abbot's deep voice was easily recognisable. The second male voice had to belong to the gendarme and finally there was a crystalline female one. From their tones, I imagined the marshal was in his forties and the woman at least ten years younger. The Abbot was enraged for their unexpected visit and, above all, because they had forced his monks to give them access to the monastery without his authorization. The marshal asked him to calm down, but the other wouldn't listen to reason and harangued them. The discussion became increasingly heated and, at that point, the whole monastery could easily hear their debate. A year after that episode, I still perfectly remember the spontaneity of their every word.

The Abbot was furious and, in a voice that resounded to the upper floors, shouted: «Do you realise that you have come here accompanied by a... by a woman? This is a monastery and maybe you're accustomed to the presence of certain people, but, we live exclusively a life of prayer instead.»

It was then that the inspectress earned my respect by giving her best. «I'm sorry for you» she answered back. «A life of futility, I'd say, for all your prayers didn't earn you immunity from a devastating accident. Nonetheless, everyone is free to manage their own existence as they see fit, provided they have no regrets at death's door.»

«Not me. But maybe you should revise your *modus vivendi*» the religious shouted.

«Don't worry, Father» she cut short, «I manage my life on a par with my sexuality: freely.»

I hardly held a laugh and regretted I couldn't see the scene but, judging by the long silence that followed the inspectress's statement, the Father Superior must have risked a heart attack. Apparently, not even the gendarme was moved by the elderly man, on the contrary, he insisted that, according to their previous surveys, the crime had been perpetrated by two SS men. One of them, after the monk in charge of the pharmacy had cut off a couple of his fingers, lost his *Totenkopfring*: the ring Himmler awarded his best officers. Before dying, the Cistercian defended himself by brandishing a wide-bladed knife, that was found at the crime scene. At least this was the woman's reading of the facts, which opened yet another quarrel with her interlocutor, who refused to accept her and all her insinuations. The Abbot repeatedly swore that he had never given shelter to criminals and that he would have never let a Nazi in his monastery. Really? So what was I doing in there? I soon gathered from their chatter that the *Totenkopfring* belonged to a certain Otto Heyder. I didn't know him, but I tried to keep that name in mind all the same. At the end of their meeting, the Abbot had to accept it had been arson. I was amazed when I learned that St. Bernard's linen was in the medical school next to the pharmacy, and not in the pharmacy library, as I expected. A moment later I heard the chairs scratching the floor: that meeting was drawing to a close and I had to leave or they would have caught me eavesdropping like an impertinent boy. I was dying to see the inspectress and her partner's faces, so, supposing they would take the stairs to go back to the ground floor, I slipped in the first corridor and waited there.

The woman crossed the threshold of the study followed by the gendarme, while the Abbot shut them out of his office unconcerned about good manners. I was a few feet away from the two, in a windowless hallway leading who knows where. The woman's crisp perfume miraculously managed to overcome the mouldy smell of the monastery. I saw her from behind. Pity. She was about five feet, four inches tall and had a small but pretty figure. I saw her tidying her auburn hair under an elegant hat and, judging by the satisfied look of the gendarme, I deduced that her face was as pleasant as her body. But then, how could a man not be pleased with such an extraordinary and singular model of womanly resourcefulness?

I ran to the east wing, alone. I imagined that Mariano was already sleeping like an infant. My Zeiss still had four more photos available, but I didn't want to waste them. When I reached the doorstep of the medical room, I stopped to take in every detail before entering and inspecting the rest with the same attention. And so I was in the place where the linen had been kept, finally. I still didn't understand why the founding fathers had allocated it to the school. My only certainty was the reason for the concealment: its "heathen sinfulness".

I placed a hand on the wooden shelf that ran along the wall and stared at the frescoed ceiling where a sun cast its golden rays over the four cherubs at the corners of the room. After the collapse in the pharmacy, even that painting had suffered some damage but nothing irreparable. While I was quickly sketching the layout of the rooms a crunch made me jump. I turned suddenly and saw Mariano at the top of the stairs. He told me that he had given up his nap to assist me and I tried to show him my gratitude forcing a smile; he realised it, but he stood by, stretching his neck to look at my booklet. I noticed that I had written the word "Pharmazie" on the notebook and hurried to rub it out before the Cistercian would notice. That carelessness could have cost me dear.

We spent a while checking the furniture and the anatomy books stored in the closets, then he addressed me: «May I ask you a question?»

«You may.»

«What do you think of medicine and surgery?»

«Such a question already implies an unorthodox position on the topic, am I right?» I asked promptly.

Mariano looked at me wide-eyed and, between a stutter and the other, he tried to excuse himself for the impudence.

«I infer that you don't share some of your superiors'

views. But don't you worry» I reassured him, «I'm not your superior, nor would I forbid my subordinates to have their own opinion if I were, so feel free to express your ideas in my presence.»

The monk sported his best smile while avowing his passion for the subject, confessing that, however, it would have been better to avoid such topics in some places.

«Ah, right, I see. You abide by medieval precepts around here! The Abbot considers doctors as bold and equally reckless men, who meddle in God's work. He must have been impressed by the Fourth Lateran Council's decisions, but someone should remind him that more than seven hundred years have passed since! So, brother Mariano, I'm telling you how I see it: theology and science are part of the same divine plan and unless we believe they are related, we'll never feel fulfilled.»

I couldn't understand why I was trying so hard to enlighten the poor man's mind; perhaps I hoped that, if he changed his life, he would feel a better man, or perhaps I did it just to get more information about that place, which was leaving me somewhat perplexed. I didn't quite understand what hid among those worm-eaten shelves, in those dark rooms, where dust and pieces of plaster had fallen from the ceiling and taken the place of work tools.

«Look» he called me, «on this rectangular table, they would perform surgery in front of the students. We were forced to move it to this side for fear that the roof would cave-in and damage it.»

«So was this table once in the middle of the room? Under the frescoed sun?» and heedless of his confirmation, I looked up at the work of art above me with different eyes. «Now I see why the Abbot and all his predecessors have been keeping the school rooms locked up for years!»

Mariano eyed me up, stunned, and insistently asked for an explanation. Could I ever confess to a Cistercian that the godly light illuminating that room, and his life, too, belonged to the Aten and not to Yahweh? I hurried and took a photograph, then, on a new page of the notebook, I copied the huge Egyptian solar disk, whose rays opened into as many blurry, almost invisible, hands.

Mariano hesitated and looked around before speaking. «There is another reason for the interdiction of this school, but it's kind of a legend whispered amongst the younger monks and the lay brothers...»

«Well?»

«It seems that, up to a century ago, some monks periodically devoted themselves to certain alchemical rituals» he explained.

«What else do you know?»

«That they were the direct disciples of the Desert Fathers. It is rumored that each novice had to undergo tough tests. Of all the students, only a small number could dream of becoming a disciple. It was a tradition handed down from the fifth century. Nothing else is known, except that the school was closed up when one of them was accused of witchcraft and the most unconventional texts were burned. With one exception...»

«Saint Bernard's linen» I said without thinking.

«You know?!» he was surprised. «They say that the Virgin was so beautiful her persecutors were urged to spare her. I wish I could see her! How is it even possible that you didn't catalogue it somewhere in Rome?»

It was pure truth, not a myth. That linen had the power to overcome human will, to conquer whoever held it in their hands. I wasn't the only one to succumb to Isis' charm.

The sun was sinking below the horizon and my time was running out. I was close to completing the sketch of the room when we heard voices at the bottom of the stairs. Mariano explained that the gendarme and the inspectress had specifically requested to return to the site of the fire before evening.

«I have no intention of meeting those two: my superior has never looked favorably upon their interference in certain affairs» I invented.

«Don't worry. This way» and he showed me a secondary way out. «However, you need to know that they won't be leaving before a couple of days and that their accommodations are right next to yours.»

I decided to leave the monastery that evening, so I greeted Mariano and he, well aware we would never see each other again, said goodbye and uttered a "thank you" that even today makes me wonder whether he followed his true ambition as a doctor after that, or gave it up and continued living in the shadow of that monastery.

Germany – Berlin, September 23, 1937

I was in Berlin on the morning of September 23rd to meet Dietrich at the Ahnenerbe headquarters and give him the photographs I shot at the monastery. He disapproved of Hauptsturmführer Otto Heyder's conduct to retrieve the cloth as much as I did. Nevertheless, he concluded with a cynical "it's the outcome that matters".

When I left the office, I stepped on the first bus and got off at the corner of Hedemannstrasse and Wilhelmstrasse, where the headoffice of the German National Socialist Workers' Party was located.

At that time, around ten in the morning, there were many passers-by along the streets of a Berlin that was all decked out and ready to welcome Benito Mussolini. The city was changing, even the shop windows had been rearranged in view of the event which, it was said, would attract millions of visitors. There was a strange euphoria in the air, by which, however, I was unable to let myself be carried away, although a historical meeting between the Führer and the Duce was certainly to be expected. Honestly, I deemed an agreement between those two to be quite complicated: they would court each other, then move away, like in a relationship with many dark sides. Also, there was a widespread belief that Joseph Goebbels opposed that pact and that the coming and going of Italians in our country bothered him, especially after the persistent rumour of a new anti-German trend urged by the Catholics and Jews of the peninsula.

I ran to a nearby club where I was to join Karl and, since my day was going to be busy with meetings and appointments, I hoped he wouldn't keep me long with his chatter. Eventually, it all ended up in him wishing me a successful mission in Egypt and giving some vaguely paternal recommendations. I perceived his satisfaction for my choice to work with the Ahnenerbe, though he considered my presence beside Angelika not very reassuring. We left with a greeting and a promise to meet again for a beer upon my return.

I got home just before noon. I had already packed the suitcase and only the "one-off piece" was left to fit in: the linen, which I had placed between two wooden slabs. I had the odd idea of shoving it in the upper hollow of my study door. I raised my arm and touched the top of it, then plunged my fingers into the groove to pull the two strings the slabs were attached to. I made the panels slide simultaneously inside the slot, then separated them and looked again at the beautiful Black Virgin, in my eyes, the alchemical emblem of the origin and the matrix of all things.

After notifying me of his arrival, the driver waited for me in the street, leaving the engine of a splendid Adler running. I hurried and put St. Bernard's linen in its place but, as soon as I crossed the threshold, I found Romy facing me.

«Hello, what are you doing here?» I asked, surprised to see her at the door of my house.

«So you're leaving again without saying goodbye» she scolded me.

I mentally went through the apology repertory in my vocabulary, but found nothing appropriate, least of all convincing. «I have to go, I'm sorry. There's so much confusion in my life right now that I don't think I can give you all the explanations you deserve» I tried to patch it up expecting her farewell hug. She turned her back on me instead, and walked away taking a side street without even saying goodbye.

I ran after Romy and found her in the book shop down the street. While she was absently leafing through a novel, I whispered in her ear: «I'm not going to war this time. Yesterday I slipped a note under your door to tell you of my departure. Didn't you find it?»

«Of course I did, that's why I've come.»

I understood that I wouldn't solve the situation in a minute, but my conscience wouldn't allow me to leave, knowing that she was angry. I followed her through the shelves after avoiding the bookshop assistant's inquisitive gaze.

«So why are we arguing again?» I asked in a whisper.

«I don't know» she replied dryly and, without saying anything else, sneaked out of that place.

I followed her, still carrying the suitcase that kept getting stuck in every corner of the shop. Something about that conversation eluded me. «What does that mean?» I snapped when I caught up with her. «I'm here because I don't want to leave knowing you're angry and you're telling me you have no idea what's swirling around in your head?»

«Off you go, be quick, or that man will leave you behind» she said with a hint of a smile. «I wish you luck,

112

wherever you are headed. But, please, be careful.»

At that point, I placed my luggage on the ground and sighed. «Talk to me, Romy, or I won't go. What's so important that you needed to tell me?»

She highlighted the earnestness of her thoughts with a sad sigh. «You know all too well what I'd like to tell you.»

It was clear, it had always been to both of us that we weren't just friends and that we hadn't been for a long time now. I had developed the belief that lasting, strong and close friendship between man and woman could only exist in preteen age. There was a boundary beyond which that honest and equally profound feeling had to abandon its naivety and rearrange itself, or disappear altogether. I was in a tricky position, to say the least. I had resolved to never let myself go when I was with Romy; our relationship was special and had to be preserved, so I didn't want it to step beyond the line of that hypocritical friendship. I didn't mean to hurt her, yet I had done it, as if my attempts had produced the opposite of what I hoped for. It was terribly unfair: I thought that taking yet another dead end in my life would have protected her from misery, on the contrary I had caused her more pain. I was already haunted by so many remorses that I couldn't bear that one, too. That's why I had always been barricading myself behind an unpleasant cynicism, but that day I decided to go beyond that. I realised that although my universe was continually at the mercy of the most absolute chaos, she was the only safe haven I could always retreat to. She looked at me with graceful eyes so full of melancholy that, I am sure, they could deter even an army from its purpose. I caressed her face and lingered on her splendid heart-shaped mouth, which had never been so close before. I let myself be tempted and finally surrendered to the allure of her lips. I kissed her for a long time, tenderly, oblivious to the comments of passers-by walking behind me. I had harboured that desire for so many years, that I wasn't willing to relinquish it very soon, but from the bliss of that pure gesture, I only got a great deal of confusion and all my efforts to find something appropriate to say were useless.

«Go, your girlfriend and your job are waiting for you» she froze me. «If you weren't so damned unpredictable, I wouldn't love you so much. I really must be crazy» and she kissed me again before getting on the first bus and disappearing from my life once again.

Her last words were like a shot in the chest. I stood there motionless, staring at the traffic and wondering when and if I would see her again.

We picked Angelika up before taking the Reich Autobahn, the highway which would allow us to travel comfortably and at high speed for the most part of our journey. I was not told why we couldn't travel by train, but after all, I wasn't interested in the means of transport, but in the destination. Our Adler travelled fast, reaching sixty-five miles per hour on some straight stretches and I liked that brisk pace. Angelika, on the other hand, didn't have the same opinion as me and would have preferred a comfortable railway carriage by far.

That endless ribbon of concrete cut through the landscape like a placid river and encouraged to enjoy the driving. It was an innovation that amazed and filled us with pride: a majestic work based on the Italian model, whose construction had employed over one hundred and twenty thousand workers. A smart move in favour of Nazi propaganda, which had won the approval of the masses.

Like most at that time, I saw in that endless road, the future of Germany, its genius and its industriousness.

We stayed overnight at a hotel in Garmisch or, more to the point, Garmisch-Partenkirchen, after the two municipalities had been unified for the fourth edition of the Olympic Games.

The director welcomed us enthusiastically and promptly clapped his hands to draw the porter's attention. After registering us in his hotel guest book, he proudly gave us his best vacant rooms and assigned me the same accommodation, or so he claimed, where Franz Pfnür, gold medalist in alpine skiing, had stayed the year before. Although I liked winter sports, I replied with a cliché smile because, after sitting in a car for almost nine hours in a row, I would have happily rested even at the cheapest boarding house, giving up all comforts except for a bed.

Italy – Genoa, September 24, 1937

After crossing Italy's border, we finally reached the harbour of Genoa, the beautiful *urbs maritima*, surrounded by two strips of land, to the east and to the west, and protected by mountains, which mitigated its climate. I couldn't even imagine how many famous people and how many hopeful emigrants had trodden that pier. The lively bustle of eloquent gestures and sounds, told about the many people longing for a new haven for their lives. Centuries of history overlapped by that sea, whose blue waters flattered my gaze, while the ready-to-sail imposing ships showed the excellence of Genoese shipbuilding industry. I would have loved being on that same pier centuries ago, when its features resembled a sea-view emporium, when people negotiated for the purchase of precious artifacts and yearned for exotic destinations and knowledge. "Exotic destinations and knowledge". The words echoed in my head reminding me that I, too, was one of that handful of men who were ready to set sail for a recognizable location, yet were looking for a rather ephemeral revelation. I looked up to the clouds and thought about the Sator. Ready to leave Europe to grasp a troublesome truth, I knew I could only find it on the opposite shore of the Mediterranean. I convinced myself I wasn't chasing a utopia: I had in fact to uncover a conspiracy against an ancient knowledge, that could potentially undermine the foundations of the great monotheistic faiths.

St. Bernard's cloth had become my guide along the path that would lead me to the Sator and to enlightenment. Different Egyptian gods had been represented, and later concealed, in it: Amun, Horus and Isis. I had gathered that the depiction was a pseudo-map that would suggest to me where to go to recover that heritage of wisdom belonging to the Shemsu Hor, Guardians of Horus. That is why, I intended to take Angelika to Luxor, Edfu and Philae, since those three cities were directly influenced by the worship of the deities painted on the linen. Once on the spot, I hoped to find the link between the Sator text and the culture of the ancient Egyptian priests.

I dismissed our driver, while Angelika and I were waiting to board our ship. Due to an alleged mishap, there was a delay, but finally, after several hours, we were ready to leave Genoa and Europe aboard a medium-sized vessel.

We found ourselves on the main bridge watching the Italian coastline recede. While the other passengers euphorically greeted their families and friends still standing on the pier, Angelika took my hand and I immediately understood that her hopes were as tied to that trip to Egypt as mine. She looked at me, so proud and confident as to rouse a wholesome optimism in me. I had become, to all effects, a scholar of the Ahnenerbe, a man of the foundation. I felt proud of that. If I had succeeded in my enterprise, and I had brought the matrix , the origin of the Sonnenmensch, back to Germany, I would have realised not only Himmler's vision, but my academic dream as well.

Egypt – Alexandria, September 27, 1937

When we reached Alexandria, we went to the station and waited there for the local guide to arrive. The sea trip from Genoa had been rather comfortable, but extremely boring.

We had been waiting for over an hour. Angelika was fanning herself with her hat and snorted impatiently. I, on the other hand, was enjoying the gardens in front of me, embellished with light marble fountains that stood out in the middle of that green oasis. The flowerbeds were well-tended and delimited by low flowery borders that seemingly aimed to "westernise" a bit that barren land.

After about two hours, a well-dressed olive-skinned man approached us. «Professor Wagner and Fräulein Blumen?» he finally asked with a smile that he could have spared us, given his loathsome teeth. «I'm Khaled and I will be your guide throughout your stay.»

We hadn't arranged for a stopover along the route between Alexandria and Luxor. We would stay in the latter for a few days, and then head to the island of Philae, provided that Dietrich didn't decide to cancel the expedition ahead of schedule for lack of results.

King Farouk's Egypt could flaunt just the illusion of its independence from the British government, as it was still heavily conditioned by it. I learnt from Angelika that, thanks to the good relationship between the Reich and the extremist Arab world, the Ahnenerbe had conquered a circle of trustworthy partners in Egypt, Lebanon and Jordan who, although not belonging to the official lists of the affiliates, were working to all intents and purposes for what they considered a mutual benefit: anti-Semitism. Indeed, there had been many positive comments in Arab newspapers and congratulations on the Führer's takeover. Islamic fundamentalist fringe and the Hizb Misr El-Fatah, better known as the Young Egypt Party, born to oppose the British Empire, immediately welcomed the Nazi ideal with open arms. In recent years Palestine had become no less than a small Germany. During a cross-border visit, Khaled himself had been surprised at the numerous swastikas his neighbours had hung on their walls. The Reich program had first encouraged the emigration of Jews to Palestine and then, the risk that it might facilitate the creation of a Jewish state had forced the Führer to sign an alliance with the Arab world. At that time, the Egyptians Khaled called Muslim Brothers had gone so far as to attribute heaven to Allah and earth to Hitler!

After about half-an-hour trip, our southbound train to Aswan terminus had to stop at a halfway station, due to a breakdown.

A slight wind lifted that talcum-fine sand, which would stick to the sweaty skin and seep in the fabric wefts. Also, I was surprised how high the temperature still was in late September. Most of the foreign travellers, embittered by the heat wave, were willing to spend a fortune on low quality fans, so that the merchants ended up filling their pockets without even having to bargain.

The carriage had overheated a little too much for my

liking, so I went out to get some fresh air. The landscape around there was of no interest; not even the sight of the local laborers struggling with a pile of luggage on rickety carts could arouse my curiosity. They looked like many mediocre industrious ants, endlessly replicating gestures and paths inherited from their predecessors: it was the Egyptian custom and I guessed that some people didn't even aspire to a different employment. The heat was truly hellish. I just wanted that damned train to leave. In Germany that would never have happened and I was beginning to harbour a dislike for the locals, especially towards Khaled, who would always display his moronic smile.

Tourists travelling along the Nile valley preferred trains because of their reliability, so there was never a shortage of local men and boys around, ready to serve them in exchange for a tip. Unfortunately the Egyptian railways had chosen that very day to ruin their good reputation. The train departed several hours later and, while Angelika checked the documents and the itinerary again, I let my thoughts drown in the memories of my first trip to that extraordinary land.

At that time, my parents and I had sailed up the Nile aboard a beautiful river ship. I remembered well my mother painting the landscapes during the voyage. I had loved that breathtaking nature then and I was now once more fascinated by the combination of water, sand and greenery.

As our train was running to make up for the delay, dozens of herons flanked it in a blaze of sprightliness. People working in the fields paused at the passing carriages and even the buffaloes stopped plowing, curious about the iron giant that was transporting us from one side of the country to the other.

«Madam, sir» said Khaled after a while, «do you prefer a car or are camels good, too for your trips out of the city?»

Angelika looked at him bewildered. «I thought it was all planned already, equipment included, but you only got us train tickets it would seem!»

«Keep calm» I said, «for now a car and some tools will be enough. We will think about the rest when necessary. We may also need shovels to remove sand and debris, then water and food, of course. You should arrange for that as soon as possible.»

«You won't excavate without authorization, or better, you won't even move a stone!» he answered me back.

Angelika's impulsiveness overflowed before mine. «You have been paid handsomely to comply with our requests, so try to be more obliging.»

«It's not part of the deal that you would start any excavations» replied the other, upset, «so I'll just show you the places, act as interpreter with the locals and nothing more.»

I lost my patience then and there and I used his disrespect for Angelika as a pretext to clarify my point of view in a less polite way.

«Don't you ever address her using such manners again! Is that clear?» I snarled at him pointing the forefinger towards his face. «We do not intend to remove archaeological finds anyway, that's not the purpose of our trip and certainly it wouldn't be easily done by two people alone. But we may need tools to free the vehicle from the sand, in case we get stuck in the desert.»

Khaled nodded and, when he went out to talk to the conductor, Angelika told me that she didn't like his company at all.

«We have no choice» I pointed out, «you should rather blame Dietrich and the foundation, which favour expeditions to Europe over ours. It's clear to me that they don't expect much from us. The Egyptian is only a tourist guide; it's not his fault that the Ahnenerbe didn't equip us properly.»

«We will get nowhere if we cannot let our researches range over.»

«Let time run its course» I calmed her down.

«I'd like to remind you that Dietrich doesn't accept failures.»

«Should we fail, I'll take full responsibility, don't doubt» I reassured her.

It was four o'clock in the afternoon and we were travelling along the railway line next to Fayyūm when I met Khaled's surly gaze.

«The people you're working with, professor, don't have any scruples about seizing other people's property» began the Egyptian.

«I'm telling you again for the last time, Khaled, I'm not a thief» I stated, still keeping calm, but when he dismissed me with a grimace of disbelief, I put diplomacy aside and ordered him to cut it or he would regret it.

«Are you threatening me, professor?»

«You got it right. You're here to be our guide, not our nursemaid» I replied nervously.

The Egyptian preferred silence to conflict and then, when the train slowed down its running, he asked us to wait for him in the carriage. «I've got an errand to run» he excused himself before disappearing.

«I've got an errand to run» echoed Angelika. «I wonder what he can have to do around here: there's nothing out here except for sand and dates!»

«We're not in Berlin, princess and, in this regard, I'd suggest you reconsider your attire» I said.

«What for?» she asked me looking at her blouse perfectly matching her skirt. She crossed her legs with the intent to thrill me. «Um, better something cosier or are you suggesting a lighter garment?»

When I saw her chirping, I replied amused: «Here women wear the hijab, the Islamic headscarf. Although it's a shame to cover you up, I think a pair of pants would be more appropriate for desert outings.»

«Rather than worrying about my clothing, you should think about retrieving Khaled. I guess he left us here because you scared him to death» Angelika scolded me amused, but right then the Egyptian came with a wicker basket on his shoulders containing goodness knows what.

The train left half an hour later, running along the stretch parallel to the Fayyūm oasis. Some children were travelling on carts loaded with dates and towed by unhealthy donkeys, which would lose their balance at the wagons' passage. In that region, the real wealth was plantations and orchards. The peasants were intent on working in the fields: men, women and children seemed only small white spots on that immense vegetable plain west of the sacred river. It was quite difficult for me to understand how, two thousand years earlier, that area, today agricultural but artistically unproductive, had been able to nurture talented Coptic portraitists.

Egypt – Luxor, September 28, 1937

The day after our arrival in Luxor, we visited the temple of Amun, where the merciless sun blinded tourists and annoyed even the Egyptians, who, despite everything, persisted in begging among the columns of the hypostyle hall. I was irritated by their presence everywhere: it really seemed like they had the gift of ubiquity! A young man even tried to sell me some old photographs of the temple taken in the last century, when the works had not been carried out yet.

Angelika shared my intolerance: she had given a biscuit to a child and now he was hounding her. I thought I'd offer him two cookies to leave us alone until the end of the tour and as many to chase away the other tormentors. I gave him one in advance, while I promised the rest on the way out, as long as he honoured our agreement. Thus we gained some time, and Khaled began to tell us, with minimal mnemonic effort, the vicissitudes of that temple, once considered "the harem of Amun".

The glyph of the ankh (☥), key of life, was everywhere, even between the paws of two hawks that held it over the sovereign. "To whom life is given", *rdì ankh*, was repeated endlessly on every wall writing. The Egyptian recited pages and pages of his school books, omitting the details that made that cult site unparalleled. We were just curious tourists to him. His simplistic comments ended up embittering Angelika who, luckily for me, felt compelled to point out the aspects Khaled left out, thus helping me to learn precisely those details that would make the difference. She was good, I had to admit, but I don't think she was guided by her love for history or her ambition, rather by the passion she put into everything, that ardour that made her irresistible.

We talked animatedly about that numeric symbolism predating the teachings of the Pythagoreans by thirteen centuries, about the number as divine creation and once again about the *Maât*, the Egyptian Harmony. The whole building was by itself a hymn to symmetry and balance, yet nothing I saw assisted me in my search for truth and Sator. Everything turned into mental pictures, images without names nor captions, that I was attaching to the album of my memory while ignoring its meaning. I realised that we had to reverse course: this wasn't the path to follow to solve our riddle.

«Angelika, we are on the wrong track. This is not how we'll get to the bottom of it» I confessed, irritated by the fruitless visit. «We're not here to see the sights!»

«You said that we needed to start from Thebes! Here we are, in Luxor, the ancient Thebes. The linen must be read as a geographical map: Thebes, Edfu and Philae, that is, Amun, Horus and Isis.»

She was right, that had been my idea, but I was no longer so sure I had interpreted the linen right.

«Yes, I know» I was resigned, «but maybe I can't find the answer because the question is wrong. Our research is too wide ranged, we need pin-point accuracy instead.»

«So, where do we start? I can help you translate everything, but I need some guidelines. Do you really think

I'm going to read every inscription between here and Philae? What are we looking for, then?»

«We seek the *Maât*, the Way of Horus and the Secrets of Isis» I replied curtly.

«Nothing else?» Khaled interfered humorously.

«That will be enough for the time being, thanks» I replied smiling and then, unknowingly, I found myself at the base of the most ambiguous portrayal I had ever analysed from a historical-religious point of view: the conception of Amenhotep III.

At the time of the Eighteenth Dynasty, Amun's pre-eminence over other deities was so deeply felt and his worship so profound that the sovereigns were considered "sons of God", not only metaphorically: the scene of the divine birth cycle in the temple was a clear proof of that. The god Amun had been depicted while fertilising the queen in an image of pure conception, although the hieroglyphic part described the insemination more realistically.

Angelika sensed my interest in the portrayal and came closer to clarify some aspects I was unaware of at the time. «Amun prevailed over other deities as a result of a theological machination» she flaunted her knowledge. «They associated him to the Sun god and he reaped the hymns formerly dedicated to Râ. Amun thus became the king of kings, the *Netjer Netjeru*.»

Fascinated, I contemplated Amun's grace in moving the *ankh* closer to the queen's mouth, to offer her the life, and I meditated on the message: offspring ensures eternal life, immortality. What a beautiful image! So I wondered: the secret of the cloth and the Sator was hidden in the children; maybe it was them who guaranteed eternal life and not a sacred text, or a litany as I believed. I carefully

126

reread my notes which, under that sun, were discolouring like my enthusiasm. The question swirling around my head was always the same: if Amun is the Sator, or the sower, then who is the Rotas? In my previous studies I had postulated a correspondence with the Aten, pharaoh Akhenaten's solar disk, but something was still eluding me, for the term Opera remained meaningless. I knew that on the path of truth, many would be the misleading indications but, man, in that place all my intuitions were doomed! Yet the linen and the Sator were born in that sacred environment and the writing on the cloth proved that: under the throne of the Virgin, the letter A of the word Amen was merged with a kind of I, as if to underline the Egyptian name of the solar divinity: Imen. In ancient Egyptian Amun and Imen are the same, so Amen and Amun have been, for at least five thousand years, the same word. Who can deny the validity of Aristotelian syllogism? If the word Amen means "certainty" for a Jew and "so be it" in liturgical expressions, for history it has always been synonym of the Sun god, Amun. It was all so clear, but I didn't understand why the joining link between the Old Kingdom, the Sator and linen was materially not to be found yet. I was so frustrated by my inability to grasp a logical conclusion that my facial expression showed it too.

«You'll win this fight, I'm sure of it» Angelika reassured me, taking me by the arm.

We were staying in a cosy guesthouse in Luxor, which had recently been renovated and made more attractive for foreigners; nothing to do with the Shepheard's Hotel in Cairo, but definitely not as many British people gathered there, which did no harm.

At the entrance and in the areas intended for

entertainment, the green flags of the Kingdom stood out, while the large dining room was the only area lacking them. Its furnishings, partly Arab and partly Western, had been skillfully matched to conquer the European and the native as well. The clear ceiling was illuminated by dozens of small windows that lightened the room and its elegant wooden hues. The rest of the hotel was a mixture of colourful tapestries, wicker armchairs and nineteenth-century furniture: a pleasant hodgepodge, distant from my everyday life. The building had a large facade overlooking the gardens where guests lingered to discuss business and sip karkadè in the evening.

The director was an Egyptian, who delighted in offering the ladies homemade perfumes, oils and herbal teas and was prone to smiling. He was a very friendly man, although he tried to make an impression by wearing a costly monocle. He could be spotted from afar: he always wore jacket, tie and vermilion fez. When he saw me tinkering with my Zeiss, he suggested to go develop my films at the laboratory of an Austrian, who had worked on the excavations in the Valley of the Kings.

After lunch, I decided to follow the director's advice and went straight to the photo studio in Karnak Avenue. I was greeted by a jovial man who lavished me with useful suggestions about my next shots. The first pictures developed were nothing but images of the Theban temples, insignificant for my study but interesting for their documentary value. To be honest, if I had even suspected I had captured something really intriguing, I wouldn't have gone to a man who, for over a decade, had been flanking English and American Egyptologists.

It was about six in the evening when I repeatedly

knocked on Angelika's bedroom door. After a few minutes I heard her running barefoot and remove the latch. With a slight and captivating smile, she invited me in.

Despite it was sunset, the room was still very bright, surrounded by a suggestive and kaleidoscopic atmosphere. However, I felt the need to wander with my thoughts, so I went out to the balcony, my gaze upon the horizon mirroring in the Nile waters. The day spent amongst the monuments had been more disappointing than ever. The analogies with Christianity, as well as the Latinized text of the Sator, were now taken for granted and I would do nothing more than rehash obsolete theses instead of unearthing something new. The stagnation in my study was frustrating.

«You can't get to the bottom of it, can you?» Angelika asked me, moving the shirt away from my chest to massage my neck.

I nodded, hinting at a tense smile, but she was thinking about something else.

«What's up?» I asked, perplexed by her gaze.

«I'm just contemplating my man who, apparently, is rather thoughtful» she replied, lighting a cigarette.

Then I watched her in a different light and realised how far apart from each other we were. Unlike me, she was ethereal. Opposites attract. Conflict and harmony find their way to compromise in every man's life, so I hoped that through the union of our personalities, sometimes at odds with each other, we could achieve the goal of knowledge. Frankly, I was no longer so convinced of that. Yet, somehow, while brooding over that predictable existential philosophy, I found an alternative for the study of the Templar magic square. «The Sator is an Egyptian text. I mean, its words are written in ancient Egyptian» I claimed.

Angelika blew a smoke ring that climbed up to the ceiling vanishing along the way. «It doesn't make any sense. Sator doesn't mean...»

I put my hand gently on her lips and she stopped talking. «You don't have to translate the word as you read it or see it written, because it would be impossible to find another matching it exactly» I explained after interrupting her. «It's necessary to reconstruct the five words and pair them with the Old Kingdom Egyptian from a phonetic perspective only. Think of *Sator arepo tenet opera rotas* and make their sound consistent with the archaic language. Maybe the magic square is just a wrong transliteration!»

Then she went to sit in a rattan armchair and nervously sucked on her cigarette. «They'll argue you've been manipulating the text and say it's an arbitrary translation and your whole study will lose credibility as a consequence» she brushed her hair aside and got all nervous.

«Wake up, Angelika, it's almost impossible that such a text stayed unchanged for millennia. The transcript must be corrupt, it can't be otherwise» I claimed, strongly convinced.

«Why?»

«Because there's no language in which it makes sense. *Sator arepo tenet opera rotas* is more like a tongue-twister! But, if we looked at the Sator as an Egyptian text, and rewrote it phonetically first, later analysing every single line of the square, then we could get something interesting from it, I'm sure. I'm telling you again: don't think of the word as it is pronounced in Latin, but in ancient Egyptian. What word or group of words could you connect it with? Please disconnect from your reality for just a moment! I need your help now» I told her, excited.

Angelika's face lit up and her eyes seemed more vivid than ever. «Something quite like Sator and with similar pronunciation… Uhm, it could be translated as "her son, Horus" or "the daughter of Horus" or even... oh, my God, the combinations are endless!»

«Come on, you're doing well! We have no reference glyphs, so just think about the sound of the words» I shouted.

«And if it was *Saw tw Râ*, then it would mean "beware of Râ" or "protect Râ" and maybe a hundred other alternatives» she exclaimed springing up from the armchair to run to the small desk where she kept her dictionary. I saw her leaf through the yellowed pages moving her fingers quickly.

«We will examine everything, even though there will be only a few plausible solutions once we read all five words consecutively» and I noticed that her face began to show a certain satisfaction.

She threw her arms around my neck and kissed me, leaving a taste of the cigarette in my mouth. «Do you think that even the original of this pseudolitany had its geometric representation like the five-by-five square?» she asked me right after.

«No. I suppose that, in the beginning, it was rather just a prayer passed down orally. The Romans, during their occupation of Egypt, may have learned that rigmarole but, since they had no alphabet letters with a similar sound, they possibly attempted an analogy between the two languages. When it was transcribed in Latin, it obviously lost its meaning or rather, it still made sense, but only for those who had learnt its original version. We are seeking that meaning, the matrix of its text.»

«You have convinced me, but now you need to let me work or I won't be able to convert the text within an acceptable time» she said, pushing me towards the door. «And you should also review...»

«The linen, of course, I know; it's possible I have to follow another path to study it. I must be led by that image only and refrain from presuming I can decide how to interpret its message.»

«I will inform Dietrich of the new developments as soon as we have the text ready» she concluded, shutting herself inside her room.

At dusk I found myself at the dock, staring at the majestic river ships slowly bobbing. You could hear the music on board and see the coming and going of the guests elegantly dressed for the gala nights. Beautiful women displayed their coquetry for their partners, and flaunted typically European evening outfits, leaving their shoulders bare and cleavages covered with voluminous necklaces.

I needed to think and all that buzzing annoyed me, but the Nile had something magic about it, a beneficial influence I didn't want to part with. Its slow, immortal flow dragged my thoughts with it. Those who have never seen it, cannot realise how much peace and harmony are diluted like pollen in its waters. Some moments are unique and, sadly, they leave too soon for us to be able to preserve their delight along with the mere memory of them. I loved the Nile because of its blue color and the unusual movement of the waves, and yet I believe there was more to it: I was also attracted by the thousand-year old history it had been involved in. I spent more than an hour there and returned to the boarding house only when tiredness made the landscape lose all its appeal.

That night was hot but not too much and, if my mind had not been burdened by conjectures, I would have slept soundly, provided that somebody had silenced the guest next door, who was snoring like a boar.

It was two o'clock in the morning when I finally left my bed and that mattress that gave off a nauseating smell of incense and dust with my every move. I decided to concentrate on the linen. I had not yet told Angelika that I had brought the original with me: she believed that I had returned it to Dietrich that day in Berlin. I was afraid that its new hiding place had already deteriorated it, so hurried to check its state of preservation. I had inserted it between the lining of my jacket and the outer fabric, only secured by its upper end. Since I had left the bottom open in order to consult the linen without taking it out, I slided the lining upwards in the hope it hadn't slipped out. It was still perfectly intact.

Once again, I dived into those faces, sacred and profane at the same time. It took me a while to realise that, my arrogance had made it impossible for me to investigate that work thoroughly. I didn't realise before, that the awareness of one's own ignorance brings one closer to wisdom, and that only the foolish boasts about his absolute knowledge. I had been a fool and, just as all my certainties started losing ground, I was able to spot a way out.

That linen had bewitched me. The light stroke, sometimes imperceptible, the more and less subtle hues, the chromatic combinations between complementary colors, all small tricks used by the artist and then geometric shapes that impelled the observer to complete a compelling visual path: that was its magnificence. It was right then that I recognised an initiatory journey in it, like for the Gothic cathedrals. Staring at that image, I compared myself to a humble pilgrim guided by an enlightening hand. The linen of St. Bernard was then transmuted into a symbol, or maybe even an initiation labyrinth. The attainment of God was the highest aspiration and the Sun was both the beginning and the end of that path. In a few centimetres of cloth, Râ, Aten, Amun, Horus and Isis, Mary and Jesus, all appeared and yet the solar disk dominated every other element and was the true and only protagonist of the linen. Every character represented in the depiction was inextricably connected to the sunlight. I soon realised that I trusted in that symbol, too, which gradually embraced me, leading me through an internal journey. Suddenly Angelika's words seemed decisive: "Only at a later stage Horus became the son of Isis and Osiris, in the beginning he was the Horus of Be'det, the son of the Sun god." The linen might very well be the emblem, a document proving the alliance among the main religions having alleged solar origins: Islam, Christianity and Judaism. But how could I possibly explain the Ahnenerbe that the Jews might inherit the knowledge of the Sonnenmensch much the same as the Germanic race? I preferred not to linger on that just right then because I had something else to think about. I studied the linen over and over again until its message was clear to me, then I put it away safely and left my room to knock on Angelika's door in the middle of the night.

«Cool it, Alexander, or you'll be sectioned! The residents of Tiergartenstrasse are not very sociable» she mocked me, referring to a well-known Berlin psychiatric hospital.

I burst into her room. «It's all in the covenant of the main faiths» I declared while sitting on her bed. «Thebes, Edfu, Amarna, Philae are leading us astray. We need to focus on Heliopolis and Elephantine.»

She yawned, rubbed her forehead and immediately afterwards lit a lamp, whose light flickered like a candle. «Why are you talking about Heliopolis and Elephantine now?»

I hesitated before answering to follow her with my eyes as she laid down on the bed, then I reached her, speaking more clearly: «Because the former is the city of the Sun god, now a Cairo district, while the latter...»

«Housed the temple in honour of the Jews' god: Ya'u, Yahweh...» she deduced as if suddenly all numbness had abandoned her.

«Exactly» I replied, smiling with satisfaction at how attuned to each other we had grown. «There's no need to go waste time on the island of Elephantine, I just needed the coordinates of its geographic position. We are headed elsewhere and now I know the destination: I have two points, so I can extrapolate the third. That is the Way of Horus, from Râ to Yahweh, from Horus to Jesus. Horus is the son of Râ, Jesus is the son of Yahweh. The third geographic point is obtained by tracing a sacred triangle, whose hypotenuse is built on the number five, which is the Way of Horus, that is, the distance between Heliopolis and Elephantine. The sides are long four and three respectively. The third point will therefore be located west of the Nile at a distance of four units from Heliopolis, Râ's dwelling, and three from Elephantine, Yahweh's dwelling» I told her all in one breath.

«Why should the third point be west of the Nile and not east?»

«The sun dies in the west, therefore, if the west is the Land of the Dead, it's over there that we'll find the sacred texts of the immortal Sun-Man, of our Sonnenmensch, because that's when we'll need them. Inform Dietrich of the new developments as soon as you can and tell him to give us more time. Tomorrow, in the morning, I'll talk to Khaled about the change of schedule. I need time» I said to her slightly authoritatively.

She smiled maliciously. Leaning against the bed headboard she was holding her bent legs pulled together and then, her gaze fixed on me, she slowly stretched them out, ending up showing me more than I had hoped for. When a strap of her negligee surrendered to the movements of her body, and slid down the arm discovering her breast, I turned off the lamp and thought of nothing else but her.

Egypt – Luxor, September 29, 1937

I lay with Angelika until the sun caressed her hips like it would do with desert dunes. In the light of the new day, I thought more rationally about us. We were different, but we attracted each other so passionately that any word was superfluous. Angelika was gorgeous, yet she couldn't soothe my inmost anguish with her lover skills. I reluctantly had to admit that she was only a sort of miracle drug, which could alleviate the pain but not cure the disease. There was something missing in our relationship as well as in all the others I had had until then. I was wrong to believe that the right woman would show me the way to redemption; I couldn't forgive myself for what I had done and not even a woman like her would distract me from remorse.

«You can't imagine how much I would give to know your thoughts right now» she whispered to me noticing that my gaze was resting on her legs, but my mind was actually focused on quite other issues. She got up from bed, her grace resembling that of Venus rising from the waters, and got dressed, but when she saw I was heading towards the door, she looked disappointed and asked me where I was going. I smiled, told her to meet me on the veranda for breakfast and said no more.

Along the corridor I came across Khaled, who was coming out of his room.

«So it was you, next door! Damn you, I couldn't sleep a wink last night because of your snoring!» I shouted at him, but without rancour.

He glanced toward Angelika's door, then looked at me mockingly. «I don't think I'm the reason for your insomnia, professor» and snickered as he went downstairs to the ground floor.

I wondered what he was doing around, at that time of the morning. He didn't seem particularly wary, however his ways still didn't convince me, so I followed him outside the boarding house and I saw he was tinkering about along with a coarse fellow. I decided to tail him to the latter's bazaar and found out that they were in business for the purchase of shovels, tanks and other sundries that would come in handy for our outings. Everything seemed to be in order and, at that point, I cut the paranoia and went back to check again the geographical triangulation that would lead us, so I hoped, to our destination and ultimate goal.

Egypt – Luxor, October 2, 1937

We had spent several days in Luxor to give Khaled time to arrange the expedition to the Dakhla oasis: it was there that I had decided to take my travelling companions. It was a pretty inconvenient change of plan because of the route. Khaled would have gladly traded the three hundred miles by car for five days on a camel's back, but what caused him the most distress was my request to have an aircraft available on the spot. That chap had connections all over the place, but finding a plane in Dakhla was no easy task. The money I granted was incentive enough for him to try harder and, three days later, we were leaving Luxor and heading for Balat, in the western desert.

The cars were ready in front of the boarding house. Angelika and I would be following the Ford driven by Khaled, who, in engaging the first gear made it grind. I immediately figured that it wasn't going to be an easy trip. His car repeatedly jolted forward for a dozen feet and then took the road finally heading west.

As I had foreseen, the Egyptian was a very bad driver.

«At this rate, I have doubts that we will arrive in Dakhla anytime soon. He makes his car leap like a grasshopper!» commented Angelika pointing at him.

After about twenty minutes we were already in the

desert, driving along the old caravan track. My instinct as a pilot had to surrender to the obvious lack of any other on-board instrumentation on the car, except for a speedometer: I was driving a strained crossbreed. Not to mention the merely aesthetic aspect! The man Khaled rented it from had stripped it of its bonnet to ease engine cooling. On our part, we had jam-packed every inch of the vehicle. In the rear area, a large loading deck was crammed with luggage, tools, and drums of water and fuel, sticking out of the car top like monuments. Since the cockpit could only house two people and Khaled was travelling alone, we had also jammed his passenger's seat with things.

The first two hours ran smoothly and we stopped only to refill the tanks and cool the engines a bit, but real hell began when the Egyptian decided he wanted to follow us. He drove right behind, sinking, along with his car, into the cloud of dust raised by ours. He got stuck into the sandy ground about an hour after the departure: he was so inept.

I stopped the car and, when I saw him hitting the gas, I swore at him. «Idiot! You're making it worse!» I shouted at him, gesturing for him to stop the engine.

«I'm sorry but I couldn't see anything. I had sand in my eyes!» he apologised, mortified, when he saw me getting out of the car.

«All right, all right, but now let's get it out of there. We have to remove all the stuff to make it lighter. Come on, help me» I ordered him. «When we move again, I will be following you and, in any case, this wouldn't have happened, if you had kept the right distance from our car.»

«It will take ages to unload and just as much to load everything back on the car! Alexander, we'll be risking falling behind schedule» Angelika reminded me, visibly annoyed.

«It's not like we have many other options, is it?» I replied, embittered by the situation and by her foolish remark.

After three hours, Angelika showed the first signs of hysteria.

«We're going too slowly. If we don't get to the set destination before night, we may fall victims to desert raiders!» she exclaimed clinging to my arm.

«Raiders? Hmm, I might make a good deal and sell you to their boss. Maybe I'll manage to get a couple of camels in return» I said to release the tension.

«Not funny at all, you hear me? For a joke like that, I might even decide to deprive you of the pleasures of our intimacy.»

«I don't believe you» I replied as I glimpsed her laughing furtively and stretched out my hand to run my fingers through her hair. I couldn't imagine that, shortly after, Khaled would get stuck once more and thus kill even the little hilarity I had left in me.

«Again!» I shouted at him exasperated, banging my fists on the steering wheel before getting out of the car. «Flies and locusts, give me everything but you! You really are a plague of Egypt!»

The Egyptian waved at me apologising as I approached with a certain martial aggressiveness.

«This time the car ended up in a pit» he justified himself showing a smile as childish as his intellect. «I had my whole front sunken and with the sand in my eyes I couldn't see anything.»

«I'll punch those lizard eyes of yours, see if you have a good reason not to use them, then!» I exclaimed furious. «Look what you've done, you moron! How do we get it out now? Let's hope the suspension hasn't broken, or we'll have to leave it here» I grumbled, squatting to check.

My throat was parched like a clump of desert dirt and I felt anger burning inside. Up to that moment, though, I had been able to check my outburst and vent through words only, but when I saw him sitting on the ground and staring at me dumbly, I understood that I had run out of patience.

«There's nothing to do!» he also had the courage to tell me, shrugging.

It was immediately clear to me that he wouldn't lift a finger to help and so I grabbed him by the tunic and hoisted him from the ground. Khaled goggled and his eyes nearly popped out of his head. I threw him against the car door and punched him in the face. Oh, what a relief! The Egyptian brought a hand to his mouth to make sure no teeth had gotten knocked out, then quickly picked up a spade and started shoveling without uttering a word. Never have I seen a more vigorous worker!

I can't say how much sand we shoveled that day. I felt it crunching under my teeth, scratching my neck and face. Whenever I moved my head, it fell from my hair into my eyes and mouth. No matter how hard I tried to clean myself up, it was never enough and, when I realised it was too late to resolve the situation, I suggested setting up the camp for the night. We would have to figure out about the car the next day.

Egypt – Western Desert, October 3, 1937

It was the best time of the year to cross the desert: the sky was clear and the air dry. Sometimes a breath of wind rose, so that small whirlwinds appeared and then disappeared quickly, leaving no trace of their passage. The firmament was glorious, embroidered with millions of stars. If it hadn't been cold, I would have lain down on the sand and spent the whole night enjoying that heavenly vision.

We had plenty of blankets, and yet Angelika kept crawling into my arms to warm up. I reckon her trembling had more to do with the thought of sleeping in the desert rather than with cold air. Also, as soon as the temperature dropped, there was no lack of unwanted guests and scorpions and snakes started creeping into our clothes.

Just before the sunrise, a small fennec, white like the moon, approached our tents. I was on watch when it appeared like a ghost before my eyes. I studied it with curiosity, stood still so as not to frighten it and hoped it would come closer. Seeing it was all fearful, I thought I could lure it with a crust of bread. Much to my amazement it accepted it. It was rather hungry and devoured the meal in a few minutes. I then slowly approached the big-eared little fox, which stood still for a while studying me with its lively eyes. When I reached out, it backed away at first, then I almost petted it, but eventually it was scared away at the sight of Angelika.

«I'm sorry» she said, mortified.

«Me too. This is the first time I had ever seen a fennec and it seemed quite sociable, too.»

«Maybe she was a female in heat!» she remarked, offering me a drink. «I confess I don't like petting animals: they stink!»

«No more than Khaled» I whispered when I spotted the Egyptian stretching, after his sleep.

We shoveled a never-ending quantity of sand, the Egyptian first among us, but the Ford only resurfaced after noon. The metal was hot and when I sent Khaled to swivel the ignition crank handle, the car gave no sign of life.

«Stop it!» I warned him, «or you'll fill the cylinders with sand.» I carefully studied the different components and swore several times while tinkering with the engine. «Damn you, Khaled, you covered even the coil in sand, but it should work now. Try again.»

The Ford suddenly revived and, with it, our optimism seemed to reinvigorate, too.

«A professor, a pilot... and even a mechanic» Angelika winked at me.

«And a puncher, too!» Khaled added.

I put my hand on the Egyptian's shoulder: he was massaging his jaw, still sore from the day before. I apologised for overreacting and he smiled at me, at least until his face ached again.

As we crossed that scorching landscape between Luxor and the Dakhla oasis, I scanned the horizon well, deluding myself that I could instantly find, among that fine sand, the solution to the linen and the Sator. Angelika kept suggesting new interpretations for the text, including a real invocation to Râ. In her opinion, there may have been a connection between the term *Opera* and *per-aa*, the pharaoh, as well as between the word *Rotas* and *rwt-taš*, that is, the border gate, but that was only the most simplistic interpretative hypothesis. She had also examined a combined transliteration of several words, and then even more enticing solutions sprang to her mind such as: *Man, temple of Horus, he ascends towards Râ; the land of the gods is the home of the rising Sun.*

Many were the alternatives that fired us up, but none of them could be confirmed.

«What do you think you'll find here in Dakhla, a new code?» she asked, unbuttoning her blouse to find some relief from the heat.

«*Lux in arcana*» I answered; «the light in the recesses of history, that's what I'm looking for. I hope to find a place which may be the depository of our origins and where a sort of ethnic, cultural and religious mixture of humanity has occurred at some point.»

We continued our journey at great speed until we had to face a more challenging section of the track, where the insidious and looser sand sported its wonderful barchan dunes, shaped like crescent moons. In that area the desert had taken on a warmer hue and the undulations sculpted by the wind plunged onto the remains of ancient buildings, perhaps from Roman times or more recent, which protruded from the ground in memory of a more glorious past. The last stretch of road, however, was easy and the sunny desert landscape finally gave way to the colourful oasis.

Angelika was using her beautiful legs as a desk: paper

sheets, books and a small ancient Egyptian dictionary were piled each onto the other. She was going over her notes, comparing the words by assonance, but she needed more time and more peace of mind to ponder over all the several combinations. Unfortunately, I couldn't ask her more than she was already doing.

Khaled honked his almost aphonic horn and pulled over our car shouting: «Balat village is near. I'm going to take you to a friend of mine who can cook the molokheya better than my mother. I'm leading the way» and slammed on the gas pedal.

Angelika wrinkled her nose. «Molokheya?! The name doesn't encourage me.»

On the contrary, I liked the idea. «You should try it, it's a very good vegetable soup» I explained.

«Do you know the local recipes, too? You'd even be able to cook them, wouldn't you?»

The fine sand at our feet alternated with grains and pebbles, that rolled down to the rocky plane. On it, buildings were perched, some of them slender, some others massive, but all with tiny doors. The windows of Balat houses were little more than slits and the entrances, at least as much mysterious as its inhabitants, disappeared in that maze of walls and stairs whose substance vanished in the shadows. It was an Islamic village that had remained unchanged since the Middle Ages: an array of corridors and raw brick walls, evocative and hypnotic in an equal manner.

As in a lithograph by Escher, I got lost in the contemplation of that architecture, perfectly symbiotic with the surrounding landscape: I found it impossible to tell the beginning from the end of it, since every corner ushered to everything and nothing at the same time. In that place I had the impression of floating over an almost ethereal world. It was an absolutely unique feeling.

Khaled approached a heavy wooden door and pounded on it energetically. Anwar, the burly landlord, didn't wait for us to knock twice and welcomed us in enthusiastically, like someone who meets old and dear friends again. He explained that he used to rent his abode to foreigners, especially British and, in recent years, many Italians, too.

The floor of the building was a bit uneven, the walls crude and crumbling, yet that house was remarkably bright and unusually charming.

Angelika immediately noticed the small wicker sofa, chock-full of cushions embroidered with well-made ethnic decorations, and sat on it trying to soothe the backache caused by the trip. Before taking us to our rooms, Anwar offered us some warm karkade.

I was amazed by the salt-flake-coated walls, which transported the guests into a forest of sorts: the mix of those differently coloured mineral panels recreated the effect of being surrounded by bark. I had never seen anything of the like and I appreciated the eccentricity of the creator who, to make the house even more welcoming and evocative, had placed dozens of lanterns everywhere along our passage. That evening Aysha, Anwar's wife, a Nubian with delicate features and slender hands, lit all those candles and their flickering light was able to conjure up a fairytale aura, permeated with a warm Arab atmosphere.

In the late afternoon, Angelika joined me on the terrace and caught me absorbed in reading. I had lit a candle that barely illuminated my writings, but I persevered in fighting against both the tiredness and the approaching night.

«You look like a poor devil with that unkempt beard and hair, you know? That linen is absorbing all your energy. How can you hope to determine the exact coordinates of a place from those maps?»

She sat down next to me, picked up some sheets on which I had jotted down the coordinates and some others with different textual combinations of the Sator, then she sighed loudly. I could foretell her uncertainties. «Um, I must confess that I still think the magic square is very far from the cloth. I don't have a clear idea and the foundation insists on evidences, but how can we provide the Ahnenerbe with explanations, if we doubt our work in the first place?»

I took off my glasses and placed them slowly on the wooden table. I looked at her after massaging my eyes, which I felt burning like hot coals. «I stopped doubting. St. Bernard's cloth is an alternative means to the Sator to pass on the same concepts. I told you already. I studied that linen as its author wished me to do: from one divinity to another, from an ancient era to a more recent one, and travelling across its weaves like a pilgrim on the way to the sanctuary. So I had the confirmation that Râ is the glue of all great religions and that, learning about Isis and Mary, you see them overlapping with the Great Mother. As you reveal the way of Horus, you interpret the teachings of Christ. As you learn to love the *Maât*» I paused and caught a glow sweetening her eyes «you can aim for eternity. But what we are about to discover might not be appreciated by the Ahnenerbe» I confessed at last, cooling my tone.

«I don't understand» she tensed up.

«The farther I go, the more my allegations of antisemitism appear groundless to me. The linen is proof of that. I mean, it doesn't exclude the Jewish religion at all, indeed, it even merges it with the others. Perhaps the Sator and the cloth exclude us and our superiors from understanding them, but I don't rule out the possibility that in the past they welcomed men of Israel among the chosen ones.»

«Stop it, what are you raving about?» Angelika exploded, leaving me speechless. «You said it: the Sator is a code devised to preclude the unworthy from earning the eternal life and, if I'm not mistaken, you underlined the hatred of the Egyptians for the invading people, the Hyksos, the Semite shepherds. You are recanting everything now? Why are you doing that?»

«Because I'm seeking the truth» I replied, raising my voice as I pounded the table with a punch that made the candle drop to the ground.

Angelika was transfigured by anger, I had never seen her that way and thought I was talking to the wrong person, it was like another woman, with identical features, had taken her place.

«Then look for your truth in the right direction, or all of your brilliant intuitions will be worthless» she replied despotically.

«Do you think you can frighten me? You, a puppet in the first place, want to become my puppeteer, now? Knock it off! You're pathetic» I answered her, sitting down.

At that point, she got back to her old self, as if she suddenly came to her senses. «I don't want to miss this chance to stand out» she confessed. «I have devoted my life to studying, I'm not cut out for breastfeeding snotty children and cooking meals to a devoted husband. I'm a woman who doesn't comply with the party's stereotypes. But, let me say, if it weren't for women, the party wouldn't be so great today and Adolf Hitler wouldn't be so charismatic. I wish to carve out a space of my own within the Ahnenerbe and sooner or later I will make it» she concluded with a sigh. «You know I believe in your capabilities, but...»

«Should I ever hinder your career with my theories, you wouldn't hesitate to hush me for good.»

«I didn't mean that. Take my advice, Alexander, learn to lie or you won't survive.»

While she recovered her composure, I experienced the exact opposite. Damn it, she made me feel like a puppet in the hands of Dietrich and his cronies, so much so that I even doubted all of her simpering lovemaking. I felt so much anger building up inside of me because of that argument that, in the end, I decided to speak up once and for all. «Bear in mind that, if I find out something, something truly extraordinary as we all hope, I won't settle for a compromise to earn a pat on the back from Dietrich. I won't do it, either for the Ahnenerbe, or for you» and grabbing my notes, I took the stairs and left her there to meditate on our quarrel.

The moon was already high in the sky when a good smell of freshly baked bread spread across the house, accompanied by a chant wailed to the four winds by Anwar, who was improvising as baker and singer both.

Other guests had arrived that evening and the whole family had to work to satisfy all customers. I preferred avoiding meeting them, even though Anwar had reassured us that they weren't British. Last but not least, after dinner, he and Khaled started ranting and raving like strays while smoking hookah, so I decided that it would be wiser to wander around the garden than watch their show.

I walked for a long time, mulling over the choice I had to make between taking the way of *Maât* or Himmler's. I looked up at Angelika's room and noticed that her light was still on: we both had a lot to think about before going to sleep.

Egypt – Balat, October 4, 1937

It was morning. The greyness of the walls soon changed to a cheerful orange that crept into the room from a small ogive-shaped opening. An eight-pointed star had been carved into the wooden shutter. I rolled over onto my side, felt the lack of a feminine warmth and realised it would no longer be Angelika's. I didn't bear any grudge against her, but I did not want to have her beside me either, it was as if a handful of words had erased a month of passion. I soon turned my mind to Romy and to that kiss, whose sweetness I still felt. I reluctantly left my bed, but preferred using my time to plan the future rather than dwell on the past.

I took the razor out of its metal box, removed it from the cleaning fluid and went to the mirror. I had let my beard grow a little in the last few days in the hope it would protect me from the sand, but, if truth be told, I believed it could carry away my impeccable soldier's look, in exchange for that of the scholar's. The attempt had failed. I placed the blade on my face and cleaned myself up from that carelessness that, to be honest, I had to recognise as a foolish rebellion against the obvious: I was a soldier, a murderer of the Reich. No other role would ever overcome what I was: the "Führer's Greyhound".

When I left the courtyard, one of the two Ford cars had disappeared, along with Khaled, whom I saw about half an hour later in a car in the distance. The Egyptian stopped the vehicle, lifted a cloud of dust and proudly turned to me: «I have a gift for you, professor Wagner!»

«I'm sorry, I do prefer women!» I answered, but, obviously, he didn't understand the quip, which I didn't bother to explain.

«I bought food, drinks and labor. That's why I'm late.»

«You're always late» I retorted, eyeing the workers he had brought with him with some hostility. I hated surprises, and those two looked more like a mishap than a brillant idea.

«These men will save us time and prevent you two from wreaking havoc.»

I rolled my eyes exasperated. «Listen, buddy» I explained after a sound sigh, «we'll stick to the rules, but stop bothering me with this matter of unauthorized excavations. There are dozens of private expeditions from Alexandria to Aswan whose aims your government doesn't even know, yet you play dumb because they fill your filthy pockets with huge *bakshish*. So please cut the hypocrisy! You will get your dues, don't worry, but now start the engine, follow me and shut up.»

When Angelika got into the car, she realised I no longer was the travel companion of the day before. I'm not sure, but I suppose she felt unwelcome on board and stayed silent. She didn't even ask where we were heading to and I didn't want to waste time chatting.

We skirted Balat, with its narrow and sandy alleys, and drove westward along the caravan route for about thirteen miles until, without warning, I abruptly slowed down to turn right into the desert. I checked the compass and then the map to assess the distance covered. I couldn't spot a cultivated plot for miles. By then, the oasis was far away and we were surrounded by bizarrely shaped rock formations. I chose an area of compact soil to stop.

Angelika cleared her voice with a little fit of coughing and asked me what margin of error I had with the triangulation.

«I don't know» I answered her, «but I guess at least two, three miles from this point.»

She goggled. «How many? A season's digging wouldn't be enough to survey the whole area!»

«Sorry to disappoint you, doll, but it's the best I could do with the equipment at hand!»

«Do you know what that means? That means we have almost forty square miles of surface to search!»

«Then we'd better get to work without arguing, don't you think?» I replied and offered her a shovel.

«Come on, get real, Alexander, it's like looking for a needle in a haystack!»

My patience ran out instantly. «Listen, which side are you on?»

«What kind of question is that? It's obvious!»

I stuck my shovel into the ground and peered at her severely. «There's nothing obvious in this matter» I said, «and if you really want to know, you don't seem so "obvious" anymore, either.»

«You should rather worry about Khaled, not about me» she replied, arrogant. «He changed his ways too abruptly. Here he comes. Speak softly.»

Suddenly, even the sound of her voice seemed annoying to me and I replied with rancour: «Yes, but at least he has the reward as his excuse. While you... what's yours? You've changed, Angelika, and I don't like that.»

It was like her reply got stuck in her throat, because she hesitated several times before speaking. «I'm afraid of Dietrich, okay? I'm afraid of what you're going to tell him, that's all» she confessed. «We cannot make mistakes. Once you are ousted from the Ahnenerbe, you're doomed, you become an amoeba of society. For the first time in my life, I was given the opportunity to participate in a foundation expedition. My dream is coming true! So far, my work has only been about words and symbols recited by heart, but now, thanks to you, I can prove my skills. I don't want to claim any successful outcome that I didn't earn, I'm happy to be your assistant in this adventure. It's sure more than I could hope to achieve on my own! If you quit, you also drag my aspirations with you» then she ended the conversation when she saw the three Egyptians approaching.

I didn't feel like showing her any sympathy: I was confused and disappointed at the same time. From then on, I would go my own way and ignore anyone who came between me and my research.

We spent the whole morning searching the surrounding area without any success. The heat was unbearable and the horizon undefined because of the quavering air rising from the ground. The soil probing had been carried out unprofessionally and randomly, as it would have been impossible to properly inspect the entire area.

I gave the car step a couple of poundings to clean my boots from the sand and went aboard, disconsolate. As I gulped down water to quench my parched mouth, I convinced myself that I couldn't hope for any short-term success, although my estimate indicated the desert between Balat and Mut as the right spot. Saint Bernard's linen led to two points of the sacred triangle, Heliopolis and Elephantine, so the third coordinate would be found in the Dakhla oasis. But the margin of error was very large.

In the days spent in Luxor, I had purchased from a local merchant some particularly detailed maps, which were part of a collection dating back to the beginning of the century. The photographer in Karnak Avenue recommended them to me. Although many of those charts were creased, faded and almost undecipherable, I thought they were perfect for my study and I spared no expense.

I had redrawn the map and recalculated the route at least a hundred times. I was hoping for a confirmation, but in the area we searched, nothing could be seen but sand, sand, and more sand. No morphological anomaly of the soil, no geometric figure concealed between the folds of the desert, no rock formation caught my eye at the end of that exhausting day of work.

Angelika sighed, shrugging, and commented: «If there was anything, it would be covered in at least fifteen feet of sand.»

«A few miles west of here, the remains of a Roman settlement can be seen. Maybe that's where we must look» Khaled said, refreshing himself with a sip of water.

«This was once a popular caravan route, right?» I asked, accepting the flask the Egyptian offered me.

«Darb al-Ghabari» answered Angelika, only to make an impression. «Actually it seems there were two caravan routes. The first was short and dangerous, while the other was easier but didn't guarantee any water supply. Years ago, I met an Englishman who was carrying out a study on the Egyptian oases during the Old Kingdom. He had discovered that Dakhla was already inhabited in prehistoric times.»

156

«Interesting coincidence: a Brit is helping me out. Well, now I know there were predynastic settlements around here. I have one more chance to find my ancestral Sator, but we'll consider the matter tomorrow, perhaps after the overflight.»

«What are you going to do?» she squawked. «What if some Englishman saw you?»

«We haven't been a protectorate for over fifteen years!» Khaled interjected stiffly. «Great Britain is a spectator now, so you have nothing to fear, Fräulein Blumen. And then, around here, my Muslim Brothers know how to hold colonists at bay.»

«Yes, of course, as if the Egyptian nationalists cared about our safety!» she replied.

Those words made my ears buzz. «Until proven otherwise, it's me who is going to pilot the plane, not you. Enough for today, let's go back to Balat» I ordered harshly and peremptorily. «As for you, Khaled, please proceed as agreed.»

Egypt – Mut, October 5, 1937

It was still dark when Khaled took me to Mut, where an old man would provide us with a reconnaissance plane in good condition. Unfortunately, the purchase of the aircraft would cost us an amount corresponding to three hundred and fifty marks, meaning, three wages of the German average worker. It might have been a good bargain if it had been able to fly, but I didn't want to get my hopes up before I saw it for myself. The deal was that the Egyptian would wait for me to takeoff, then he'd go back to pick up the others at the hotel. I wanted them all at the excavation site by dawn, when the grazing sun light would reveal the desert's secret face.

The old man walked before us, limping through the cramped alleys of that far corner of Mut. Finally, we reached a square closed on three sides by crumbling walls and wreckage of all kinds. And then, the old man struggled to lift a cloth and proudly showed what he called his jewel.

I had a strange feeling in front of that heirloom. I was amazed that there really was a plane under the tarpaulin, but at the same time I doubted it would ever fly.

«Do we get it?» Khaled asked me excited.

Honestly, I was perplexed and overwhelmed by pessimism. «Keep calm. Ask him what kind of plane it is, it looks like a half-breed.»

«He says it belonged to a European» he translated, «an Englishman; it seems he had put the pieces of two planes together. One of them had crashed nearby and the other in Balat.»

«Wow, talk about good omens!» I exclaimed. «Where's that bloke now?»

«He's dead.»

«Well, exactly!» I commented, laughing to play it down.

«He flew every month to bring mail and take medicines from Luxor. Now the old man says that the plane is his.»

After I heard that, I showed more respect for that antique. Incredible. The previous owner had assembled the parts of a Sopwith Camel with those of an Airco DH4, using a twelve-cylinder Rolls Royce Eagle engine: a real jewel, just as the old man had defined it. Either the Englishman was a genius, or he was a nutter.

«I'm not going to spend more than two hundred marks, fuel included in the price, for this wreckage» I said resolutely to Khaled, who was already calculating the equivalent to offer to the old man.

After a few minutes of bargaining between the two Egyptians, the seller accepted my conditions unperturbed and, with the look of a satisfied trickster, he shouted in the direction of a shack. Immediately, some children rushed out to remove the pile of junk that cumbered the courtyard. All that childish euphoria put me in a good mood. I asked Khaled to deal with the fuel cans and the oil drums, sure that the contraption would drink more than an alcoholic. We also brought along tools for repairs and the tarpaulin to protect it from sun and sand.

I boarded the plane, then I signaled for my mate to come closer. «Grab the propeller and, when I tell you, thurst it down with all the strength you have, and get away quickly. Ready? Go!» I shouted at him trying to start the engine, which didn't really want to start, though.

It took six attempts before the engine decided to engage. Finally, that thingamajig proved to be still "alive". I put on my goggles and drove the aircraft away from the houses. The children ran after me until I took off. I heard their shouts of joy and saw them fly with their imagination: they spread their arms and chased what was only a magnificent and enormous toy to them.

Immediately after takeoff I headed east. I was amazed by the manoeuvrability of the plane and by its engine that still had yet more thrust to offer. There was only one little problem: the exhaust gas, and often drops of hot oil with it, sputtered all over my face. I tried to get familiar with the aircraft and flew over the southern part of the oasis, where there were no buildings, then I headed north, again towards Mut, to greet the kids still on the street. I flew over their homes by performing a tonneau, which wasn't a particularly difficult manoeuvre for the aircraft structure. I heard the kids below me cheering at my aerobatic feat, then, after that humble homage, I headed towards the desert, my mind full of hope.

The aerial reconnaissance over the excavation area yielded nothing but another failure. There was nothing interesting down there and, since my goggles had lost their transparency because of the oil splashes and I needed to make sure of the efficiency of the fuel gauge, I decided that it would be better to land on the first stretch of compact ground. I waited there for the rest of the group and, in the meantime, I took care of the problem with the exhaust pipes. In the toolbox I found some iron bars that proved to be useful to bend the pipes downwards, so as to prevent smoke and oil from hitting me in the face. That biplane was a gas guzzler, but that aside, it hadn't behaved badly. I stroked the fuselage as a sign of gratitude for her service, after which I sat in the shadow of her wings, disheartened by the failure.

That evening we went back to Balat in very low spirits: two days of research frittered away and Dietrich's expectations hung over us like a sword of Damocles.

Egypt – Balat, October 8, 1937

Four days had passed since we arrived in Balat and there was still nothing new under the sun. My every conviction was crumbling with the passing of the hours and the despondency painted on my companions' faces bruised my ego. After the umpteenth sleepless night, creases of tiredness ploughed across my face and, when I caught sight of it in a mirror, I could hardly recognise myself. That wasn't like me. I rebuked myself, since a man's neglect implies his resignation to fate, and so I shortened my hair and trimmed my beard, exposing my former face.

While I was dabbing my skin with a sandpapery cloth, Angelika knocked on the door. I greeted her with coldness, whereas she shot me a radiant and aroused look. Then, out of the blue, she said "I miss you", but it didn't have the effect she hoped for. Unperturbed, I went back to my occupations without any comment.

«Your silence wounds me fatally, and you know it!» she finally cried out, to compel me to talk to her. «Every time, it feels like you throw me into a deep chasm of solitude. I can even feel the ice of your glance on my skin. I exist, Alexander, even if you pretend to ignore me!»

At that point, already prey to my frustration at the recurrent failures, I remember I suddenly turned towards her and retorted: «I never pretend. And then, what am I supposed to say? In these days we haven't done anything but collide. Do you think I'm satisfied with how things are going? What the hell do you want of me?»

«I just told you what I want. Damn you and your bloody temper!» she cried in a tremulous voice.

I felt a slight remorse, then I clenched my teeth from nervousness and answered, using the only language Angelika seemed to understand: Reich's. «This is how our Führer wants us to be: tough as leather.»

«We're not talking about him, but about us. I told you that I miss you. I hope that means something to you, or would you rather see me on my knees before granting me your attention?»

That quarrel was absurd. I realised she was used to another kind of man.

«I have been impulsive the past few days, but only because I fear for your safety, in case the results of this expedition are disappointing or collide with Himmler's aims. If we found something down there and someone were to disclose your discovery, an Englishman for example, since there are so many around here, that might even affect the previous Ahnenerbe study on the origin of the Aryan race and on the anti-Semitism it fosters. They'd kill you, Alexander» she said hugging me tightly, perhaps for fear I would drive her away. «I know they would. They have already done that in the past for much less.»

I returned her embrace half-heartedly, then I replied: «They have already tried to get rid of me, and yet I'm still alive.»

«Would it really be inconceivable for you to lie to survive?» she asked crying.

«That's odd, I thought the Ahnenerbe opposed

manipulations, but maybe this doesn't apply when Rosenberg's sacred theories are challenged, does it? If Dietrich wants an answer, he'll get it, but it will be the truth and not a deformation of it. You're still in time to go back, but if you're with me, then let yourself be guided by history. Now we only have to focus on finding an iota of evidence» and I flung my room's door open to invite her out. It was time to get to work.

For a brief moment she looked at me dejected, then she turned austere, her beautiful blue eyes became icy as the polar winter and she walked out towards the courtyard. I joined her a few minutes later and saw her handing a missive over to Khaled. I imagined its addressee. As I walked staring at that letter, I bumped into two foreign guests of Anwar. I heard the man mumble a sort of greeting, whereas his pretty partner, crisp like her fragrance, scrutinized me from head to toe, lingering on my face, as if we had already met elsewhere. But I would have certainly remembered her eyes and beautiful oval face in that case. I raised my hat to greet her, while she gave a hint of a polite smile and paraded past me resolutely. Before leaving the building, I turned back in the hope she had not already disappeared through the corridors, but there was no trace of her anymore. The lack of closeness between those two prompted my suspicion about them. I ascribed that bad habit of mine to the years of Luftwaffe training when, in addition to the sense of duty, they ingrained in me that of mistrust, too.

That morning, at the excavation site, the air was cool and the horizon absolutely magnificent: a scenery that would stick to my memory as well as the emotion it aroused. The first sun rays stroked the sand heaps mounds, spectacular and changeable as they shifted from golden to shadow hues.

During the night a strong wind had surely blown: the tire tracks had been erased and the landscape looked less unyielding than the day before. Each stride marked the ground: gusts had combed and pushed around the sand, building new dunes on top of pre-existing ones. To the naked eye the area was smooth and only sporadic dips interrupted such monotony. The plane was still where I had left it the night before and, fortunately, the cloth had shielded it from the sand.

Before leaving, Angelika handed me a small black soapstone scarab: more an excuse to get closer than a propitiatory talisman as she claimed.

«I trust that luck is on our side and that it'll help us find a truth that also satisfies Himmler's ambitions about the Sonnenmensch» I declared, seeing a sparkle of new optimism on Angelika's face.

The wind was cool at that time of the day and I felt strengthened. After all, it felt good flying that old wreckage, and never would I have imagined such connection between us. I softly veered to the north, a few miles away from the excavation area, and then realigned with the reference point. After half an hour of overflight in all directions, I quit and prepared to return to base camp loaded with anger. Thus, I needed to gain height again to fly over a dune whose fine sand seemed to embrace the wind and form a crescent moon. When I got past the ridge, I saw a rock formation peeping out from the base. It was linear, very low and similar to a chequerboard. Nothing to be excited about, but I opted for another flyby. At low altitude it looked like the remains of a retaining wall, typical of old local buildings.

I was carrying a pair of red bags full of sand soaked in waste engine oil. I dived to reduce the altitude, so as not to scatter the contents and thus compromise the signaling, then I unhooked one of the two bags that would have shown the others where to go. Hitting the ground, the red canvas torn, leaving a visible black powdery spot shaped like a star.

I couldn't help reliving the bombing in Spain. I had to concentrate to shift my attention from the vision of those big, highly explosive aluminum-powder bullets, dishing out death and destruction.

I veered three hundred and sixty degrees to make sure the mark was visible and decided to keep the second bag for later flights. After a moment, I spotted the two cars below me and performed such a low level flight over them that Angelika's hat flew off.

I landed about a mile away and, before leaving the plane, I took care of the post-flight operations, usually a petty officer's job. My mind kept digging up the past, specifically, the night at Ritter's house, and the terror in his wife's eyes.

I walked to the place I flagged and soon the silence of the desert was torn apart by the arrogant racket of the two Fords appearing before me. Angelika jumped out of the car while it was still in motion, but I immediately dampened her enthusiasm exhorting her not to pop the champagne just as yet, since I still had no idea of what was under our feet.

We immediately split sectors to clean up the visible surface. The building was clearly quite large: its remains were strewn everywhere, even over areas distant from the main core. If it had been a temple, a season of excavation would not have been enough to free it from the sand, assuming it was worth it. To be honest, I thought it was the remains of a recent settlement: ruins from old houses or animal pens.

We wasted the whole morning just cleaning roughly and measuring. At sunset, after an afternoon spent shoveling, one of the two hired labourers let out a scream, so loud that Khaled thought a horned viper had bitten him. The man, however, was healthy and insistently pointed at a smooth surface under his feet. We hastened to have a look and Angelika quickly swept the slab with a whisk broom.

«Well, I'm not a geologist, but I think it's white limestone» she pointed out, quite enthusiastically. «Maybe it comes from the quarries of Tura, from Lower Egypt in any case.»

«There's nothing written on it, it's not a monument» said Khaled.

I quickly assessed the situation and decided that we had to move the block without making a big deal about it.

Khaled goggled. «I'm not sure we can make it without help!»

I froze him with a spiteful look. «There are four of us and we have got a car.»

«Thanks for your consideration!» Angelika scolded me.

«You are the driver» I replied as I went to pick up some towing ropes with which I harnessed the heavy slab of stone. «Push the gas gently» I suggested, fearing she would cause the engine to seize.

«Stop talking and let me do it. If Khaled can drive, I can do it too!» she shut me up.

It was not an easy task. At first all of us only tried pushing in the direction of the car which was gradually pulling the monolith. But it could not be moved an inch.

Then we tried prising the stone open with some iron bars and managed to chip the edge touching the ground, so we stuck the tools inside again and thrust them in deeper. The slab was lifted only slightly, but it was enough to allow an exchange of air between the inside and the outside which facilitated its removal.

Angelika got out of the Ford and ran towards us to have a peek.

«It's a hypogeum. It looks like a Roman favissa» she explained, trying to impress me.

«Or a nilometer!» Khaled contradicted her.

«For heaven's sake!» I objected. «We must be more than one hundred miles far from the Nile. What purpose would a flood measurement tool have around here?»

Meanwhile Angelika had knelt by the circular opening, roughly thirty inches large, and had put her head inside. After a few seconds, she rolled onto her back and lay that way staring at me with a blissful smile.

«Well, what do you say?» I provoked her, serious.

«I adore you, professor» was her reply and, at that point, I loosened up and smiled at her. «There's an inner lining of white limestone panels reflecting light like mirrors: it illuminates the surroundings even when the sun is low on the horizon. It's gorgeous.»

I took off my hat and leaned out of the edge as far as I could. The moonlight would be enough to cast light upon the whole room. I heaved a sigh of relief and ordered the others to uncoil the tow rope all the way to the opening. «I'll go down and have a look» I told them.

The Egyptian nodded. «Yes sir, but it can only be secured to that hook.»

«I'll fasten it to my belt. It's not so deep. I'll keep my balance long enough to touch the ground. Come on, lose some rope for me» I ordered, but immediately Angelika grabbed me by the arm.

«Wait, the main entrance should be nearby, too.»

«It took us a day to clear a three-foot opening, do you think we'll ever be able to dig up the rest by the end of the day? Look around, do you see another excavation team that can help us?» and I began to slide down the rope, gently freeing myself from her grasp. «Try not to worry, I won't leave you alone for long» I said, my tone softened.

I was in the centre of a cone whose concave walls were nearly ten feet at the base diameter. The panelling consisted of smoothed rectangular slabs cut with incredible accuracy. I was inside an inverted funnel, which touched the floor of a room without decorations, furnishings or any votive objects, thus weakening the thesis of it being a Roman favissa.

«Do you see any inscriptions in there?» Angelika shouted at me.

I looked around, but saw no sign etched on the walls. «Here on my right there's a side room obstructed by some granite blocks. Wait, it's a fan-shaped staircase that climbs up to the surface.»

I looked up and saw that the ceiling had perfectly symmetrical steps. I conjectured that the spectacularity of the place had led the builders to bury the entrance in order to preserve it from desecration. I wasted no time and took some photos, until a strange hiss caught my attention: a viper hadn't appreciated our trespass and was threatening me with its forked tongue.

«Careful! I'm going to drop some tools» Khaled's voice thundered. From above, the Egyptian dropped a shovel that ended up hitting the reptile's coils. I congratulated him on his good aim and pushed aside the animal remains with my foot.

In the meantime, Angelika had also climbed down using my technique. «Let me take a look at the staircase» she told me, studying the place for a few minutes. «We are in one of the underground chambers of a temple, that most likely stood above our heads.»

«I believe it must be a sort of nuraghic well, though, rather than a crypt, a place of union between heaven and earth» I inferred.

«But I don't see any inscriptions… I think it never had a liturgical function» she disagreed.

«What if it's just an antechamber?» I asked her, letting my gaze wander inside the room, run along the curved walls, and then rest on the point of contact with the ground. There, a change in the gradient towards the centre of the room allowed the light to propagate in every direction.

Angelika didn't reply and positioned herself perpendicularly under the top hole, then she ordered the others to move away from the opening. Suddenly she turned to me and, as if our thoughts were travelling in unison, we started cleaning up hurriedly the ground on which, we hoped, the opening of a sacred well would be.

Although the light in there was more persistent than elsewhere, it began to fade, as well as our time.

«Are you all right?» Khaled shouted, sticking his head in the hole. «Do you want me to come down and help you?»

«It's not necessary» I replied, condescent as someone who doesn't want to be bothered in a key moment. And a key moment it was indeed: the sand had covered a second limestone monolith carved with concentric circles. I took off my shirt to sweep it faster. «It's an antechamber, an environment of preparation for a ritual, a room of purification. Maybe that's why there are no inscriptions» I explained to her.

Angelika nodded, drying the sweat from her forehead. «And now? How do we lift this top?»

I smiled at her because I had already found the solution. «With levers. Look here» I answered, pointing to a small hole under her foot. «We'll take advantage of this hollow.»

«Come back up» Khaled called in a commanding voice, and lowered the hook for us to climb up. «We'll be back early tomorrow, but now we have to leave for Balat. We're not equipped for the night.»

I looked at Angelika and realised that she was exhausted and I was too, so we accepted his advice without hesitation. We knew the next day would be a great day.

Egypt – Dakhla, October 9, 1937

Anwar had decided to join the excavation group and had descended in the hypogeum with me, Angelika and Khaled, while the two labourers had remained above-ground to operate the winch. We managed, with some difficulty, to displace the stone disk from its slot. We assumed it blocked the opening of a sacred square-shaped well.

I picked up a stone and threw it into it. We heard a thud after a substantial delay compared to our expectations and it didn't even sound like water.

«Well, Khaled, it's not a nilometer» Angelika decreed with satisfaction. «I could possibly admit to the hypothesis that five thousand years ago this was a fertile and luxuriant area, but I don't think a river has ever crossed these lands.»

The two were debating about what was and what wasn't possible while I, after leaving the bag next to the opening, lowered a lamp into the well thus silencing their chatter instantly.

Some holes had been chiselled in the walls. We immediately noticed there was a string of them positioned at regular intervals and it was easy to deduce that they had been used as slots for wooden rungs, now rotted. I asked Angelika to keep an eye on my bag while I climbed down to inspect the well. Khaled handed me a safety rope I tied at the waist. He and Anwar would support me if I slipped, so I held on to the edge and slid my foot in the first hole in the wall.

The well, like the stone top that had occluded it, was not up to our expectations: it looked anonymous in all respects. I confess that in those days my enthusiasm came and went with the same regularity of Berlin buses, so that I felt the thrill of the discovery extinguish like a candle in the wind. In a moment of distraction, and frustration, I misplaced my foot and slipped for a few feet before finding the grip again. I grazed my fingers but then came to a stop and saw something new before my eyes: endless polychrome inscriptions, impressive for their formal completeness.

«Angelika!» I shouted when I saw her leaning out of the top hole.

«Are you okay? What happened to you?»

«I'm great and there are inscriptions down here!» I replied, my voice still croaky from the damp hot air.

«Wait a minute, it's not possible that there are inscriptions in a well» said Khaled, «the water would have worn them away!»

«Do you see any cartouches?» Angelika asked at once.

I cleared my throat: my voice had become hoarse because of the sand and the heat of those days. «The water never got in here, because there are no signs of corrosion on the walls. I'm afraid I can't see any cartouche either. I'm going in deeper now» and I let myself go a little further down.

That well seemed to be bottomless. Angelika and the Egyptians soon disappeared from my sight and I found myself completely alone. In the bowels of that alleged place of worship, where darkness served as both ceiling and ground, the lamp soon became the reassurance I was still alive. I abseiled down deeper and deeper until a tunnel opened in front of me. I approached the light, but couldn't assess its length. I gave myself a push, tying not to put too much strain on the rope and that swaying allowed me to reach the opening on the side wall of the squared shaft.

The tunnel was narrow and climbed upward, leading me to the unknown. I had gone in very deep, and was no longer certain I would be able to go back without help. The smell inside was difficult to describe: a stench of mould and thousand-year-old dust. Hit by the light of my lamp, I could watch as it hovered and then settled again on me like pollen. I walked on, undaunted, and went up that nondescript duct I don't know for how many feet, gasping and fighting leg cramps. It took a few minutes before I could enjoy the view of a large room, which my lamp was unable to illuminate in its entirety. Although I felt pains in the calf, where the large scar was still visible, and my lungs burned for lack of air, I walked quickly along the perimeter of the chamber, and I imagined I would need Angelika's help to understand where I was.

I went back down the passage, but when I reached the junction with the well, I heard a rustle and then some stone rubble falling. I looked up and grinned when I saw her sliding down the rope a bit awkwardly.

«I must admit that you're reckless» I commented.

She looked down at me. «I was afraid something had happened to you. You have been down here for ages!»

I suggested that she swing to get closer to me, so she gave herself a good push sideways and I grabbed her on my first attempt. It had been so long since we hugged each other that way, that I felt somewhat gratified in embracing her again. I immediately realised, though, that the emotion was only the result of that little success, reopening the game with the Ahnenerbe. She smiled at me gently when she gathered from my gaze, that we could put many of our misunderstandings aside. I invited her to follow me along the tunnel and, when we reached the new room, I heard her moaning. I thought she was going to pass out when I saw her kneeling, but I was wrong: she was just catching her breath.

I approached an indefinite coloured wall, shiny like a mirror, and turned to her with a proud smile. «Well? Not saying anything?»

Angelika held her lamp close to the panel, which was made of unspecified material and formed a right angle with a large shale wall. «There are no engravings that can help us with the dating of this room. The finish of this huge slab... it's wonderful, but doesn't help us much to find the sacred texts of the Sonnenmensch we're looking for» she commented, a little disappointed.

«Do you know what your problem is?» I finally asked. «You judge by appearances.»

She looked at me, her arms crossed. «Are you implying I'm superficial?» she asked me, offended.

That squabble amused me, because I was already foretasting the finale. «Sometimes.»

«Look who's talking! I judge by appearances while you don't, huh? Would you have me believe that you were stricken by my intellect when we first met?»

«Of course not, but now I'll show you how superficial you are» I went on, somewhat proudly. «Look at this wall carefully: it's made of glass» I explained just before increasing the intensity of the lamp.

The slab shone and the finish was nearly perfect. To the touch, we could only perceive slight irregularities on the surface, small scratches, which however weren't visibile with the naked eye. It was in fact about a hundred transparent polished pieces, placed side by side with almost absolute precision. Even now I still happen to rethink about the emotion of that moment and still wish to go back then and there. The sacredness of that place was blatant and the discovery amazing, to say the least, but surprises weren't over. Across the room, at the far side, there was a sort of stone throne, right in front of the shale wall, which was entirely covered by the image of Isis seated with little Horus on her lap.

«Don't you notice anything familiar?» I asked, lighting up the representation.

Angelika dropped her arms along the hips while she was gaping at the wall. «Alexander, this is identical to that of St. Bernard's linen!»

«By the way, where did you leave my bag?» I asked her all of a sudden, worried about the relic I kept in the lining of my jacket.

«Don't worry, I entrusted it to Khaled.»

I totally lost my temper. «I asked you to take care of it personally!» I shouted. «Dammit! I'll tell Khaled to lower the bag and more lamps. Don't move» I ordered, annoyed by her carelessness.

It took me only about five minutes to climb down the tunnel, scream at the top of my voice to tell the two Egyptians to lower the material, and walk up to the room again with the equipment, but, when I got back, I saw Angelika crying like a baby. I didn't realise my reproach would have had such an effect, so I tried to fix it with irony. «What happened to you? Have you seen a mummy?»

«Look at these slabs» she said touching the glass wall with her fingers, «they are engraved on the back!

Everything here got lit up in a moment, it's… it's gorgeous and unfathomable. The text on the walls is endless!»

She wasn't crying over what I had said, but because of what she had seen. A strange light had surrounded the chamber and awakened it from its sepulchral greyness. Honestly, I was confused by the revelation myself, but satisfied with the discovery, too. I immediately looked for the source of the two beams of light which, weak and yellowish, left the entire room in the dim light while emphasizing the smooth wall only.

The engraving on the back, only a few millimeters deep, refracted that faint glowing beam running along the wall, and gave a three-dimensional effect to the inscriptions. The artist who had worked on those slabs, apparently made of glass, had engraved the glyphs from the back, and then fixed them to the supporting wall. In that way, the panels appeared smooth on the outside and the light, hitting at an angle, highlighted the engraving on the side against the wall. Thus, even if the outer surface happened to be somehow scratched, the hieroglyphics would stay protected on the back forever.

«It's like someone turned on the light, it happened a few minutes before you came back. They really seem glass panels, but the Egyptians could only achieve manufacturing glass paste: these are almost perfectly transparent instead!»

«Of course it's glass» I said without hesitation. «It means that, they found out how to remove other minerals residues from it sooner than we believe they did. I think our colleagues need to reconsider some dates after this discovery. I'm sure that the sacred signs were engraved on the back of the slabs to preserve them from the corrosive action of sand or from breachers' hands. Come on, read the engravings and tell me if they have anything to do with our theory.»

«Your theory» Angelika pointed out.

I sighed and moved close to her. «I thought this was a teamwork. For better or for worse, I wouldn't have gone this far without your help.»

«I only did it out of pure selfishness, if you really wish to know. I mainly helped myself» she replied with a sorrowful look. «What do you mean to tell Dietrich?»

«So what do these scribbles say?» I tried to elude her question to avoid yet another dispute, that would have been quite inappropriate there and then.

«I'm with you, Alexander, but I want to know your intentions» she insisted, holding my face between her hands.

«Are you?» I replied and saw her nod. I wasn't sure she liked my idea but, at that point, I might as well tell her my plan before it was too late. At least her reaction would have clarified many points of the matter. «I wish the whole research, and what we will deduce from this expedition, to be sent to a foreign correspondent for publication. Your name would also appear on it and we would request for the refugee status to be granted to us.»

Angelika's eyes widened as she exclaimed: «Do you want to ask for political asylum? And to whom? Where would you like to escape? Do you think the Ahnenerbe is not capable of hunting you down abroad?»

«I have made too many mistakes in the past, I don't want to pursue that course any longer. I would only go back to Germany for...» and I left my sentence hanging. It was my intention to bring Romy with me too, because I feared there might be retaliation against her.

«Darn! What's the matter with you? Is your courage

wavering in the face of your discovery? I got it, you've already made your decision. You have decided for me too.»

«There's nothing settled! We will have plenty of time to ponder the best course of action. We will decide together what to do with our lives and which direction to take, but I would like you to come with me.»

«That's not true. I'm just a hindrance to your plans, a dead weight placed between you and your future away from the Ahnenerbe. I thought your ambition would lead you to aspire to high office, or at least to high profits, but I was utterly wrong.»

«Stop talking nonsense. In that case, I wouldn't have told you anything, would I? We will talk about it at the appropriate time. We have discovered nothing yet, so let's not cross our bridges before we come to them. And now tell me what's written on that damned crystal wall» I ordered, but right then Khaled joined us and, hands in his hair, he exclaimed:

«But how can it...» and pointed to the glass wall.

So, although reluctantly, I decided to briefly explain why the engraved words were refracting the light and acquired a relief effect. «Remember that smaller opening at the mouth of the well? My bag sat on top it. When the light from the antechamber finally channeled into the slit, it came down here through that small conduit» and I pointed to the opening on the ceiling. The light beam came down from above, reached the corner of the room, then hit a small monolith, on the top of which an inclined obsidian slab had been placed. The light reflected by the polished mineral was parallel to the long glass wall and hit the slabs edgewise. Once more, I took off my shirt, a rag by then, and cleaned the surface until it shone.

Angelika had a downcast expression, yet she read the inscription on the base of the monolith in a commanding voice: *"May the darkness therefore be dispelled."* She looked at me gently, then rummaged in her bag and took out her notebook.

«Let's start from the west wall» I advised, «then continue eastward, towards the rising sun, that is, God. Khaled, come on, you too, help us!» So, while he was studying the entrance tunnel, Angelika seemed to have set aside our discussion and eagerly began to transliterate the wall texts, her gaze enraptured by both the Egyptian art and the mystery floating over that place.

I watched her while she was working. She was writing quickly for fear that the lamps or the rays coming from outside would lose intensity when, suddenly, she stopped her feverish translation and looked for me.

«They write about Horus as the son of the Sun god, whose memory lingers on the mouths of those who live on Earth and those who are yet to come into the world» she said after a few minutes of silence.

In the meantime, I had moved away to contemplate the depiction of Isis on the shale wall at the far end of the room. I must confess that, once again, I surrendered to the beauty of the Goddess.

Angelika came up to me, put a hand on my shoulder and, without saying a word, kissed me for a long time. I knew well her soft and sensual lips, yet it felt like kissing a stranger. Unable to get carried away by passion, I felt indifference prevail over attraction and took that kiss as a farewell.

She looked down and whispered: «This place is wonderful, one of a kind and it's obvious there aren't any cartouches, because, judging from the quality of the wall writings, here we're in the Predynastic period, at the dawn of civilization and perhaps a step away from your dream. I'll do my best with the translation, but many of these glyphs are unknown to me. These inscriptions represent an intermingling of styles from different eras. Some of them are proto-hieroglyphics, while others belong to the ancient Egyptian. It's such a multifaceted script I'm left befuddled. What bewilders me most are the several transcriptions on the other walls, in different and more recent languages.»

«I don't understand» I confessed disoriented. «Do you mean that the script, engraved on the back of the glass walls, has been translated into other languages? I thought that each of them dealt with a different topic!»

«I have transliterated the initial part so far, and then, out of curiosity, moved to the stone wall at the end of it. I found a demotic text, more precisely Frühdemotisch, as we call it, the oldest kind» she explained pointing to the part engraved on the wall. Then she moved away to indicate another block, «and this is certainly Sahidic. But the amazing thing is that each passage, more recent than the one engraved on the glass wall, repeats the very same sentences. I don't specifically know Sahidic, however the demotic faithfully reproduces the hieroglyphic script, as if the part, that can be directly illuminated by sunlight, and which they aimed to protect from profaners, is the origin of all the other writings, their matrix.»

I couldn't hold back a satisfied smile. «A new Rosetta Stone» I fantasized. «If you are right, this place have handed a single great theological concept out to dozens of different ethnic groups. So, the one and only religion might have been born here, within these walls. The chimera of a universal brotherhood... yes, it must be so» I mused. «In this temple of crystal and light that slashes the darkness of earth» I recited, turning my gaze to the gorgeous black Isis, the goddess and universal mother, who had guided me down there.

Angelika sighed: universal brotherhood was not what she hoped for and I knew it all too well. «I wouldn't even be surprised to find part of a Proto-Canaanite script at this point» she added, while matching each glyph with its sound and meaning, and each sentence with its transliteration and translation.

«Come on, what else is swirling around in your head?» I asked after several minutes of silence. «Something to do with my proposal?»

«No, it's the Shemsu Hor» she answered with an incredulous look. I guess I changed my expression when I heard her uttering that sentence. «Well, you might be right when you say there's their hand in the Sator, too. Also, some believe that those "Priests of Horus", or "Guardians of Horus", were fully knowledgeable about techniques which were very advanced for their time and through which subsequent generations were able to erect some monuments we haven't been able to comprehend so far.»

I burst out laughing: Angelika Blumen validating my hypothesis. That was a miracle!

«Mine is just a simple conjecture» she hastened to point out, «and you know very well that I don't believe in fairy tales.»

«So what are you doing in a place like this?» I replied widening my arms as an invitation for her to take in the immense work surrounding us. «The Shemsu Hor are mentioned in the Royal Papyrus of Drovetti. Correct me if I'm wrong, I'm just a heretical medievalist and, of course, I don't have your knowledge of the matter but, for goodness' sake, once in your life just give me your opinion, instead of that of the luminaries who wrote the books you studied on! So, do you think it could be Shemsu Hor's work or not?»

«Yes. Yes, I believe this could be their work. In fact, I really hope so. The problem is, that we know almost nothing about these Guardians to formulate a plausible theory and I don't want to ruin my reputation even before I've got one. I have no starting point to elaborate on. I should begin from scratch without having the necessary knowledge. Interpreting this place from a historical point of view is a leap in the dark, can you understand that? I believe that the Keepers of Horus have much in common with your thesis about the Egyptian litany and I know the term *shemsu* doesn't originate from the Egyptian, but from the Babylonian word *shamash*, which means sun. And I know the text on these walls refers to the unique solar religion, to the only god, whose son, Horus, has come among men.»

«I like that, go on» I urged her, enthusiastically.

Angelika pointed to the lines she was about to translate from the top to the bottom. «Be prepared for revelation, Herr Professor» she said, clearing her throat. «*The Time of Râ. And Râ said: "I am Râ; Râ, who bestoweth life. The God who came into being from himself, is what he is and what he is not. It is not by childbirth that I was born. I am the only One, the Lord of heaven. Thou cannot behold me with thy own eyes, but I am he, Râ, the Father of the Gods, the one who is on his mountain. Such am I: I am my name and my name is God. I am the one who speaketh to thee. Do not be negligent towards what will be revealed to thee: every plant perisheth but not the word. This is a teaching. Hearken! Tell the truth, observe justice. Respond thou not to a good deed with an evil doing and the evil will not come upon thee. The luck of the unjust lasteth not. Show not thyself contemptuous, glorify not thy soul and it will not be torn apart. Give unto thy fellows. This is the tenet for thou shalt not die again. He, who hearkened to me, giveth thanks. What was commanded, was pronounced and I am satisfied"»* and with a smile she turned to me. «I hope you enjoyed it.»

«Indeed!» I replied while a shiver was still running down my spine for what I had heard. «We are in the place of initiation the descendants of the Shemsu Hor used, to select the elite members, the chosen ones. This is truly the Templar Crystal Temple, where everything has been set up for humanity!» I exclaimed, but she looked puzzled, waiting for clarification. «Since back in the days of king Baldwin of Jerusalem, the knights knew the sacred values that now I know descend from the *Maât*: Truth, Righteousness, Harmony. The Temple *Militia* itself should have kept all those noble precepts, as well as the Wisdom that arises from the understanding of the past and the future. Unfortunately, some in the *Militia* didn't understand those values and devoted themselves to slaughtering the infidels, thus leading the Order to its ruin. The Crystal Temple represents the union of ancient and modern wisdom.»

«Is that why you're here, professor?» Khaled, all covered in white dust, asked me as he slid out of the connecting tunnel. «You feel like you need to combine what you already know of that modern wisdom with the most ancient Egyptian one, right?»

«Not the most ancient, the most esoteric» I said, amazed by his speech.

«Why would anyone hide something like that? Why not openly declare that we all descend from the same stock, whose faith was based on the worship of a solar god? I don't feel upset by your revelation; why should others be? You told me that the genesis of the universal creed is written on this glass wall. The One God presents himself to his creatures and dictates his guidelines to the world so that humankind can live in harmony and earn eternal life. What's so terrible about it?»

In my own point of view, there was something visionary about universal brotherhood. «Let me explain it to you: uniting what's different is still a difficult task after millennia of wars and manipulations, especially so, after countless crusades. The great faiths have drifted apart too much and a discovery like this won't be enough to reconcile them.»

«There is something you should see before you go on with the translation of the texts» said the Egyptian, leading the way. «Follow me into the tunnel, lie on your back and read the engravings on the ceiling.»

Angelika snorted. «Get out of the way, so I can lie down on the ground. Come on!» She pulled him out to stare at the ceiling. It only took a few moments before she squealed with excitement. It was the first time I saw her that way.

«Tell me what it says. Come on!» I cried out, elated.

«Here is your invocation: *Iu em hetep, Sau Hor! Iu ek uâbet!*, that is, *Welcome in peace, Guardian of Horus! You are pure!*» she exclaimed in a broken voice.

«Guardian of Horus? » I repeated, dazed.

«Yes, Alexander. Guardian of Horus: *Sator*, or better, *Sau Hor*, guardian, custodian, keeper of Horus, in short, Shemsu Hor» she repeated, quickly exiting the tunnel to jump on me, joyful.

All our disagreements disappeared at once. Heedless of the Egyptian's comments, I lifted Angelika from the ground and kissed her. «We found the Temple of Initiation and understood that the Sator is the Guardian of Horus, but we still don't know where to start to find the twelve texts of eternal life, the Sonnenmensch» I summarized, thoughtful, but enthusiastic at the same time. «Let's get back to work immediately, the air is beginning to run out down here and we have no time to waste.»

«I don't think this room has ever been used for any ritual and I want to point out that the Shemsu Hor are just a legend» said Khaled, as if he could boast a knowledge of the subject equal to mine and Angelika's. «The mere fact that the Guardian of Horus is welcomed at the entrance, doesn't mean that this temple was built by the priests themselves, nor that their descendants ever existed.»

«You're such a jinx!» I rebuked sitting on what looked like a stone throne.

I was worn out by the heat and the many questions troubling me, so I tried to relax on that seat, which was anything but comfortable. It was a rather unremarkable block of stone, whose only peculiarity was the hawk with folded wings which was engraved on the back. That kind of representation, Angelika explained to me, was usually placed on beds or pallets to ensure peaceful sleep. The symbol of the resurrection was also visible on the back: a strange *djed* with only two levels. Although the throne had been obtained from a monolith, taurine paws were roughly outlined on its base and its seating surface, perfectly flat, suggested that it belonged to the Predynastic period.

All of a sudden, Khaled, inexplicably out of his mind, shouted that he had found signs of desecration in the back wall. Behind me there was a fake door without seals, where a breach had been opened.

«The violators ventured as far down as here. Damn, they destroyed half the wall!» exclaimed the Egyptian. «I can't explain how that happened. There were multiple profanations, judging from the siliceous stones used to close up the opening. It's not a tomb or we would have found some clay seals. There's nothing to resell, no valuable object to remove and, if there were any, it wouldn't have been possible to climb up the well so easily.»

I glanced at the door and sighed. «Cool it, Khaled, and help me remove the rubble. It is a desecration in all respects and then, what would a fake door to the Hereafter be useful for if this were not a tomb?»

The light beams illuminating the large walls went out suddenly, then came back. The Egyptian complained about his helpers' behaviour: «And to think that I explicitly asked those three out there not to block the entrance!»

I instinctively looked askance at Angelika, who stiffened. Khaled, meanwhile, was doing all he could to remove the last boulders that blocked the fake door and he had already stuck his head in the opening. A breath of hot air made him shrink back.

«Wait!» Angelika shouted as she ran towards us. «Above here it is written: *Beware! Heaven and Earth are about to fall because of you, for you shall not stand before Him.*»

«I don't believe in curses» I replied and entered first, lowering my head and stopping on a sort of ledge on the back of the wall.

Khaled shone his lamp on some inscriptions and read aloud: «*You have been granted trust, yet you are a transgressor. Wherefore you shall return into darkness!*»

In an instant, I saw him sinking and grabbing my legs not to get swallowed by the chasm that had opened under his feet. The last thing I saw before falling down was the terrified expression of Angelika, who tried in vain to catch hold of my arms.

Khaled couldn't cling to me for long. I felt him lose his grip and heard him scream as he disappeared into the dark. A dull thud, then nothing more. I miraculously managed to stop the fall spreading my legs and pushing my feet against the walls.

«Khaled! Khaled, can you hear me? Hold on, I'm coming to get you» I shouted at him without having the faintest idea how to get out of that situation. I tried to see the bottom, but with every movement I risked sliding even further down. The pain in my calf and knees was taking my breath away and tiredness would soon exacerbate the precariousness of my position. I shouted again and again, and the Egyptian answered with a groan only after the fourth call.

«I can see a light switching on and off» cried Angelika. «Maybe he's not able to move, but at least he's alive. I'm going to get some ropes to rescue you.»

A moment later I was tied to the rope that Angelika had secured to the seatback of the throne and was lowering myself to retrieve the Egyptian. Several feet further down I saw him: Khaled had hit the bottom of that second dry well. I set foot on the ground right next to him and was disconcerted by the sight: instead of water there was a pile of human bones, which seemed to lose solidity under my feet and dragged me deeper and deeper. When I felt I was being swallowed by the ossuary, I limited every movement of the legs and tried to understand what state my companion was in. Khaled was in a foetal position, his limbs broken. I had seen so many people die, several by my own hands, and yet, at the sight of the Egyptian lying that way, I felt an unfamiliar pity for him. I approached the corpse to close his gaping eyes. Under my feet the bones kept crumbling like cookies and a chill shiver ran down my spine. There was nothing I could do for Khaled, so I grabbed the rope and was climbing back up quickly, when I saw a side tunnel at half height: that well, which we would later name "Pit of violators", was an exact replica of the first.

«Alexander, what are you doing?» Angelika scolded me from above as she saw me lingering.

«Khaled is dead» I replied.

We could no longer continue the inspection: the accident was one of our problems, the other was the lack of air. We had been down there for too long and were losing clarity of mind, so we decided to get back above the ground before it was too late. I thought about the possibility of recovering the Egyptian's body, but it was far too deep down for it to be brought back to the surface and, also, we would have risked that others would end up like him.

At the exit, I explained what had happened to Anwar, who wept over his friend's death. I saw him pick up a fistful of sand and let it slip between his fingers, while sorrowfully uttering some incomprehensible words. At the end of what I imagined to be a prayer for the deceased, I showed him the plan of the temple I had sketched on my notebook, specifying the exact location of the body. The Egyptian looked at me dejected and realised that there was no chance of bringing his dead friend back outside. The matter was utterly troublesome: because of the accident, Anwar would certainly ask for the intervention of the authorities and we would have to give up the expedition permanently. I read a strong anxiety in Angelika's attitude and I couldn't blame her: we really didn't need that setback.

Anwar muttered something to the other two Egyptians,

who nodded repeatedly. She held my arm fearing a sad epilogue for our mission and all its dramatic consequences, but, to our surprise, Anwar begged us not to mention the mishap to anyone else. We would be resuming the exploration the next day as if nothing had ever happened: that excavation wasn't authorized, he had already had hassles in the past for some burial finds sold on the black market and his helpers had to wait for the end of the expedition to receive the rest of their pay. It was clear that his statements hid much more, but I didn't investigate, because that was clearly the perfect solution for everyone.

As we were on our way back, the tiny homes of Balat, which I recognised from afar, seemed like a vision to me. We were raddled because of the fatigue and of the accident, but a deliberate optimism was gradually making its way among us. Angelika was calm and, despite everything, she seemed to have retrieved even her most brazen sensuality.

Egypt – Dakhla, October 10, 1937

On the morning of October 10, we went back to the excavation site at the crack of dawn. Angelika and I abseiled into the temple down to the "Pit of violators", where Khaled's body still lay. We didn't need to reach the bottom, because the access to the side tunnel was about halfway; nevertheless, the stench of Khaled's rotting corpse had made the air unbreathable already. We only spared ourselves the macabre sight.

Twice we had descended a well and walked up a narrow and high passage, stretching towards the unknown. It was as if that place made us relive the same moments and feelings over and over again, as if there was no way for us to escape from that reality and go back to our lives outside the temple.

We were in front of the first wall inscription of the tunnel which, to our great surprise, had nothing to do with the previous ones: *Terribilis est locus iste.*

Angelika turned to me, dismayed for that inappropriate Latin text. She demanded an explanation with a rather bewildered look. However, that sentence didn't seem so incongruous to me, even though I felt a thrill at its sight.

«There's no doubt that this place is terrible and frightening» I told her, «others have experienced that before us. But what if it also were venerable and wonderful?»

«Does *terribilis* have other acceptations in Latin?»

I suggested that she look further down. «*Omne datum optimum et omne donum perfectum desursum est, descendens a Patre luminum*» I recited by heart. «Every good and perfect gift is from Above, coming down from the Father of the heavenly lights.»

«Have you already memorised it?» she was astonished.

«I already knew it: James 1, 17. That's also the opening of Pope Innocent II's Bull, which granted enormous privileges to the Templars. The *Militia* must have passed here after 1139, when *Omne Datum Optimum* was issued.»

«The Father of lights? Did they worship the Sun god?»

«At least according to my heretical theory» I stated just before climbing a steep flight of stairs.

She smiled and shook her head, staring at me, amused. «I adore you when you upset my every certainty. I know this is not the right time to go into detail, but I want you to know that, before Khaled's accident, I finished the translation of the text in the glass room.»

«Well?»

«The part I had transliterated was an actual introduction of God to his creatures, remember? A sort of genesis of the cult, so much so that it began with *"The Time of Râ"*.»

«Get to the point, Angelika!»

«The rest heralds the coming of Horus, his role on Earth and that of his mother, Isis. I'll quickly read the rest to you: *The Time of Isis. "Râ spoke to me: Hail to thee, Lady of Beauty. Life is by thee, Isis, thou art the star that cannot die. My son's heart is joyful: he is in thy womb and carrieth the Maât. To him Heaven and Earth and his name will be eternal. Horus is his name, the young God. I am with you, for the love he inspireth is the love I foster. His protection is my protection. Fierier is his fervour than the flame of fire. He will tread his lake as he wisheth. Ah, if the Earth abounded in his fellows! Horus, thou took Heaven, thou inherited Earth. Thou art a god and thou shalt be a god with no rivals, thou shalt walk the sea shod with sandals, thou art pure as he who is in his pyramid. Behold Horus, gods, his spirit cometh from the Father!"*

Here is the third and final part of the translation: *The Time of Horus. "I am he who loveth his father, the beloved blood son of Râ, Horus whom Isis bore. The one whose name was created in the womb of his mother, the son of Râ, from whom cometh what is and what is not. It is on the horizon that life and power have been given to me. I am vested with the great role that Râ entrusteth to me. I open the gates, I open the paths. In the form of Râ I will enter, as Horus I will leave. I have come to be thy protection and in the same way as Râ liveth every day, I will live after death."*

This explains the linen of St. Bernard and the depiction of Isis in that context. Horus is the heir of the Sun god in all its forms. Think, Alexander, of the pride of Isis as the mother of Horus, *Baefemjt*!»

That last word reverberated in my head like a gong. «What did you say? How did you call Horus? That thing you said in Egyptian» I said shaking her by the shoulders.

«That the spirit of Horus comes from the father, *Baefmjt* or *Baefmet*, it depends on the pronunciation» she repeated without understanding what was spinning in my head.

«Baphomet!» I exploded with joy, «Baphomet, the Baphomet of the Templars, and Isis is their star, she who cannot die!»

«For the Egyptians, Isis was Sirius, in the constellation of Canis Major... so what?» she wondered.

«Then raise your eyes» I suggested, illuminating the vault with the soft light of the lamp. Every single nook of that place was surprising. We felt like children in a toy shop, where we could play with every item on sale without any restrictions.

A starry sky was painted above our heads and each star matched the most rigorous geometric standard. The golden ratio between the segments of the five points expressed the link between heaven and earth, for the pentacle has always been the earthly element, along with the man, whereas the number five has always meant the union with the divine. The man inscribed in a circle with his limbs extending outwards emulated a star.

«If man is directly involved in this geometric framework, why do some people connect the five-pointed star to evil?» she asked me childishly.

«Unfortunately, that is a more recent legacy. Its meaning changes according to the orientation of the apex: if the tip points upwards it symbolises good, if it's upside down it represents evil, but if you really want to know my opinion, it's just nonsense. An ancestral symbol such as the pentacle is a mere emblem of the union between God, man and the forces of nature; at the same time, it represents the five senses as well as the intercourse between the two sexes. Ignorance makes it a negative sign, especially if you think that for several centuries it stood for Christ's five stigmata! Speaking of stars, which one was the morning star for the Egyptians?»

«*Sopdet* or *Sepet*, if you prefer: Sirius, it's always her. Isis was their morning star and the queen of the decans, that is, the thirty-six stars to the south of the solar ecliptic.»

I still remember that instant of fulfilment, that feeling you get when, finally, after years of study, you suddenly unravel the tangle of questions.

«The knights idolised her, yes, they revered Sirius, and for the early Christians that star represented the Sun of

Truth, the omen signifying that a messenger of God was coming. Now it's all clear to me: Isis announces the Truth, the *Maât* and the coming of her son. The chosen Templars, those initiated into the ancient wisdom by the heirs of the Shemsu Hor, revered Isis as the Morning Star and Horus as Baphomet.»

She nodded. «Râ inseminates Isis, just as the sun fertilises the earth and makes it fruitful. Yes, this is the first and true place of union between Heaven and Mother Earth, later ones followed its orientation, its harmonic principles, its sacred writings engraved in the glass room.»

«It may well be one of the first cases of theogamy in history. I wouldn't be surprised if there were one hundred and forty-four stars upon this ceiling, like the number of the chosen ones admitted to the Heavenly Jerusalem» I replied, staring at the largest of the celestial bodies depicted on the ceiling. «To each star its man, or woman. Five points, because five is the number of God and the number of Jesus, from its Greek acronym. *Ichthýs* comes from the Greek word for "fish". It's funny that for the Celts the fish symbolised Mother Earth instead. The connections between the great cultures are countless.»

«You're going off the beaten track, professor, there's no connection between the fish and the goddess.»

«If you rotate the fish symbol by ninety degrees, it turns into a perfect representation of the female womb, and I think the *ankh* can also be.»

«The *ankh* is the key to life and that's it. Don't you always turn everything into a matter of sex! Just move on before Anwar abandons us down here and let's try to recap everything to get a clearer understanding.»

I epitomized our journey as an initiatory path towards revelation. We had entered an inverted cone antechamber, penetrating the earth through a bottomless well. We had moved away from the light, only to find it again in the glass room, where the sacred scriptures had taught us how to live according to the *Maât* to gain immortality.

«Yes, then we knocked down a fake door to access the second shaft and then the tunnel we're in. We are violators, Alexander, we need accept that» she commented, smiling.

I considered her words. «Originally, the door behind the throne was open, I'm sure. Those who didn't know the place, or were not led by a priest, ended up in a trap, but could venture farther and try their luck. This is not the way to the Underworld, but to the knowledge of Shemsu Hor's great secrets. It must be so.»

Angelika smoothed her hair and wiped her sweat. «The limestone used for the building is excellent and the finish, well, you've seen it for yourself how accurately cut it is. Probably the two factors contributed to the thermal insulation of the temple. Considering the temperature variations between day and night, it's amazing that there are no cracks along the walls and no landslides happened. Also, considering its position, and the total lack of depressions on the surface, it's easy to assume that it has never been directly affected by floods during torrential rains. Even though the western desert is less rainy than the eastern, potential difference in temperature means that we would still have to be careful in handling possible finds we may discover. The transition from a closed space to the open air is enough to turn them into a little more than a pile of dust in our hands. That's why a conservative action is often necessary before removing them from their location.»

And while she was chatting on, I was thinking about

what to do with our discovery. I can't quite explain what state of mind I was in. Sometimes I wondered if it wouldn't be better to go back home empty-handed. What would I tell the Ahnenerbe? Or rather, how would the foundation exploit those wall texts? Would I ever be able to persuade Angelika to let go of everything and go along with me to publish our discovery abroad?

Soon we were in front of a door, and my every conjecture was instantly shattered. A winged solar disk was depicted above the arch. Those who had come there before us and scratched the corridor walls, had gone as far into their criminal work as to carve *Haec domus Dei est et porta Coeli* right next to those masterful friezes.

Angelika was furious. «How could men like the Templars understand the meaning of all this? How could they associate this temple with the House of God and the Gate of Heaven? They would have needed to be able to interpret the texts in the glass room first, but it's no easy task for us even today, let alone in the Middle Ages!»

«I've explained that already, maybe a priest showed them the way!»

«The Shemsu Hor must have sunk really low if they allowed their heirs to pass certain knowledge on to shady characters as the Templars!»

«Don't decry the role of the Order in history» I reproached. «They were condemned because of a conspiracy, and in any case there's good and evil in each of us, too. This is the temple of revelation. For centuries, millennia, we have been searching for our origins as men, as children of God and as worshippers. We are now in the *omphalos* of this knowledge, which fuses different ethnic groups, religions and worlds. We are not talking about the Aryan race here, we are talking about mankind. Maybe that's precisely what you can't understand. It's not absurd to assume that the Templars were initiated into the utmost knowledge by the descendants of the Shemsu Hor, just as we cannot rule out the possibility that a similar fate also befell Saladin. Sometimes a very special bond is created between two conflicting factions, opposites attract, you know, and antagonism is not necessarily due to cultural diversity.»

«If initiates of the solar cult from all ages and ethnic groups reached this place before us, where are the documents proving that great wisdom?» she asked me twirling around the place to show its emptiness.

«You're such a demanding woman! Aren't you satisfied with the few hundred hieroglyphs from the other room? These walls, these pictographs, the geometry of this place are part of that wisdom. It's all around us! Symbolism is the language that allows man to communicate, to get in touch with God. You, of all people, should understand the value of all that. You study hieroglyphs, and what are they if not immortal symbols of God's work? Maybe initiation rituals were performed here. The entrance hall was a chamber of purification and in the glass room the sacred laws were to be learnt.»

«Rituals? Seeing is believing, and so far I haven't seen any papyrus!»

«But it is not to be excluded that certain teachings were handed down orally. We might not find any script at all. Even Pythagoras forbade his followers to leave writings to posterity. Why do you think he did that? Such a wisdom cannot be left at the mercy of just anyone, that's the reason of the Sator. But now look ahead and get ready for the revelation» I told her pointing to the new room with no pictographs.

We walked on to a perfectly circular room, whose geometric rationality would have enraptured even a Pythagorean, provided that the knowledge of those exceptional mathematicians didn't stem precisely from that place. In the centre of the room stood a huge conical monolith with a rounded apex, very similar to a *menhir*. It was dark and slightly speckled, Angelika assumed it might be diorite, like the ring-shaped stone around its base. The top of the ring, engraved with the names of the decan stars, surrounded the central block encircling it like a wedding ring on its finger. The floor was pure alabaster and blended with the colour of the walls. Such exceptional architectural minimalism made that place timeless, as if essentiality could make ancient and modern coexist in harmony.

In that monolith in the centre of the *omphalos*, Angelika saw the Ben Ben stone, that is, the primaeval mound that gave birth to the Sun god. «Do you know what these writings mean?» she asked me, like a little conceited know-it-all. «That this stone ring is a very old star clock. It was used to calculate the hours of the night and was quite accurate at it. I don't think anything like this has ever been found before.»

I didn't pay too much attention to her because, at that moment, the geometry of the place engrossed me more than its function. «This room is a copy of the Râ glyph and also of the Heavenly Jerusalem» I concluded, out of the blue. «The top of the circular wall ends with a step that joins the base circle to a square, from whose corners a ribbed vault starts and divides it into four ribs; it's…»

«Oh my God» she interrupted me, «it's squaring the circle! An anticipation of Ahmes' papyrus. I think you were right about Pythagoras, too.»

Even increasing the intensity of the lamp, we still couldn't see the upper half of the dome, so I decided to climb on the ring in the centre of the room and from there on the *menhir*.

«Careful!» Angelika cried when she saw me slip.

«It's OK, everything's under control. You won't believe it, but I think the dome is also made of glass. Its lenticular shape must have evenly distributed the load of the sand weighing down on it, and prevented it from collapsing.»

Everything followed a logic I trusted I had grasped, so I compared that place to a Gothic cathedral, which has its base on the ground, but stands out towards the heaven of God and not towards the sky of men. I knew that initiates build their temples on earth so as to imitate the temple of the Great Architect as closely as possible. Each stone in God's cathedral speaks of divine rationality, which is Harmony. Each of them is a sacred book, written with the help of the Creator's weights, numbers and measures. I turned to Angelika resolutely. «Saint Bernard knew well the precepts of the *Maât*, now I'm absolutely sure of it. The intersection point of the axes is the centre of the Earth, and there is the altar. This is one of the earth energy cores, or was when the temple was built» I inferred.

She looked at me in disbelief. «What is the place of revelation in Gothic cathedrals?»

«The whole journey is.»

«Alexander, there are four corridors leading out of this chamber, one of which is the one we came from. There's not enough air to inspect them all! Choose one.»

I was agitated and dripping with sweat. «Damn. The north is the beginning, the initiation, and sure enough we came from there. We come from the night of knowledge, from the starry sky» I explained checking my compass and turning west. «To the west the two principles merge: the masculine, solar, with the feminine, lunar, but it is to the east that you'll find the *Sancta Sanctorum* where the Master's Chair is to be placed» and I pointed to that corridor.

«Look at the floor» Angelika shouted at me, tracing with her index finger a fissure running along the large alabaster slab. Beside the line, a short hieroglyphic text would lead us to the truth. «*Sator* to the north, that is, the Guardian of Horus, and *Arepo* to the east, that is, *Ra pu*, the "*word*"!»

«Quick, let's check the other axes starting from the central monolith. What do they say?» I hurried to wipe the inscriptions, my heart in my throat.

«Here, I found *Opera* and *Rotas*! *Per-Râ*, meaning the "*house of Râ*" and *Ruty tasc*, therefore the "*border gateway*". Hey, where is the *Tenet*?»

«*Tenet* is the fulcrum of the Sator... try and find it in the middle. Look on the monolith!» I yelled at her. «Horus, of whom we would be guardians, is the Word, while in the House of the Sun you find the door to the Hereafter. You have to listen to God's word to earn eternal life and this is possible thanks to Horus. That's what Sator means!»

Angelika rushed to read that last line and smiled when she realised she had dismissed the most plausible translation. «Alexander, we are treading on the sacred Earth, the *Tenet*, for the Egyptians *Ta-Netjer*, the "*Land of God*" is our *Tenet*. Come on, it's time to take a look at the corridor, too» she told me entering the eastern tunnel. «Follow me and lower your head, or you'll get a migraine.»

And she was right: in the first section the ceiling was no more than six feet high, and then it became even lower near a door, whose lintel was at neck height, as if to impose reverence to anyone who crossed the threshold.

The narrow granite passage led to a new room, whose ceiling featured an inverted staircase that joined with its twin on the opposite side, in a truss about sixty-five feet high.

Angelika was walking ahead of me quickly until, upon reaching the new chamber, she suddenly stopped in front of a large collection of wooden caskets.

We didn't believe our eyes. Hundreds of boxes were placed side by side in a variety of shapes, sizes and friezes. The lids had beautiful polychrome depictions on a plaster base, still perfectly preserved. It was extraordinarily mesmerizing being able to examine them in the light of our lamps. The structure supporting them was a stone shelving from which all the caskets protruded by about a few inches. They rested on nets of vegetable fibres woven in the shape of diamonds and whose ends were tied to the holes on the sides of the support.

Angelika stroked a casket in the way she had often caressed me. «It's amazing how everything has been preserved in such good state. To prevent damp from forming, the Shemsu Hor chose not to plaster the depository» she told me.

«Let's open one» I suggested peremptorily.

«Wait! Hold your breath for a second because sometimes the fumes can knock you out, especially if there are resin-coated objects inside. Chemical reactions can be as deadly as the traps devised to protect these treasures.»

I was in a weird awe of the creators of that place and I felt like an ungodly man for snooping into their archives without authorization.

The casket I was holding in my hand was spectacular, slightly pink and shiny; the lighting was scarce but at first glance it seemed semi-transparent.

«It looks like alabaster, but I'm not sure.»

«I think it's calcite: it's easy to find and suitable for this kind of decorations» I replied, leaving her gobsmacked.

«I didn't think you also knew about minerals!»

«A former date of mine was a mineralogist.»

«I should have imagined that, but to get out of here with all this stuff, I would have preferred you had seduced a sorceress! Hey, wait before taking out what's inside. We can't pull it out on the spot. We need some damp cloths and a few hours. Be careful.»

I smiled at that joke. «Angelika, we don't have either enough time or much air. It's not like an ordinary excavation, with experts just waiting to take the documents to analyse them in their laboratories» I replied.

«We could spoil the content! What if there were the sacred texts, the Twelve Doors, inside one of these boxes? Do you know how much damage was caused to the papyri by people considering themselves professionals? Do you want to open it and possibly pulverize the documents inside? And what will we tell Dietrich then?»

I suddenly lost my patience, perhaps because that name irritated me, or because of my longing to learn if I had gone down there for a valid reason or for just some writing about Egyptian ordinary business. I shamelessly threw the box open and realised that it only contained a fistful of sand. «Scheiße!» slipped out of my mouth.

Angelika blanched from disappointment and suggested that I open another one, and then one more. «Damn! Which of these thousands of boxes is the sacred text in? Tell me, Alexander!» she shouted at me furiously. «Oh, my goodness, you still have no clue! I thought you already had an idea about what to look for. So the linen only helps to find the temple, but not the sacred text to elevate man to the Sonnenmensch?»

«Shut up! Be quiet, for a moment!» I snapped back
nervously, as I was trying to mentally rework all the steps
of my analysis of St. Bernard's linen. Had it helped, I
would have willingly banged my head against a wall: my
brain was an insignificant blank sheet right then. She kept
muttering and sputtering like a teakettle, making me so
furious that I threatened to fill her mouth with sand if she
didn't stop it. When the silence allowed me to be calm
again, what was a blank paper sheet suddenly tinged with
the colour of an idea.

«There's a mistake on Saint Bernard's linen» I suddenly
came out, «the acronym of Christ is misspelled and it
cannot be a coincidence. Also, the triangle before the
Ichthýs may symbolise a letter "delta", while the other with
the tip pointing down represents water in alchemy. Two of
the five Greek letters are wrong, so that word doesn't
make sense... unless you flip it one hundred and eighty
degrees pivoting it around the middle letter!»

At that point Angelika tore out a white page from her
notebook and handed it to me along with a pencil. I
immediately transcribed the exact acrostic, ΙΧΘΥΣ, and
placed it next to that of the linen, ▲ ΙΧ Ο ΙΣ ▼, then I
rotated the sheet and showed it to her in a new form: ▲
31 Ο ΧΙ ▼. «Delta thirty-one, what does it mean to you?»

She brightened up. «Sirius!»

At that point the mosaic started to take shape: "delta
thirty-one" indicated the Morning Star, Isis for the
Egyptians and the Virgin for the Christians; the circle was
the fulcrum; lastly, the Roman numeral "XI" I associated
with the eleventh house of the zodiac. Sirius and Aquarius
were linked together. If we reveal the role of Isis as the
Universal Goddess, Mother Earth, Virgin and mother of

Horus, it follows that it will be possible to achieve enlightenment only in the Aquarian age, when the world will be ready to know the answers it has always sought. Aquarius marks the end of the age of Pisces, that is, of revelation, and opens that of knowledge and awareness about our origins, hence the new Age of Inner Light. Whoever interprets the Sator discovers the role of Horus, the word of Râ and the existence of the Shemsu Hor. Whoever understands the linen reaches the Crystal Temple and reveals the genesis of the solar cult.

«I believe that the wrong spelling of the acronym for Christ is the reference to the sacred text we're searching for, and indicates where to look in» I concluded after I calmed down. «And this acronym could also be one of the first evidences of Arabic numerals in Europe!»

We hurried to find the spot of the shelving marked with the hieroglyphics of Sirius: a triangle similar to the delta letter, a loaf of bread and its determiner, the five-pointed star, at the end of them ($\triangle \; \frown \; \bigstar$). The tension in the air was almost tangible and we were both afraid we would end up with just a nice gift box and no present within.

«Here it is!» Angelika cried, exhausted by the search.

«At long last! Let me take a look before picking up one of the caskets» I said, moving her away from the shelf.

«Well? Do we start opening them all or do we aim at a target?»

I picked up several containers and scrutinized them carefully, then put them back in their place. «Let's open number eleven and hope for the best.»

Angelika looked for the container matching that Egyptian number, then stretched her hand to pick up a wooden box weighing approximately six pounds. She asked me to help her, we placed it on the ground and removed the lid with the trepidation anticipating a great discovery, or a bitter disappointment.

«Yep! There's something inside!» she exclaimed cheerfully before checking its contents.

I had given her my water-soaked shirt to moisten the sheets so as not to damage the fibre and she had slowly performed the procedure before unrolling them. «Papyri in... but what...» she stammered, staring at me, bewildered.

«What? Isn't that what we should have expected?» I asked, impatient for her answer.

«I don't understand. I was expecting Hieratic, Egyptian demotic or something of the like, but these dots in succession make me believe that it might be a Meroitic script. I must discuss it with other scholars dealing with artifacts from the Kingdom of Kush. Are you sure it's the right document?»

«I don't even know if the acrostic indicates the sacred text!» I replied.

«Okay, I'm starting to feel the lack of air. Let's get out of here, then we'll see what to do» she suggested, panting. «At any rate, we found the archive and we now know that not all the boxes are empty! We'll come back and take our time to check the remaining ones.»

We retraced the path backwards; I helped her to climb the rope up the two wells and, after a long time, perhaps forty minutes, we reached the initial antechamber again, where Anwar should have been waiting for us. But he was not there.

My watch, in fact the only one we had, had stopped working, so it was impossible for us to know how long we had remained underground. Luckily, the Egyptian had bothered to anchor the ropes we would use to ascend to the Ford winch outside.

I asked Angelika several times how she felt, but she always replied that I didn't have to worry and yet I saw she had a ghostly white face and was sweating profusely. I helped her into the harness and then I shouted to the workmen, who I hoped would still be at the mouth of the temple, to operate the winch for the ascent. Meanwhile, I put my bag on my shoulder and got ready to follow her.

«Finally! Some air! » I heard her exclaim as soon as she got out in the open.

I waited several minutes before she appeared at the entrance. She had the waxy complexion of someone who is about to faint.

«Are you sure you're okay?» I asked her again. I saw her nodding unconvincingly, then she suggested I tie the casket to the rope. So, I did.

The box, small but heavy, was slowly hoisted to the surface and, while I was following it with my eyes, I thought of the Sator script found in the *omphalos*.

«Now we'll help you up» she told me.

Angelika moved away from the opening while I was already climbing up, when suddenly the winch stopped working and I found myself swinging midair in the void of the anteroom. The weight of the bag on my shoulder made me unsteady and I had to adjust my balance several times to avoid falling. The sand, at the edge of the opening, fell on my face blinding me, I spat, trying to shield my eyes and, finally, I saw a figure silhouetted against the sun.

«Haase!» I shouted at the top of my voice, instantly realising the reason for Angelika's attitude from earlier.

«Surprised, Wagner?» he asked pointing a gun at me.

«Not so much. Have you come this far to get the job

done?»

«Actually I'm here to retrieve the beautiful woman who has accompanied you» and with a satisfied smirk, he pulled Angelika closer, while she didn't even have the courage to hold my gaze.

She had betrayed me and I felt stupid for hoping, even for a moment, that her loving displays of affection had not been just the result of a brilliant actress's virtuosity. «Like I said. I'm not surprised» I replied from the bottom, trying to hide my frustration. «Just out of curiosity, Angelika, what did you write in your latest letter to Dietrich? Not the telegram you sent from Luxor, but the letter you gave to Khaled when we were in Balat.»

«I only let the leaders know that we were failing and that it was appropriate to look elsewhere for the sacred text. I didn't imagine what their intentions were nor that they would send...»

At that point I let my anger explode. «You're a liar! I know what you wrote. You told the old man that whatever truth I'd ever found, I wouldn't let it be manipulated to serve the interests of the foundation, and that if I disclosed my new interpretation of the Sator and the linen to some newspaper, I would wreck all the studies of the Ahnenerbe on the origin and the superiority of the Aryan race. Am I right? You and your ambitions can go to hell! You don't deserve to be here.»

Angelika leaned so further in towards the inside of the antechamber that she nearly fell inside. «I tried until the very last to make you understand what was the right thing to be done, but you only listen to yourself!»

«Myself? I had found the solution for you, too!»

«Come on, Wagner, lovers' squabbles don't suit you» Haase ironically commented, wearing a grin I would have gladly wiped out with a gunshot.

«Lovers? I just have sex with women of that kind » was my reply.

«Let's cut all the chit-chat» he said and with a gunshot severed the cable: a hiss and the rope fell into the void, dragging me with it. The impact with the ground knocked the wind out of me and caused me a pang in the hips.

I heard Angelika's cry, but it was too late; I saw her leaning out to make sure I was still alive, but Haase drove her away and, with a wave of his hand, ordered a subordinate to throw the corpses of the other three Egyptians inside, too.

Anwar and the two hired labourers rained down on me and I just barely managed to step aside from their trajectory. When I looked up again, I saw another SS beside Haase slapping Angelika. My eyesight was a bit blurry, but I was sure I had never met him before. Haase defended her and threatened his comrade. I was confused and didn't understand what had happened, until I saw, next to Anwar's corpse, the canteen she had always had on her.

The limestone slab was repositioned and darkness fell once more into the antechamber. In a handful of minutes, what was supposed to be the temple of knowledge had turned into a banner of death. In those days, the souls of four Egyptians joined the ones of the ancient profaners, and soon mine would follow.

Egypt – Dakhla, October 11, 1937

I could keep my eyes open with great difficulty and felt the sand scratch my limbs as absolute darkness enveloped me. My breathing was laboured and the backache was as unbearable as the prospect of death: I had been buried alive.

I rolled onto my side and bumped into the corpse of one of the two Egyptian men. My heart thumped. I shrank back to lean against the wall and tried to pull myself together. I thought that, despite my misfortune, it felt like someone wanted to give me another chance, for I was spared from falling straight into the endless pit. Nevertheless, I was trapped. Thus, since there was no other exit besides the one they just blocked, I soon deemed my previous hope of survival to be utterly groundless.

Several times had I imagined what it would be like to die, to find oneself in front of the inevitability of fate and, just when that question was about to be answered, I let myself be touched by fear. I suddenly felt all my unforgivable sins bear down on my conscience with their irrefutable verdict: death. Yet, in the middle of all that dejected overthinking, I was able to recall the moments when life had been all too kind to me, and Romy came to my mind. Her image was so clear in my memory as if I had her by my side. I hoped she would never know about my end. Better to vanish into thin air and leave our loved ones the hope that we are still alive, goodness knows where, rather than just give them the certainty of our death. In my case, I feared what the Ahnenerbe men would tell her about me. Death is nothing compared to the dishonour that can be brought to your name.

I reached out for the bag with the lamps and lit one, then pushed the corpses of the Egyptians aside and slowly got up. I staggered from the severe migraine and waited a few minutes before moving forward. I resolved that, if that was to be my tomb, I would at least open the remaining caskets in the archive. So, in the face of fate, I joined the few remaining ropes and twisted them around the bodies of the Egyptians to use them as ballast. I wasn't proud of myself for that, but I had no choice. I estimated that they would weigh at least four hundred and ninety pounds altogether, about two and a half times my weight, and I thought I had to take the risk. I secured the other end of the rope to my waist and lowered myself into the endless pit at a very slow pace so as to avoid tugging too much on the three bodies I was bound to.

Although the pain had forced me to stop repeatedly, I reached again the *menhir* room, this time alone. For the third time I treaded the same path, but now I looked at it more like a penance than an initiatory journey. I was seized by a slight nausea at the idea that, just a few hours earlier, I had found myself in that same place with Angelika, still foolishly trusting in her good faith.

I climbed on the diorite ring and from there up to the central cone. Again. Having nothing left to lose, I tried to escape with a crazy expedient, before going to hole up in the archive to wait for my end. I grabbed the Walther and watched at it resignedly. I told myself that if I hadn't been hanging from a rope before, I would have used all the shots against Haase. At that moment, however, I decided to point the gun at the heart of the dome above me. I was standing on the monolith with my arms outstretched towards God and, instead of begging him to spare my life, I was threatening him with a firearm.

Honestly, I didn't have the faintest idea either how many feet of sand were above my head, or how thick the dome was. It wouldn't have been easy to shatter the canopy and, if that had happened, there would have been a very few chances to escape before the collapse.

My semi-automatic gun had seven rounds available and one in the chamber. I pulled back the slide to save one shot, so that when the desire to take my life would prevail over my survival instinct, that bullet would at least spare me the agony. I held it in my hand, and looked at it respectfully, then I put it between my teeth. I was ready for my last attempt before surrender.

I fired repeatedly and, after the first series of shots, I replaced the empty magazine with another seven-shots, then fired, and then I did it yet again one last time.

The dome above me, which I hoped was made of glass, was not even scratched. At that point I gave in. The ammunition were finished: twenty-one rounds and it was still perfectly intact. I felt transfigured by anger, worn out by that betrayal that I thought I had averted and, to vent my rage, I hurled my weapon towards that canopy, as ominous as it was tough. Even the last hope had vanished and God had finally found a way to punish me. I got off the large rock block and sat on the stone ring to drink the drop of water left in the canteen that Angelika had thrown me. I picked up the Walther and loaded it with the last bullet, the one I saved for myself. At such times, the thoughts swirling around the head are endless, but what bothered me most was the regret for not being able to get my revenge.

I was sitting there, dejected, when something slithered down my neck. I jumped, expecting to find a snake behind me, but didn't see any reptiles nearby. I quickly realised what had happened and ran a hand over my shoulder blade: there was nothing crawling, except a thin stream of sand that was hitting me. I looked upwards and deemed it wise to take off. I rushed to the nearest tunnel, but didn't have the time to cross the threshold before the upper part of the ceiling collapsed making a shocking racket. Without looking back, I reached the opening that led to the archive. I managed to miraculously escape the avalanche of sand and debris but, in my haste, forgot to bend my head before entering the room, so I hit violently against the lintel. Until then, my forehead had been the only part of my body that was still unharmed. I swore, but didn't stop running to the nearest corner of the room. I took cover behind a stone shelving, but the cloud hit me all the same, filling my lungs. Although I tried to cover my face, I was gasping and thought I wouldn't survive. I held my breath for only a few seconds until the dust settled on the ground.

My lamp had gone out for good and I could no longer see anything. As if that weren't enough, most of the caskets on the shelving, behind which I had found shelter, had fallen over me. It took me a while before I got rid of them. Groping, I dug until my fingers bled, but I finally opened up a passage through the sand that was blocking the only exit.

A thin beam of yellowish light hit me in the face and I

breathed a sigh of relief, imagining that I had won that battle too. I left the Shemsu Hor archive to return to the *omphalos* and contemplated the half-destroyed dome and the room flooded by the sand of Dakhla desert. For the umpteenth time, I wondered what God had in store for me and why he kept on sparing my life. It was then that I realised I had to thank him for his mercy, rather than judge him for his work. I squinted and opened my arms wide to soak up that glow, as intense and warm as the ardent kiss of a beautiful woman. I stood there, motionless, to enjoy that sun, that immense God who had enlightened my path from the beginning and who was allowing me to be born again.

«I told you that we were the good guys here, but you didn't believe me!» thundered a stern voice from up outside.

I well remember that I jolted backwards: I didn't expect to find someone waiting for me. I seemed to remember that timbre which, fortunately for me, had nothing to do with Haase's. I shielded my eyes from the light and saw a wiry man with a keffiyeh on his head. When he turned and let the sun light up his face, I recognised him: he was one of my kidnappers. Two other silhouettes promptly joined him, one of them was female.

«Grab the rope, professor» the woman invited me with a typically Italian accent.

I didn't need to be asked twice and, with the bag over my shoulder, I climbed up to the edge of the canopy, where the two men lifted me by the arms.

I was dazed and unable to find a rational explanation to that rescue, but that was okay. I watched the woman, who tucked a lock of hair under her dotted headscarf, then I studied her partner and recognised them: they were the two guests of Anwar's. Looking at him more carefully, he also reminded me of the papal gendarme I had seen in Tuscany. The pain in my back and calf was a trifle compared to the severe headache that seemed to worsen over time, nevertheless I was still able to disguise my discomfort very well.

«The marshal and the inspectress?» I asked them knowing the answer.

The woman was amazed and frowned at me. «How do you know?»

It wouldn't have been easy for me to explain the whole story of my visit to the monastery and, frankly, I had no intention of doing so. I had met her elsewhere, too, but I couldn't quite relate her appearance to that of any other woman I had met on the street or in places I regularly went to. Despite that, her demeanour and her crisp perfume, still perceptible despite the scorching heat, were familiar to me. I knew I made her feel uneasy while I stared at her, struggling to try and recall our previous encounter. A moment later it struck me like a bolt from the blue: she was the girl from the library back in Berlin, the one Gottfried was infatuated with. It had always been her! «You were spying on me when you were in Berlin!» I suddenly exclaimed pointing my finger at her.

«Sehr gut, Herr Professor» she replied with a mocking smile that displayed perfect teeth.

«It's clear that it's not thanks to Mussolini's policy to approach the Arab nationalist world that you're here, but thanks to the Vatican, Ms...»

«Annunzi, Lorenza Annunzi, and my colleague is marshal Gianni Orsini of the Papal Gendarmerie.»

Meanwhile, the local tall man had rappelled down inside the temple to check the conditions of the archive, which, because of me, was completely submerged in sand. When he resurfaced, he shot me a disapproving glance, which I didn't pay much attention to. I sat on the ground and dodged the giant's disapproving stare to address the woman and the gendarme.

«You can speak in your own language, if you deem it appropriate» I told them as I snatched a canteen from the marshal's hands and then took a long sip of water.

«We want the linen back, Wagner» were the first words of the marshal who, judging from the look, reciprocated my dislike for him and his face as round as a full moon.

«I already know that, your Egyptian friend tried to kill me to get it back» I replied dryly. «It was you that night, right?» I asked the tall man.

«My name is Abdel Ahad, professor Wagner, and I'm not a murderer. If I had wanted to kill you, we wouldn't be here now. I never intended to harm you, but only to persuade you to give us the cloth of Nūr šamši Alliance, as I had already explained to you at the time.»

The man spoke calmly and compellingly, and his ways had a soothing effect on the listener. I didn't appreciate that, though. He was staring at me insistently. Tiredness was playing nasty tricks on me, because in those seconds that I spent looking at the enemy, I felt prey of his will.

I got rid of the bag to proffer it to the small beautiful Italian, who had motioned me to hand it over to her. She opened it and took out the handgun, which she casually tossed into the pit. And that was the last I saw of my faithful Walther PPK!

«There's no linen in here! Will you make up your mind and give it to us or shall we throw you back inside?» she said almost amusingly.

«Here it is. The cloth of the great Doctor of the

Church, Bernard de Clairvaux» and I entrusted it to her, after taking it out of the lining of my jacket. «I hope my present is to your liking.»

Annunzi thanked Heaven the relic was recovered still in good condition, but she marvelled to see me so compliant. I could read it on her face. I guess she expected a reaction from me, a refusal at the very least, but that was what I wanted too: getting rid of the object that had enslaved me.

Abdel Ahad took the linen in his hand and recited a few words in Arabic, then he addressed me politely. «The woman who was with you, professor, stole some scripts from the archive and ran away with an SS officer, whom we unfortunately know: the Obersturmbannführer Franz Haase. Am I right?»

«If you knew so much, why didn't you arrive faster? That would have saved me the bother and, perhaps, prevented me from destroying part of the Egyptian historical heritage» I argued, shaking off the sand that had stuck even on my eyelashes.

«All in due time» he replied, imperturbable.

I was starting to get annoyed. «Oh, great, so you don't care about this temple, not even you!»

Abdel Ahad smiled softly, noticing my disapproving look, while Annunzi, decidedly, approached me, her step quiet and smooth, and took my notebook from my breast pocket. She read quickly and complimented me on the drawings I had made of the inside and outside of the temple. Unfortunately, I had lost everything else, including the camera that Haase and his people had taken away along with the cars.

Abdel Ahad wanted to take a look at the small diary and, only after a while, he spoke with the same unblinking face: «The one you call Crystal Temple has been, for

217

millennia, the cradle of indoctrination of the greatest men who have ever trodden the Earth. Egyptians, Hyksos, Romans... people of all eras and ethnic groups, gender and age. They were the pillars of Nūr šamši Alliance. Many have had access to the temple, but few have contemplated its treasure. There was a time when the Shemsu Hor ruled these lands. Today the archaic teachings are the prerogative of their descendants and of the few chosen who are still alive. The temple has been built over several eras, in subsequent stages following that of the first Keepers of Horus, from the Predynastic period throughout the conversion of the Egyptian population to Christianity. That's why there are scripts in different languages inside, including Coptic, but all strictly compliant to the precepts of that ancient caste. The sacred texts of one of the Twelve Gates of the Hereafter, now Ahnenerbe's target, have been sitting undisturbed for millennia in the archives of this temple. I'm sure that your friend has taken at least one document belonging to our legacy with her. Now I'm asking you to help us recover it for your own good, and that of the entire world.»

I inquired him about who he really was, although I was starting to get an idea of that. «You're helping these two Italians, but you don't work for the Vatican. So would you be one of the chosen?» I asked, a little rudely.

«Come on, Wagner, tell us where that witch is heading. We can't waste any more time» the woman cut short.

«I don't have the faintest idea. Luxor, perhaps...»

«Don't talk rubbish, professor!» took over gendarme Orsini, irritated by the chit chat. «We need to retrieve that document before it reaches Germany and you will tell us where to find it.»

«Well, if I were you, I wouldn't worry. It is undoubtedly

worth a lot, but it's not one of the twelve sacred texts they are looking for.»

«Where did you take the document from, professor?» Abdel Ahad asked me.

I got tired of being interrogated so I demanded answers from them, or I wouldn't cooperate any longer.

The Egyptian's unconcerned gaze, scanned the horizon, which was beginning to darken. «I found some interesting deductions in your notebook: our Sator, the Universal Mother and the Templars all guided by the supreme laws of the *Maât*» he said. «My forefathers did much to help mankind throughout the Golden Age and yet, after more than seven thousand years, there are still those who are trying to make their way through history to extrapolate their own wisdom, the one leading to the eternal man, the superior being, the Sonnenmensch, as you Germans call it. A beautiful dream for Himmler, a nightmare for human race. Does everything appear clearer to you now, professor?»

«Would you be a Shemsu Hor?» I asked without much conviction.

Abdel Ahad stared at me as if he wanted to penetrate my mind, grasp my every contrition, and that made me nervous. When he made to get closer, I instinctively shrank back, but then, I don't know how or why, I surrendered to his will. I felt his right hand on my forehead as he pressed his index and middle finger between my eyebrows.

«In a few moments, Alexander, you'll no longer have a migraine» he told me, setting all formalities aside.

«I don't believe in magic. Tell me more about the temple» I asked firmly.

«No, we have to see about Haase!» Annunzi exclaimed

instead, as she and Orsini motioned to get into the car. «Abdel, damn it, your evangelization can wait. Also, I remind you that you're trying to convert a sinner. Come on, let's not waste any more time!»

«No, I want him to know» the Egyptian said.

«What a foolish Shemsu Hor!» she commented. «The Nūr šamši Alliance is compromised precisely by the discovery of the man you're trying to save from perdition. Get moving, Abdel!»

«No, he must know» he insisted, as if he owed me something when, in fact, I owed him. «In the first centuries of the Christian era, many gathered here, seeing as these stones represented an unparalleled site of worship. It was a sort of transition chamber between the ancient creed of the fathers and the modern, a breeding ground for the proselytes of the new religion that was spreading in the country. The temple and its archive were regularly used until the eleventh century when, due to the moral and cultural bewilderment, the entire cult area was banned, by the Islamic, the Christian and the Jewish factions, for fear that it would harm each of the three faiths in such a delicate moment in their history. It's preposterous that they jointly agreed upon such a decision at the very time of their greatest hostility. That should serve as proof that no dispute is ever irreparable. The small overground building was dismantled and what remained of its bowels was soon buried by sand and debris. A few centuries later the temple and the archive were restored and other chosen men were trained: artists, scientists and souls of pure spirit. The Shemsu Hor draw disciples from all faiths, religions and nationalities, as long as they are guided by the *Maât* and enlightened by the halo of the Sun god. Now you know that our God summons all men, and teaches them respect for their fellowmen and for life. Full awareness of the laws of nature gives human beings wisdom and eternal life. However, not all men are able to appreciate the value of the sacred texts and to use them appropriately.»

I must confess that he had earned all my attention and was nearly persuading me of his good faith, nevertheless my natural distrust prevented me from trusting him, or anyone else, for that matter. Maybe he wasn't a real Shemsu Hor, but as an impostor, he looked extremely convincing.

«Are you afraid they could be misused? Their publication would invalidate all dating, would lead to scientific chaos and to a new unrestrained enlightenment» I inferred, indulging his interesting farce. «Yet, I'm convinced that if the world knew the true origins of faith and science, as I have known them, if we helped them understand, then we might avoid other conflicts and...»

«Some scripts would be distorted. Alexander» he said, shifting his tone from solemn to fatherly, «I know your motivations are not driven by National Socialism, but the masses are not ready to accept certain messages, yet. We are drawing closer to the time of full awareness of our origins, but it's up to us, Shemsu Hor's descendants, to decide whether or not to make such writings known. The revelation will occur in the Age of Aquarius, that's for sure, but there's still a long way to go and it won't be either you or your discoveries that will anticipate it.»

That man showed a deep knowledge of the subject, he was also a skilled orator and perhaps that peculiar talent of his was getting me confused. Was he lying or not? Was he pretending to be some kind of druid or was he really able to read my mind? Did he want to redeem me or threaten me?

«Look at me, Alexander» he told me and, for the first time, he took off the keffiyeh he was wearing, showing me the legacy of his alleged ancestors: an abnormal, narrow and very elongated skull. He was completely shaved, in some places there was a slight regrowth, although much of the head lacked hair bulbs altogether.

I had no longer believed in coincidences for some time and, at that point, I had to admit that his gifts transcended human abilities and his claim of being a Shemsu Hor was more justified than ever.

«Oh my God!» Annunzi inadvertently remarked. «I didn't think you had...»

«I swear I'll stop complaining about my incipient baldness» Orsini commented amused and, for the first time, he gave up his frown to indulge in a joke.

«Wise Mandhur, my maternal grandfather, was like me. Big elongated eyes, gaunt face and a genetic dolichocephaly. Unfortunately, as a child, I found it difficult to accept this impairment until I realised that it was a gift. It was precisely my grandfather who told me about the Shemsu Hor and their blood running through my veins. My ancestors saw the dawn of Egyptian civilization, the one we call Zep Tepi and you Europeans call the Golden Age. Mandhur initiated me into their secrets when I was twelve and I have been pursuing the Way of Horus and righteousness ever since. I'm the keeper of the Eleventh Gate. For this reason, Alexander, I have to ask you to tell me which text is about to be handed over to the Ahnenerbe.»

«I already told you: not the right one» I repeated confidently.

Annunzi smirked. «Did you trick them into taking the wrong relic? Did you deceive your mistress and Haase?

You redeemed yourself just in time then!»

«Look who's talking! I thought you had to take vows to get to your position, but I was wrong, apparently. Tell me, what is a libertine like you doing among priests and nuns?» I asked her, meeting the marshal's wild gaze. «Don't worry, I'm not going to eat her up!» I made fun of him, seeing as he was on the warpath.

«I'm a civilian and don't have to abide by ecclesiastical rules, so...»

«Is that an offer?» I provoked her to understand what she was made of, although I had already got a taste of her temper when I was at the abbey. She tried to hit me, but I anticipated her reaction and stopped her hand in mid-air.

Annunzi growled at me. «So, if I want, I can also beat the shit out of you and then decide whether to go confess my sin or savour it. Don't you tempt me, brunet» she concluded, annoyed by the grin I couldn't hold.

I looked her in the eyes and was sure I was facing a tough cookie who, nevertheless, succeded in earning my respect. «The script belonged to the section marked with the hieroglyph of Sirius but, before Angelika could notice, I switched caskets» I admitted, averting my eyes from her to stare at Abdel Ahad, who suddenly seemed surprised. «So I got it right!» I deduced.

«How did you assume it was Sirius? There are hundreds of sectors for each archive and you chose Sopdet! Which Sopdet?»

«The false acrostic of Jesus Christ on the cloth preceded and followed by two triangles, giving the clue you should rotate it, so I thought I'd turn IX O IΣ into "Delta 31 and XI" using the central letter as a pivot. Since Sirius is the thirty-first decanal star, I asked Angelika Blumen to look for the sector corresponding to the morning star, which was only logical.»

«Quite an imagination you have!» commented Annunzi, resting her hands onto her hips. «Among hundreds of shelves, you found the right place where to search.»

«Let's say that he got close, but, due to his haste, he didn't notice a detail: there are shelves marked with the hieroglyph of Sirius and other shelves marked with "Sirius Eleven", that is, the Morning Star of the Eleventh Gate for the Hereafter. Alexander» the Egyptian told me, «luckily for us, you chose the wrong sector. This means that, with or without your stratagem, the Ahnenerbe would have retrieved a document unrelated to the Eleventh Gate, but I thank you for your cooperation nonetheless.»

«Yes, but despite his mistake, he made it to your archive decoding an incomprehensible linen!» Orsini commented still incredulous.

Then Abdel Ahad addressed me again solemnly. «You have made an initiatory journey, you have understood the *Maât*, then you have been able to make out the *Uat Hor* in the linen, and the Way of Horus has led you here. This is our initiation, you are now a neophyte, Alexander Wagner, make us proud of you» he told me, but I didn't understand what he meant. «However, despite your perceptiveness, you need to know that the text of the Eleventh Gate is very complex, and it, in turn, has therefore been subdivided into one hundred and forty-four chapters.»

«Assuming that the Ahnenerbe is going to come back to take everything, the remaining sacred doors would still be missing and I imagine they are located in other temples built who knows where. Aren't you afraid that they might succeed sooner or later? They hired many scientists, far more renowned than me and now they know how and where to look for...»

«Do you really believe that?» he asked me seriously. «Then I will tell you that the greatest riches are buried before the eyes of their seekers. And that does not only concern precious objects, but also treasures such as knowledge, love, happiness. It's not nature that deprives us of such jewels but ourselves. It's not about finding, but about joining together, *Gàmos* precisely, and for those who don't understand the meaning of brotherhood, the Twelve Gates of the Afterlife, or the sacred texts of the Sonnenmensch, are just museum pieces.»

I noticed that the marshal was shaking his head like a horse shooing flies. «I don't think it's wise for you Shemsu Hor to still use this place now that its coordinates have been disclosed.»

«Calm down, Gianni, my men have already been warned. Saint Bernard's cloth is now compromised, we know it well. As a matter of fact, from now on it will only be a mere object of worship and will withhold no other secret than his pagan birth. You have opened an investigation into its disappearance, though. Lorenza, tell your superiors that our covenant is still true as the light of God, but discretion will gain us more time to prepare for revelation. Close the file on Wagner and the linen, burn the coordinates of this place or a hunt for the sacred texts will soon begin and it will shake the Papacy to its foundations as well.»

I was anxious to get all the answers to the questions that had recently crammed my brain. «Had the linen been censored by Saint Bernard? I need to know.»

«Ah, you don't easily give up, do you?» Annunzi exclaimed impatiently. «The cloth was brought to Europe by the Desert Fathers in the fifth century, but, at the time, it bore the original depiction with Isis, Horus and Râ.

When Sylvester II ascended to the papal throne, the Arabic numerals were introduced in some convents that kept scientific documents. The concession was also given to the monastery on Monte Amiata, as chemistry experiments and surgery were carried out there. It is believed that, around the Year One Thousand, the monk in charge of the relic decided to write down on the linen the location of the sacred text in Dakhla. Since he couldn't indicate it conspicuously, he associated it with the acronym of Christ with the alterations you mentioned. Saint Bernard understood the meaning of that linen, studied it, suggested a reworked version of it and...»

«He was initiated into highest knowledge» Abdel concluded, «like so many others before and after him.»

«Thanks for the clarification, gentlemen, but now I have to stop Angelika and Haase. Do you want to come for a ride with me, redhead?» I proposed, smirking.

«Don't act all braggart!» Annunzi replied. «What the heck do you mean?»

«That I will soon fly over your heads. In this regard, I need one of you to help me start the engine» and I motioned the two men to follow me while I moved away paying no attention to their calls. When we crossed the barchan dune, huge and reddened by the setting sun, the others were amazed to see a plane camouflaged under a sand-coloured sheet.

«Do you really think we'll let you go on your own just because you gave us the linen?» cried the woman.

«I don't have enough fuel to get to Luxor, so where do you reckon I'm going to go, since I have no other means of transportation?»

«Lorenza, you stay here with Abdel» ordered the marshal, worried about the outcome of the overflight «I'm going with him, so we'll retrieve the last document, too, and leave the Ahnenerbe empty-handed.»

«You know I can't drive and neither can Abdel!»

«Then I'll go with the professor» the Egyptian offered.

«Forget it! No way!» I replied, pushing him away, «it'd be like having a bullock on board! You'd better give in and follow me from the road, if you can» I concluded, climbing up and wearing my glasses. «Come on, Orsini, turn that propeller and stop nagging me» I told him.

«Wait!» shouted the woman who resolved to accompany me, contrary to her colleague's opinion. «I'd like to inform you that I'm aiming a pistol at your nape. One wrong move and I'll slay you, as soon as we land» she yelled at me as I was already taxiing along the beaten sandy track.

«And where would you lay me?» I punned at her expense as I was taking off. The situation was starting to become comical, so much so that I heard her screaming in panic. Discovering I also had a euphoric streak was interesting, although I imagined it was only a transitory luxury conceded by my nature after years of absolute rigour. Maybe that was also thanks to that amusing woman and her pseudo-unbending attitudes, as well as her typically Italian-flavoured exclamations.

«Bastard!» she shouted at the top of her voice as she found herself upside down after the barrell roll.

«And now that you've become familiar with the flight, let's go catch Haase. What do you think?»

«Goddamn you!»

«Curses won't work with me!» I replied, turning quickly to find Haase's cars.

It took me about ten minutes to spot the smoking vehicle from afar: one of the Fords had overturned and ended up at the edge of the road.

«They left it behind! How do you plan to stop the other cars?» Annunzi shouted, tapping me on the shoulder.

The aircraft didn't give us many options. «Fuel is running low» I explained, «I have no weapons aboard, so I was thinking I'd land onto them.»

«Are you out of your mind? Don't you have a machine gun?»

«What are you talking about! It's a transport plane, not a war plane!» I exclaimed.

A trail of dust rose in front of me, indicating there was a car ahead. It was them. I decided to dive and fly low in front of their car to slow down their run and force them to stop.

«Are you crazy! Oh, good God!»

«Great idea, it's a good time to pray. Hold on tight!» and I plummeted into a dive, but at that very moment the engine misfired and my blood froze. It couldn't be happening again! I had learned from the Sauerthal accident not to underestimate those first hints of breakdown. Once again, the engine seemed to give up and then I no longer had enough thrust to overtake the Ford, so I decided to land on top of it.

I heard some shots.

«They do have machine guns, they're not beggars like us!» Annunzi shouted to me in a shrill, worried voice.

«So, use your damned handgun against them, instead of pointing it at my head!»

«I'm fairly busy trying not to fly away!» she replied, screaming at the top of her voice.

«Then brace yourself for the collision» and I plunged even lower.

I cannot remember her exact reply, but it wasn't an

elegant comment. I flew low-level some more until, with the plane undercarriage, I hit the car. It swerved and I was able to regain altitude while one of the passengers unloaded his magazine on me. A bullet grazed my face, but I didn't relent and slammed again into the Ford, smashing it completely.

Those shots had damaged the plane and I was flooded by a hot smoke that blacked out my sight. The undercarriage was stuck and the car was dragging us with it, but the ride ended when the biplane banked to the side and, although I had vigorously pulled the control stick towards me, there was nothing more to do. The wings rammed into the ground, throwing metal splinters everywhere. The metal sheets bent like paper and Annunzi's cries were probably heard as far as Balat. The Ford stopped shortly after, smashed by our plane weighing on the roof.

When I got to the ground, my back was in pain and my arms were sore; I took care of the woman and helped her out the aircraft. She was still shaking as she threw herself onto the sand to bless it. I turned around just in time to see a man, still trapped in the vehicle, aiming the machine gun at us.

«Down!» I shouted and grabbed Annunzi to push and roll her to the ground.

It all happened in a few seconds. I drew the handgun from the holster the woman had on her hips, turned to the car and fired, hitting the man in the chest. His body, pushed backwards, collapsed like a puppet. I stood still for a moment, just to make sure the shooting was really over. Then I approached the car, which was in a terrible state, and stole the weapons from the two occupants, breathing a sigh of relief: Angelika was not on board. It may have been foolish of me to wish I had failed, but for no reason in the world did I wish to find her lifeless in the cockpit.

I turned to look for my fellow traveller. She was still lying on the ground, goggling at me. She remained silent until, imperturbable, I placed the two machine guns next to her feet. I looked at Annunzi and, with a tired smile, I handed her out the stock of the handgun, thanking her for letting me borrow it.

«Thank you for saving my neck and praise to your quick reflexes» she said in a softened tone while brushing the sand off her. «But where can your other friends from the Ahnenerbe be gone?»

«Under the circumstances, I believe they are headed north to Cairo, and these two cars only served as a diversion.»

«If you hadn't destroyed the plane, we could have changed course instead of lounging around, waiting for a ride» she complained.

«I ran out of gas: that's why I rammed the car.»

Annunzi burst into a loud laugh and I realised that, after all, she was not the unfriendly and cold woman I thought she was in the beginning. «Indeed, you have an aggressive but creative style, I have to admit.»

«Maybe it's the Italian portion of my genetic code.»

«Definitely the best part» she commented before sitting down on a boulder to take off her boots.

She confessed she hated the place and, even more so, the fine sand that ruffled her hair and filled her shoes. She made some room for me on her stone when she realised I was exhausted.

«Once we reach Cairo and find your friends, we'll go our own separate ways. It will be us and the Shemsu Hor to deal with the retrieval of the last text of the archive. I know that you're neither the instigator nor the perpetrator of the theft of St. Bernard's linen. Get out of this country as soon as you can, professor.»

«I have a matter to settle with the Ahnenerbe. I'm not ending the game now just because I'm still alive.»

«Pride kills more than stupidity.»

«Then I'll die, but not before facing the enemy.»

«You're speaking as a soldier now.»

«That's what I am» I replied proudly, because, right then, the professor had to step aside and let the soldier deal with the matter.

«No, you're a good professor in my eyes, and a crazy pilot, too. Get away now, while you can.»

«Assuming I wanted to» I replied, «and this will never happen as long as Haase and the others are alive, where do you think I can go to? Germany? Dietrich's men wouldn't hesitate to kill me. Spain? They'd be happy to know that one of the men who heroically bombed the small town of Guernica came back to seek asylum. Italy? The Duce would hand me over to his brotherly German *alter ego* without hesitation and finally, the Vatican? Ah, right, Rome! You who are from there, do you think they would welcome an alleged thief of a holy object?»

«Do you have family in Germany?» she asked me with a gentleness I had never seen in her before.

«Only friends» I replied sadly, «whom I fear I have endangered. If the Ahnenerbe knew I survived, they would retaliate against them. I need you to help me stop Haase and Angelika before they get back to Germany. They must not leave Egypt and if Dietrich is here to collect his text, then here will be his tomb, too.»

The woman sighed, resting her elbows on her legs as she let her head dangle, probably to relieve the tension in the neck.

«I liked your confrontation with the Abbot» I said, out of the blue, wishing to break the ice for good with her. The topic, though, could build a new barrier between us, but I decided to risk it, because engaging with Annunzi quite enticed me.

«You were at the monastery! I didn't see you.»

«I was outside the door when you and the gendarme were meeting that holy man of the Abbot» I explained sarcastically.

She looked at me in disbelief. «Fantastic! We were one step away from the enemy and didn't even know. Uhm, so were you eavesdropping?»

«Not exactly. Let's just say that your shrill voice spared me from doing that. Ah, and for your information, I don't blame you for losing your temper. You were magnificently pitiless on him. I wonder why he didn't excommunicate you on the spot!» I grinned.

«Ah, I suppose you're referring to that remark... well, to be honest, I lied brazenly but, to win a fight against people of the like, you have to scandalise them, so I thought I'd play the "pleasures of the flesh" card. You know what I mean» she declared unembarrassed.

We laughed together about that incident at the monastery and, later, we lay down on the sand, waiting for our companions, who, apparently, had decided to take their time.

Egypt – Balat, October 12, 1937

At the crack of dawn on that unusual Tuesday, I left Balat for Cairo with the two Italians, Abdel Ahad and some of his most trusted men. We were travelling on flatbed trucks, more uncomfortable than the back of a dromedary, but I was glad I didn't have to drive. I went to sit on the cargo bed and indulged in thoughts. I still couldn't bring myself to accept Abdel's identity, but all that "harmonic asceticism" of his was giving me ever more cause to believe in him. Besides, considering the latest events of my mission, not least the dirty trick Angelika played on me, I also began to seriously doubt my acumen.

It's not easy for me to explain what I then felt for that woman, who kept messing with my mind, nor what real feelings had brought us together before her betrayal. From the beginning, ours had been a purely hedonistic relationship, which made our intercourse all the more passionate, as we increasingly gave in to our voluptuous impulses. Indeed, there had never been any romantic entanglement between us, yet I never expected such disregard from her as to wish I was dead.

We had been travelling for about forty minutes when Annunzi, who sat in front of me, began to ask me questions. Some of them were harmless, while others required answers still too compromising for me and to which I refused to reply. Her interest in Himmler's foundation was equal to the one I had in Shemsu Hor's secret documents, so I decided to play a game with her: one question apiece.

To begin with, when it was my turn, I demanded to know what agreements tied her, Orsini and Abdel Ahad. The woman hesitated at first, but then, eager to find out about the guests at Wewelsburg, she complied with my request and confessed she worked for the Prelature of the Mysteries of God, better known by Catholics as Arcana Dei, founded in Trento in 1929 by His Excellency Monsignor Schulman. She was ordered to visit the abbey by her immediate superior, who had sent her to the monastery as a laic assistant for the investigation on the fire. Since the authority she had been given on that occasion was anything but canonical and, since the Arcana Dei was an exception and was not appreciated by the other prelatures the Church officially approved of, she explained to me that she had earned all the Abbot's malevolence, because he didn't have any episcopal authority to refuse his cooperation. Long after, Annunzi herself decided to admit that their debate that day had been the result of a strategical psychological torture, designed to make the Father Superior disclose every detail of the life of the monastery in recent years and to recover all the documents relating to the various guardians of the linen throughout history. I remember well how furious she was when I mockingly compared her to a cardinal of the Holy Inquisition.

On that occasion, I wondered about the reasons that had prompted Monsignor Schulman to send her instead of a priest, then she herself clarified her position, atypical in many ways: Giordano Ettore Annunzi, her father, had been a famous restorer, who died some years before. Abdel Ahad had met him in Milan in the late 1920s when the artist was engaged in the restoration of the Basilica of San Vittore al Corpo. At that time, Annunzi didn't even imagine that he would be offered to work on the restoration of some sacred art pieces of "apocryphal" origin. The linen of Saint Bernard was clearly one of them, listed in both the directory of the Shemsu Hor and that kept by the Prelature of the Mysteries of God. Needless to say, if it had not been for Giordano Annunzi, very little would have probably remained of that linen today. When the previous abbot of Monte Amiata monastery realised the precarious conditions the artwork was in, he informed Rome, which for centuries had been secretly entertaining a relationship of mutual benefit with the ancient Egyptian priestly caste. At that point, worried about the fate of the relic, they hired Giordano Annunzi who, not only knew how to repair the ravages of time, but studied it from an artistic and historical point of view, too, just like I had been doing.

Having said that, it's quite understandable what interests had connected Lorenza to the Guardians of Horus and why the Arcana Dei, of which she was a secular member, had chosen her to recover the "family" linen, which was the joining link between modern Catholicism and its concealed Egyptian heritage.

We had discussed enough about the matter. Neither of us intended to say any further, so we opted for a healthy and restorative silence. However, that illusory peace only managed to soothe my ears but not my mind, which jumped from thought to thought invariably tripping over Angelika. I was wondering what she was doing with Haase and if she had already given herself to him. I was more embittered than jealous, I didn't even know how to judge my own mood but, as I closed my eyes, her image was displaced by that of Romy, whom I pictured sitting on her sofa and reading a book. I missed that sweet smile of hers that slightly arched her lips and had such a beneficial effect on me.

When we reached Cairo, after the countless hours of travel by car and the ones by train that followed, Abdel Ahad assigned us some rooms in a hotel near the city centre.

The air in the room was unbreathable on that late October afternoon and I was forced to go out onto the balcony to survive the swelter. As a result, I found myself contemplating the coming and going along the road, since I wanted to force myself not to think for a while. A policeman wearing a red fez, which stood out from his white uniform more than his complexion, was controlling the traffic with composed expertise, although a lady, whose features were typically European, had been repeatedly asking him for information. Many were the tourists in the city at that time of the year, and even more the people who had moved there for work. Cairo was by then a European metropolis and we were not surprised to see British, German and French people walking about the city centre escorted by local people with whom they had solid business relations.

I heard a knock: it was Abdel Ahad who informed me of the new developments about Haase and Angelika. One of his informants had seen a beautiful European woman wandering around in the bazaar of Khan el Khalili the day before. In those years, the local contact person for the Ahnenerbe was one Karim, a merchant who had made his fortune out of the Germans' wages, but mainly out of hundreds of tourists he had fleeced selling them his leaves of banana tree for authentic papyri. We didn't get to know what he and Angelika had said to each other, nor whether she had gone to the bazaar to pay off some Ahnenerbe debts, but as soon as she left Khan el Khalili market, Karim and a couple of his friends promptly shut their trades to prepare for a-few-day trip, judging by their equipment. They were rumored to be headed to Dakhla.

«Damn it, Abdel, that man is going to ransack the temple archive!» I exclaimed, but he reassured me, unperturbed: the only thing he'd be able to take from the archive would be sand, because the Keepers of Horus had already transferred all the documents elsewhere. «But how did you manage in such a short time?»

«There are many more of us than you can imagine, Alexander, and we have been working day and night. The temple is by now entirely covered by the desert sand and that man will have a hard time finding it again.»

«But the wall writings...» I insisted fearing that Karim, to take revenge for the missing loot, would destroy the remaining historical heritage.

«You have nothing to worry about, there's nothing of interest in the archive now and then again, well, there are other ways to dissuade the desecrators from trespassing that threshold» and after a sly smirk, he patted me on the back. «Now we must see to our plan to recover that one document your friends have stolen from the temple. We can allow not even one sheet to be lost. If they manage to escape us, we must ensure they return to Germany empty-handed, so that Ahnenerbe leaders can declare the mission failed.»

I thought to the material in Angelika's hands: she had

my camera and some of my notes, so there was no lack of evidence.

«Then, we'll take back all of your belongings too, except for her» he said, apologizing immediately for the unhappy comment that had clearly clouded my gaze.

Egypt – Cairo, October 15, 1937

Abdel Ahad and his team spent a lot of time studying the moves of Angelika, Haase and the third Ahnenerbe man: Otto Heyder, the officer accused of the theft from the monastery. I was instructed not to leave the hotel where I was staying to avoid jeopardising the Egyptians' plan, but, impatient to face my old allies, I was just waiting for the most appropriate moment to break cover. Abdel was sure those people weren't alone, so it was sensible to fill the fishing nets before hauling them aboard. As far as I was concerned, I wanted to devote myself to getting my hands on Haase before it was too late. There was no significant news until the morning of October 15, when the Egyptian informed us that the time had come to spring into action.

It was the first time I entered the Coptic neighborhood and I was struck by the tranquillity of that corner of Cairo, totally alien to the noisy pace of the city. It appeared to me like a small and mysterious world unto itself, capable of keeping chaos and tourism at a distance, while reserving a historical religious intimacy for itself. They called it the Old City, although it looked more like a ghetto.

We walked along a winding and peaceful street, whose

uneven paving incidentally matched the grayish and lumpy walls, which were out of square even with their own stairways. An old woman, covered by a veil as dark as her complexion, squeezed into an alley with unexpected nimbleness. We turned round the first corner, where a man in his slippers waited patiently for some passers-by to rescue him from his tedium, and spare him a glance, at the least. Although my mood was anything but bright, that small alley and that urban settlement, full of contradictions, gave me an unexpected feeling of peace. I was fascinated by the line of lanterns along the houses, the colours and the atmosphere.

We reached the southern area where, on the remains of the ancient Roman fortress of Babylon, the church of El-Moallaqa had been built. Inside that humble jewel of Christianity, invisible to inattentive eyes, Abdel suspected they were about to deliver the document, the fruits of my labour, that is, that had come into the hands of the SS, thanks to Angelika's betrayal.

We waited until late afternoon before making our move. I don't know why Abdel had us linger for so long, I assumed he wanted to wait for the local police to leave the coast clear. He was a surprising character, phlegmatic but determined and very charismatic. He could boast connections and friendships everywhere, probably even within the police in Cairo. We were cautiously getting past the inner garden but, suddenly, we were attacked by a couple of men who sneaked up on us like ghosts.

The Shemsu Hor escorting us intervened and got the better of the two attackers before the four of us could even reach out for our guns. We had been lucky: we couldn't risk being discovered before taking up position to strike. We scattered: our aim was to recover the document and not to slaughter the enemy.

Certainly other sentries were around, so we kept our guard up. Haase was a damned bastard, for sure, but I considered him militarily flawless and I was positive he had protected the area effectively. Any moment now, I was also expecting that a few members of his emergency squad would crush us in their deadly grip. Therefore, I ordered three of our men to comb the surrounding area and, given the imminence of the attack, to shoot on sight in case they heard our shots. Abdel translated my orders making weird gestures with his hands and arms, and I hoped that the others had really understood what to do. After getting rid of another of Haase's guards, we climbed the stairs to the porch. I was surprised how stealthy and prepared Abdel's men were.

The architecture of the basilica towered over us, the ever-present memory of the ancient patriarchs were even imprinted on the reproductions of those merchants who, until a few hours earlier, had occupied the area in front of the entrance.

I spotted fear in Annunzi's eyes, who, I imagined, had never had anything to do with the SS men directly. I supposed the same thing for Orsini, whose mask of imperturbability and proud resolve hardly hid the placidity of his nature. As for Abdel, who seemed to keep everything under control, it was difficult for me to understand what he had in store. Usually, I was able to guess every personality at first glance, but that Egyptian seemed impregnable. To be honest, I couldn't even figure out how old he was, and not just because of his head, shinier than a metal badge, but also because of his anachronistic manners and the sharp-witted face of a man in his fifties. There were so many contradictions in him that I was soon led to give up the investigation. Thus, I confined myself to following his decisions, of which at least I shared the logic.

Using gesturing in order not to break the silence, the Egyptian ordered his men to go the exits of the building to prevent any SS men from escaping. To another group he ordered to descend with ropes from above, in case they heard shots. Who knows, maybe Abdel trusted in my compatriots' rationality. He obviously didn't know them well.

We were in an ideal position and could count six men. I couldn't see either Angelika or her accomplice, though.

Inside the church some incense burning in front of the tabernacles of the small aisles emanated a foul smell. Given the situation, I didn't allow myself to be distracted by the architecture of the place, nor by the reading ambo which, in other circumstances, would have aroused my keenest interest. Besides, even in a less excited moment, I would not have felt at ease in there: judged and sentenced all in one go by such sacredness.

A few minutes later, when he was certain his men were ready, Abdel waved at me. The two Italians and I understood that the time had come to reach the cloister, so we moved to the sides of the exit, ready to spring into action.

«Here I am» a hoarse voice was heard from under the loggias. It was Dietrich and not Haase as I had assumed.

I saw a woman, in a typical Egyptian dress, walking towards the darkest spot. Her head was covered, but her solemn gait revealed her name like it were an identity document: Angelika Anne Blumen.

Orsini and I reciprocally signaled to be alert, for those two could not be alone, although we hadn't found any trace of Haase and Heyder. Soon we understood why: unknowingly, Angelika and Dietrich approached us, so we took the opportunity to listen to their speeches.

«The man who is to verify if the piece is genuine lives within these walls» Dietrich said in a low voice. «He's a monophysite and one of the few who can confirm whether it's really the text we're looking for. We must be sure that it's the right find before closing the deal with the pharmaceutical company. I'm happy that you went along with my proposal in the end, and put the blame on Haase... that thick head! I hope you took care of him already.»

Pharmaceutical? What were they talking about? I was taken aback and kept listening to them while holding my breath for fear I might give away our hiding place. From those few words we sensed an infinitely vaster reality than we could only remotely suppose. Dietrich had presented my study to the Ahnenerbe as indispensable for the achievement of Sonnenmensch, the immortal Sun-Man, but in fact he was searching his personal chimera: he was convinced that the Eleventh Gate could lead him to the regeneration of his worn-out body. The sacred text, interpreted and reworked by biologists and chemists, would soon become an anti-aging drug: the first in history. Certainly, Dietrich couldn't grant himself the luxury of waiting for the Ahnenerbe before testing the new formula on himself, so he had devised a plan to shorten the time by at least two years. The loss of the script would entirely be blamed on Haase and me, who had resolved to resell the piece instead of delivering it to the foundation. Thus, Angelika could take credit for both the discovery of the archive and the removal of the two traitors. Eventually, she would get the promotion she longed for, the lavish remuneration agreed with the Ahnenerbe, and the one granted by the pharmaceutical industry, too.

It was hard to believe their words. I was experiencing a waking nightmare, that story was bizarre to say the least. I imagined I was still at the bottom of that well, dead and buried, and only my spirit had soared to reach the Coptic church. In an instant, I lost sight of reality and, probably, my reason as well. My God, what a bloodcurdling feeling! My intellect was failing me, it had to be so, because that situation seemed to me as paradoxical as old Dietrich's plan.

Their footsteps approached and we were tempted to leave our hiding place when, suddenly, Angelika stopped and answered the old man's question with unrecognisable coldness.

«I wouldn't be here, if I hadn't taken care of Haase. Don't you think? After drinking my hibiscus and mandrake infusion, he's now taking a bath at the hotel. Heyder's still alive and kicking, though.»

«Don't worry, I have sent my two best men to hunt down that snake» the old man reassured her.

I was baffled and, even though I cheered for Haase's well-deserved end, I froze at the thought of what Angelika had been capable of, how lethal her coaxing could be! Meanwhile, Dietrich had opened the casket and was already unrolling one of the papyri contained inside, in all probability without understanding its meaning, judging by the monosyllabic sounds he was uttering.

«I couldn't translate anything of the text, because it's beyond my knowledge, but Alexander, Professor Wagner» she corrected herself, «took it from the section indicated by Saint Bernard's cloth. I cannot reassure you about its validity, but should this text be wrong, I know where to find the secret archive of the Shemsu Hor. Certainly, the Eleventh Gate is kept there.»

My heart thumped as she pronounced my name in that warm voice, but I couldn't help but shiver at the thought of her lies.

Abdel motioned for his men to be ready to step in, then looked at me and the two Italians, who had already prepared our weapons. With a leap, I appeared before Angelika making her startle. Dietrich didn't flinch and, with a quick nod, he warned someone who I imagined was on the other side of the loggia, ready to attack me.

«I really don't think you'll retrieve those texts!» I began and heard the deep tone of my voice echoing as if we were in a crypt.

Angelika smiled and shouted my name with an enthusiasm that caught me unawares. «Welcome. Karim has been faster than expected!» she exclaimed, but I didn't understand her words and pointed the gun at her, aiming for the heart.

«What the hell are you saying?» I asked her.

Dietrich cut in. «Everyone had to believe you were dead, professor, but we need you alive. In case that script is incorrect or we need to look elsewhere, who else can we turn to but you? That's why we sent...» the old man was explaining, then he stopped abruptly at the sight of the Shemsu Hor behind me. At that point his expression changed and his eyes became bloodshot.

Dietrich's men promptly came out, armed to the teeth, but dropped the weapons to the ground when they realised they had been outnumbered: Abdel Ahad had dozens of followers in tow, among them, former policemen that wouldn't hesitate to kill whoever would oppose the Shemsu Hor's will.

«You and your race are hypocrites» old Dietrich railed against Abdel, who stole the document from him. «Your scripts carry the solution to all problems and you won't allow drugs to be produced to heal the plague of our century!»

«People like you are the plague of our century» the Egyptian replied, imperturbable.

«You, crazy fool, don't you see that my deal with the pharmaceutical industry would deprive Himmler of his dream? I'm not like them. A medicine for cellular regeneration and for the preservation of anti-aging genes, that would be the real dream!»

«A dream for humankind, or for you?» I butted in. «Eternal youth doesn't exist, Dietrich. It's a chimera that has led many innocent people to their death before its effectiveness could even be tested.»

«That's not true» he denied approaching me furiously, «and if you weren't convinced of the value of these writings, you wouldn't be here. Think of the antediluvian patriarchs; how do you think they could live so long? Those were no miscalculations. Enoch, Methuselah, Noah and the list would still be long, but I don't need to go on because you are better at history than I am, Alexander.»

Abdel handed the box with the text to one of his men and spoke patronizingly: «No pharmaceutical company will ever be able to develop a drug for cellular regeneration using our papyri and, although in fools' eyes it may seem a contradiction, lengthening human life too much would only mean bringing its extinction closer.»

«You're lying, demon, you just want to stigmatise a miracle of science! We have Miescher's studies on nuclein and with Egyptian knowledge... Why the heck are you laughing, you foolish subhuman?» the old man was furious at his interlocutor's entirely atypical reaction.

«The one Fräulein Blumen gave you wasn't the sacred text, or are you stupid enough to believe that a few sheets of paper can explain the miracle of life? The true code of regeneration, the Eleventh Gate of Heaven, is made up of one hundred and forty-four documents and conceals the Egyptian dualism, since it is both a word of rebirth and death. There are billions of people in the world and if each of us lived a hundred years longer, the world population would increase to the point of a planetary collapse. We would be the very promoters of the apocalypse.»

«If it's so dangerous, it should be destroyed together with Saint Bernard's linen, yet you still keep them today. That cloth was in a monastery!» Angelika cried vehemently.

«You cannot see beyond your selfishness and you don't think of the consequences of your actions because you are obtuse. You are the real Untermenschen! But now, enough with the chatter!» the Egyptian commanded, avoiding the question.

Annunzi and Orsini drew their guns, in view of their possible reaction, and in a matter of seconds a man of Dietrich's, with a rash movement, freed himself from the grasp of one of Abdel's guardians and managed to snatch the semi-automatic from his captor. An inadvertent shot was fired and the young Egyptian fell to the ground. He looked around for Abdel Ahad, who tried in vain to help him. Soon more shots were heard in the distance: the recon squad had done their duty. Orsini promptly struck the murderer without killing him and then it was chaos.

After getting rid of one of my fellow compatriots, who had tried to hit me, I looked in the direction of Annunzi, who was surrounded by enemy fire. I was on the opposite side and instinctively fired my shot just before she was attacked from behind by a third man. I feared I had missed the target, because the man stood for a while, but then I saw him swing like a pendulum and realised that he would collapse to the ground in a matter of seconds. I turned around after hearing a thud behind me and saw Abdel lying on the shiny tiles, which reflected all the horror of the massacre. The Egyptian managed to get up without help and I felt relieved.

Taking advantage of that pandemonium, Angelika had vanished. When all was finally quiet again, many corpses lay on the ground. The losses were huge on both sides, but we had got the better of them. Of all our adversaries, only Dietrich had been spared and he was lying on the floor monitored by two Egyptians.

«We need to find Heyder quickly, that man is a loose cannon» the gendarme remarked.

«If I got it right, Angelika and Dietrich were playing on their own and, if Heyder's still alive, then the beautiful German woman is doomed unless she's with us» Annunzi said, turning to me.

«No!» Abdel shouted while running towards the old man. Dietrich had put to good use a moment of distraction from his captors' part to chew a cyanide pill and, despite our timely intervention, he died after a few-minute agony.

I suggested that we leave before the police arrived and, meanwhile, I turned and beckoned to the Shemsu Hor still unharmed, to help the wounded and get away from the church.

The alleys of that neighborhood, a stronghold of Christianity, were narrow and suffocating and they were even more oppressive for those who, like me, never believed in any faith. The heat was as stifling as my sad memories. In that place, devoted to pity and mercy, we were the only discordant note: in order to preserve a piece of history, we might be endangering another. The light color of those walls blending with the ground deprived me of orientation. I stopped for a moment, looking around to figure out which alley to take, when I heard a gun fire. A shudder ran through me: Angelika. I started running towards the gunshot. I don't remember in which exact corner I found her but, when I spotted her, I barely held back an exclamation of dismay at the state she was in. She lay in a pool of blood thickened by the sand. Her head was still leaning against the wall, while the rest of her body lay on the ground like a rag abandoned at the side of the road. All vanity was gone, along with her ardour, and I felt pity for the woman I had once elected as my muse. She was staring at me, but I wasn't sure she was still alive. When I was closer, she called me.

«Stay still, I'll take you away from here», I said to reassure her while stroking her face.

«Don't talk nonsense. I'm already dead, but Heyder is not. Don't let him leave Egypt, or he will tell his version of the story to the director of the Ahnenerbe» she told me, her voice increasingly weaker. I brought my face closer to hers to be able to hear her and, after a slight spasm, she explained to me that he was heading to Dakhla and that he had killed Karim, the man she had hired to save me. «Did you really think I was going to let you die over there? You know I love you. Stop Heyder and send someone you trust to take Rosemarie Meyer away from Germany, before he or anyone else uses her to get to you. Flee, run for your life, but...» She didn't finish the sentence, because the words died on her lips. Right before passing away, I felt her squeeze my hand tightly. The cold of death ran through my body making me shiver, then, suddenly, it left, releasing me from the worst feeling I had ever experienced.

I heard footsteps approaching. Annunzi put a hand on my shoulder and invited me to get away from Angelika before the local police arrived.

«If she hadn't chosen me for this task, she and many others would still be alive» I told her, holding in a strong emotion, well behind my unyielding cynicism.

A shadow stretched in front of me and outlined against the wall that supported Angelika's lifeless body.

«There's a reason for every event scarring our life» said Abdel Ahad's reassuring voice. «You have been allowed to rewrite it, move on and become a new man. For better or for worse, she helped you take a different path. Angelika will be reborn, like all of us sooner or later, and who knows, maybe her memories might make her a better person in her future existence. Now come, my friend» he said, motioning me to follow him, «it has been a sad and tiring day.»

Egypt – Cairo, October 22, 1937

We stayed in Cairo for a few days, so that Abdel Ahad could clear up some outstanding issues with the authorities.

I learnt from him that Otto Heyder had been arrested by the police just before his departure for Alexandria. I was not told how that was, but it seemed that, while he was in the midst of his preparations, the agents had found an *ushabti* in his pocket, a grave statuette of dubious origin. That evidence had earned him the accusations of both grave robbery and illicit historical artifact trade. According to the report of one of the policemen in charge of the case, Heyder had reacted violently against his arrest, thus decreeing his immediate conviction. The investigations had taken place in an incredibly short time. Otto Heyder had been found in possession of the gun whose calibre was consistent with the bullet that had killed Angelika and, since the matter was extremely complicated, the authorities had preferred to quickly wrap up the case. That's why they took the opportunity to attribute the murder of his superior, Obersturmbannführer Haase, and that of Dietrich Schrödinger to the SS officer, too. Since from the outset the Ahnenerbe top management had declared that they could not grant any official support to the operation, they would never expose themselves to repatriate Heyder.

The Egyptian authorities had also ruled out other accomplices, because there were no witnesses or documents that could prove the presence of other men of the Reich on Egyptian land.

Thanks to Abdel, I left Egypt without ever having entered it: all the documents certifying my presence in the Land of the Pharaohs would fatally disappear.

Annunzi and Orsini had already boarded the train that would take us back to Alexandria, while I preferred lingering on the platform instead. We wouldn't depart for another ten minutes and I had no intention to be sitting in a suffocating hot carriage longer than necessary. Abdel Ahad had sorted everything out for our return to Europe, and also arranged for us to board the ship to Italy, but I would have to manage on my own thenceforth. He repeatedly tried to persuade me not to return to Germany, but how could I heed his advice, when I was afraid for Romy's safety?

Abdel laughed at me and my thoughtful face, then he took a long sigh and whipped my notebook out of a pocket under his tunic. «This is yours» he said placidly.

Never would I have thought he'd do such a thing and I was more than happy for that. Nevertheless, I thought it wise to refuse.

«The archive has been dismantled. The stolen text has been recovered. Now your studies are no longer "dangerous", unless you're willing to find our new Crystal Temple too!»

«I'm not that crazy» I laughed, shaking his hand. «I'm sorry I brought chaos to your ancient spiritual world.»

«Many a question still hover in your mind, Alexander, I know. This is the time for goodbyes and for elucidations, too, if you wish.»

Those words aroused an enthusiasm in me that had been dormant for days and as I listened to his story, my desire for knowledge became even more insatiable.

«The Shemsu Hor didn't see the cell as we know it today, they didn't have microscopes, yet they had already contemplated structures such as the nucleus. Nature never wastes energy to generate useless bodies or substances, quite the contrary, it transforms and reuses. Even the soul, you know, is reemployed, though it cannot be manipulated like the human body. Should anyone generate another life from a living being without the aid of fecundation, they would obtain a new being, yes, but genetically old. Here lies the key to everything, Alexander, that is the science of the Shemsu Hor. If we used worn-out cells, proteins, mineral salts, we would only reproduce old beings. Contrarily, when, due to meiosis, ovums and sperms are formed, and their union leads to the zygote, a new human being is born, with a whole lifetime to live, despite the fact that the basic genetic material has already been used. My ancestors understood the inner workings of this renewal, they knew how to use Râ to create that vital energy, to strengthen beneficial proteins. Dietrich hoped to provide science with enough information to understand cellular regeneration. He had made deals with a German pharmaceutical industry and would have obtained not only power, but also a longer life by undergoing the regenerative drug experimentation. He was desperate: he had been fighting against a degenerative disease for years. Angelika, on the other hand, was ambitious and had big plans for the future. Perhaps, what she never told you was that she wanted you by her side and not a sick old man, even less a trigger-happy man like Haase.»

Again, I was amazed by his dialectic and, above all, by his knowledge in the medical field.

«In 1865 the University of Marburg granted me a degree in medicine. My dissertation was on human transmission of hereditary traits. It wasn't easy to be taken seriously!» he admitted smiling.

Abdel was a doctor! That man amazed me yet once more.

«Yes. It seems that Marburg is attended by brilliant and enlightened students, don't you think?» he asked me.

«You bet! But you cheated!» and as I spoke, I saw the conductor walking towards the carriages. «Tell me about the Sator before the train starts. I read the text in the temple, but I know it hides so much more. How many other ways shall I read it before I grasp its true meaning?»

Abdel performed a belly laugh that made me a little nervous.

«Ah, I never expected that from someone like you! The linen has led you along the way of Horus, you have studied a lot to come to that conclusion. There was probably a one-in-a-thousand chance that you would think to look for the third point of the sacred triangle, yet you have found the location of the temple. You've come to the presence of an ancestral Sator, and you're still overwhelmed by doubts! Admittedly, there have been many versions, for it had been modified by different generations of Egyptian priests. Nevertheless, its intrinsic meaning is the same as you know: "*Son of time, prince, resort to the house of Râ of the border gateway*"; at the time of Akhenaten, they interpreted it in the Atenism version and so it became "*This is the land of Râ, where is the Aten? In the Great House of the border gateway*". If it's still not clear to you, I can quote "*The Throne of the Great is near the Land of the Neith Crown, in the district of the House of*

254

Râ, the border gateway".»

In an instant, it was as if a bolt pierced through me. We were talking about the crown of Lower Egypt, so the border gateway was north of the Nile. In ancient times, regeneration took place in Giza! The great pyramid was considered the Temple of Râ and the Border Gateway. There the Shemsu Hor gathered to officiate the sacred ceremony of regeneration, together with the twelve Guardians of Horus and their respective sacred texts, which we today know as the Gates of Heaven, those that should give life to the immortal Sun-Man. There could be nothing more obvious in the light of the latest revelations.

«No evidence could prove your assumptions» the Egyptian replied amused, at the end of my deductions. «Unfortunately, the secret was kept by the renowned Shemsu Hor, now extinct. No one can reveal the absolute truth, since it belongs only to the gods.»

«Right. Nobody will ever do that, Abdel, although in Wewelsburg someone is eager to recreate that Border Gateway. Twelve are the members of the Ahnenerbe and twelve the sacred texts that would be associated with them. That's the reason for the castle north tower and its triangular plan. They wish to celebrate your archaic rite in the modern era!»

«Yes, I assumed that much, that's why you were the scholar who exactly suited them. But Himmler isn't striving to reach the spiritual elevation only, he also seeks the knowledge that would grant the supremacy of Führer's men over all other races. Sonnenmensch, the original and immortal Sun-Man disappeared at the end of the Golden Age. Certainly, Hitler's men won't ever be able to claim the title. But you, Alexander Wagner, what would you do if a Shemsu Hor granted you that privilege?»

It may happen that, right when you give up chasing your dreams, you are granted the opportunity to live them and that, incomprehensibly, you get overwhelmed by uncertainty. Well, at the beginning of my expedition I wouldn't have hesitated to accept Abdel's offer, but after that journey through history, and through my soul, I decided I would let myself be guided by feelings.

«A long time ago a man and his wife, who had never seen me before, saved me from certain death. I was unable to repay their gesture and I still feel I owe them. That man suffered from a serious form of hematuria. I'd like to give him my place» I said, trusting in the Egyptian's approval.

«For that you don't need a regeneration rite, it's enough that he removes salt from his meals and follows my instructions» Abdel Ahad replied in a paternal tone. «I'll arrange for one of my friends to deliver you a parcel at Alexandria station. Consider it a small gift for your friend.»

I looked at that gentle giant for the last time and took my leave from him with a pat on the back. «Thank you, Shemsu Hor.»

I stepped onto the carriage while the train was already moving, then I turned back to get him to repeat the year of his graduation: maybe I had misunderstood? But the Egyptian had disappeared already and the train had started its run towards the delta of the Nile, taking me and my questions away from that place of legend and mystery.

Germany – Berlin, November 4, 1937

The cold air of Berlin hit me fiercely in the face, reminding me that it wouldn't be my city any longer, nor would Germany be my country. It was already dark when I walked to the Sausuhlensee. I wished I could sit on its shore and watch the wildlife like I did as a kid, but I wasn't there for recreation. I filled my lungs with the air of the park, loaded with a thick smell of live wood and chlorophyll, then I quickened my pace to reach Romy's house. Anxiety merged with a strong emotion, all too similar to that I experienced before an important exam. I had not found the right words to begin with, yet, and that made me even more nervous, since I couldn't just show up at her door and brutally ask her to pack. I doubted she would take me seriously and, after all, how could I ever convince her to give up everything and follow me, when I didn't even have a future to give her far from Berlin?

Eyes down and fists clenched, I began to run relentlessly to chase worries away and avoid the imminent downpour.

By the time I got to Meyers' house the rain was just starting to fall. I waited for a few minutes, sheltered between the walls of two houses, as worn and undistinguished as that street. At that late hour, the whole neighbourhood seemed deserted: there were no cars on the road and public transport never came over there. I looked around before approaching the fence, then decided to enter from the back of the garden.

I sneaked into the house with the duplicate key that Romy kept in the saucer under a small privet pot. That awakened in me the beautiful memory of an early March afternoon, when the worst days of my life had not tainted my soul, yet. The garden mirrored the peaceful disposition of the woman who looked after it. That day I had caught her tinkering with scissors and metal wire and she had enthusiastically talked to me about her meeting a certain Fumiko, who had introduced her to the art of bonsai. Fumiko was the wife of the engineer Keisuke Tanaka, a celebrity in the land of the Rising Sun, who was in Berlin both on business and to test the waters in view of a political rapprochement between Germany and Japan. Romy was their interpreter at the time and had the opportunity to interact with their traditions, which she found fascinating.

Everything seemed to be changed since then but, in my heart, I hoped that her interest in foreign cultures could be my ally at convincing her to leave Europe.

The house was deserted and there was a good smell of fresh laundry in the air that made me feel at home. I took off my rain-soaked jacket and hat and left them in the kitchen, dripping onto the floor. I thought it better not to switch on any lamp or start the fire either, so I sat in an armchair in the half-light, patiently waiting for Romy to come home.

Unfortunately, I had no alternative to that escape plan and couldn't even afford to fail: I had to take her with me at any cost. Romy had always lived in a less cynical and brutal world than mine and, although she had often worked alongside diplomats and soldiers of various nationalities, she had been able to keep herself at a distance from their power games, and saved the "less compromising" interpreting for herself.

After more than an hour of waiting, the entrance door creaked and closed slowly, accompanied by a sigh of resignation. Romy didn't notice me when she hung her coat next to the mirror. A flash of lightning lit up the hall, hiding me in the shadows of that house. I was still sitting in the armchair behind her and looked at Romy like I was seeing her for the first time. I kept silent, hoping she would turn soon, but she didn't. Suddenly, a second bolt of lightning broke through the darkness and the rain fell violently accompanied by deafening thunder, that made her jump. She untied her hair and looked down as she took off her wet shoes. I quietly approached her, so that, when she turned again to her reflection in the mirror, she recognised me by her side, as a new flash lit up my face. Romy was disconcerted at my presence, and although I felt guilty for scaring her, I didn't say a word. She stood still, staring at me in silence. Her eyes, sad and lifeless at first, began to glow with joy when I finally hinted at a smile. I knew I didn't have much time, yet I didn't want to waste that moment. She soon released herself from my embrace and took my face in her soft hands. «My God, you're safe» she said under her breath as her eyes filled with tears.

«I promised I'd be back.»

Romy nodded. «I met Kopf a couple of days ago and he told me that you were in trouble, that you had betrayed the Ahnenerbe, that you were fomenting anti-nationalism, that they would accuse you of subversive propaganda... oh, I thought you were doomed!»

«I was, but now listen to me because we have no time

to lose. I need to take you away before it's too late. Unintentionally, I got you into trouble» and I started explaining the whole situation, but stopped when I saw her bewildered stare. I understood that she wouldn't follow me. I told her everything, almost in detail, to try and convince her. In a few minutes, she learned about the Shemsu Hor, about Angelika and Dietrich, about every aspect of my life that I had withheld from her, but it didn't seem to have any effect.

«I'm not in danger and none of it makes sense. I'm not your family and, Kopf aside, nobody knows we're friends» she replied, gesticulating animatedly and ridiculing my every fear.

I let anxiety overcome me. «They know everything about you, they know everything about anyone on German land, damn it!» I yelled and repented it immediately after. «This is no joke and I'm not paranoid. Romy, I put you in danger, and you don't know what I'd give to go back, but I can't. You really have to come with me. Please listen to me. I wouldn't ask you to abandon everything, if I didn't deem it critical.»

She stiffened seeing me bewildered. «Get out of Berlin at once, then. It was reckless of you to come back» and she vehemently pushed me away from her. «I'm not going to be your ballast. I'd slow down your escape. Leave before it's too late, this is the time to say goodbye. Bye, Alexander» she said as she opened the door for me.

«Alexander Wagner is dead. Now I'm Gabriele Ferrari.»

She widened her eyes, dumbfounded, and told me to go to hell. «All the more reason for me to feel safe, then» she replied. «Let's pretend that you're just a figment of my imagination; that I have in front of me the phantom of the man dearest to me, whom I would have begged to run as far from this place as possible, if I had ever seen him again before his death.»

«Look, this time I fear I haven't got the situation under control, maybe because you're involved, I don't know, but I'm not going anywhere without you. If you stay, then I'll stay too.»

«Who? You? Fear? Impossible» and she laughed in my face as if she wanted to exorcise her fear as well, and I knew she was afraid, because her voice was uncertain and her gaze restlessly shifted from one point to another and never met mine.

I shouted at Romy, shaking her by the shoulders. «I fear they'll hurt you to get to me. They assume I'm still alive; they're going to take revenge, because I have upset their plans and I'm about to make public some information, that will bring down their theories on Sonnenmensch and the superiority of the Aryan race. Have I made myself clear? Wake up, we're no longer two light-hearted teens!»

I saw her turn pale and shiver. «What the hell have you done!»

«Come with me. Now, immediately. Pack the necessary only and be quick. Don't turn the lights on. I'll be waiting for you down here» I told her before checking outside the windows for any suspicious passer-by. She hesitated a bit longer, then went upstairs without uttering a word.

The wait seemed neverending. I was wondering how long it could take to pack a suitcase, when, just a couple of minutes later, I heard a first thud, then a second, so I silently climbed the stairs and headed to her room. I only had time to hear her moan, when, suddenly, a chilling scene appeared before me: Karl, my dear old friend Karl Kopf, was pressing the gun to Romy's temple. Suddenly my heart seemed to come out of the chest and my breath became short at the sight of her, terrified and distressed.

«Karl!» I shouted before putting my hands up in a gesture of surrender. «Here I am, you don't need to use her to catch me.»

«I don't want to catch you, boy, I want to see you beg, how else do you think I could savour revenge?» He used the tone of someone accustomed to disposing of other people's lives and deciding their fate without too much regret or remorse. Alas, I knew that kind of intonation well: too many times had I heard it from my superiors and used it myself against the enemy.

«What are you talking about?» I asked him, still ignoring the reasons prompting his gesture.

«Are you scared, Alexander? Of course, you are! I can see fear in your eyes» and he peered at Romy, whose pleading eyes begged him to let her go. «I never expected you to be stupid enough to come back to Berlin, yet you did. You have a heart, too, after all. But you couldn't go unnoticed, of course my men recognised you» he told me. «Did you think you could come back to Germany without me knowing?»

I saw him turn the barrel of the gun against Romy's skin, so hard he bruised her. I didn't have time to come up with a plan, he would kill her in a matter of minutes. It wasn't easy for me to stay calm at a time like that, but had I failed to pause and think, she would have been doomed.

«You were my father's best friend and mine too. Where does all this hatred come from? What have I done to you?» I wanted him to lose focus, I had to let him talk, even if I didn't care about his answers. I knew he was a man with great limitations: one of them was the inability to concentrate on two different tasks simultaneously, another was his impulsiveness, which made him an easy target.

«When I look at you, I see your mother's eyes, Alexander, and that's maybe what has always kept me from hating you. But your temperament, that's all Jürgen's. His restless and cursed blood flows in your veins, and it's like you constantly reminded me that I lost the most important deal of my life because of him.»

I saw his focus weaken, his nerve slacken, and I insisted, so I would have a few more seconds to devise my next move. «What do you mean?»

«Why, don't you know? Don't tell me Jürgen never told you! Your father screwed up my contract with the Wehrmacht for the supply of solvents, claiming that my products were highly corrosive and toxic. If I hadn't resorted to my entrepreneurial genius, I would have lost everything. I reused those substances as pesticides, instead, and now, twenty years later, in spite of your father, I have the chance to resell them to eradicate all Untermenschen like you.»

«What are you raving about? I have worn the uniform and spilt my own blood for Germany! While you were selling shit to your own country. You are a subhuman, not me!» I snapped back angrily.

«Maybe, but Himmler thinks you are a Freemason, as well as your teacher Heinz Hilgenfeld.»

«Hilgenfeld is not a Mason!» I replied, approaching him within two-arm length. I would soon put my plan into action.

«I know, but I forged false evidence against him and you both with the same mastery I used for my pesticides. You're done, Wagner. Also, to stick to confessions, I was counting on killing you before you joined the Ahnenerbe, because I meant to buy the Messerschmitt at a good price. Your accident would have been perfect for my business and for my personal satisfaction. I laughed when I read on the accident report that they blamed you entirely, but I didn't feel satisfied, since you had survived and, unfortunately, the Messerschmitt had not been affected by the event as I would have liked. Thus, once again my plans had been screwed up by a Wagner. If you really want to know, though, I'm now here mainly to avenge Angelika. My lovely Angelika!» he yelled at me, clutching Romy's neck even tighter with his arm. He twisted his lips and knitted his eyebrows in the attempt to hold back angry tears. He shot me the most furious look I had ever seen: the loss of Angelika had driven him crazy and no one could have dissuaded him from his intentions. «You're like your father. You enjoy watching others trudging along while you flaunt your victories and hurt those around you, like you did with Angelika. You weren't worthy of her, yet she wanted you and I couldn't deny her my support. Unfortunately for me, my superiors also wanted to involve you in the mission and I had to give up and wait. How could you hurt that angel?» and he yanked Romy even harder until he could hear her moaning in pain.

It was the right time to risk it all. I couldn't fail. I sported a cynical laugh and replied condescendingly: «An angel? That whore I brought with me?»

Karl's anger simmered: that was what I wanted. The message was very clear: he wanted me dead instantly. As I had predicted, he couldn't contain his fury and ended up losing his mind just when he needed it the most. With a nervous jerk, he pointed the pistol at me, pulling it away from Romy's temple, who wriggled away. She was free and, with a quick gesture of my arm, I hit the hand which Karl was holding the weapon with, and moved it away from my trajectory. The gun went off and a bullet hit the wall behind me, just as I violently beat him in the face with my elbow, knocking him out. Right then, I twisted his arm so that that the weapon aimed at his abdomen and, without any hesitation, fired the fatal blow. Karl's body collapsed to the ground soaking in his own blood.

The speed of my movements was renowned both on the ground and in flight, that's why I was the "Führer's Greyhound". On that occasion, I was proud of it. He stared into my eyes as I threatened him with his weapon.

«I never wished to call Angelika with such an epithet; I'm sorry you forced me to say that to make you lose your temper. It was my only chance. Angelika was very important to me and, although she betrayed me, I would have never laid a finger on her. Otto Heyder killed her. My only fault was I couldn't reach her in time. So weird your colleagues from the Sicherheitsdienst and from the Ahnenerbe didn't tell you what actually happened. You were one of their puppets, too» I hastened to explain before he died.

«You will rot in hell, Wagner!» he shouted at me with the last of his strength.

I watched that human carcass, feeling no pity for him anymore. «That's true, but please, lead the way» and I shot a bullet to his forehead.

I remained cold and impassive in front of the corpse of the man I had considered my best friend for nearly thirty years. I felt the same as if I had killed a repulsive beast. And right then, my illusion of being changed, of having rediscovered the less petty side of myself, vanished: I recalled Adolf Hitler's words, which had been able to fill me with fervour only two years earlier: *"Flink wie Windhunde, zäh wie Leder und hart wie Kruppstahl"*. My God, despite everything I had experienced in Egypt and despite the remorse for raining death upon Spain, I was still the same damned Alexander Wagner: nothing in me had changed for the better. Before Karl's corpse, I still was *"swift as a greyhound, tough as leather and hard as Krupp's steel"*.

And now, I was to face the hardest challenge of all: Romy. She had never seen me that way, a callous and remorseless killer. I had just shown her what I was truly capable of. I imagined what she could think of me then: one of the many two-faced Januses forged by Goebbels and the other propagandists. I was sure I scared her as much as Karl did. I had opened her eyes to who I really was and I had done it in the most brutal way I knew. My heart felt heavy as lead. I remember that moment of ignominy well. I wished I could throw that weapon away, but thought I would need it to get out of Germany. I finally turned to look her in the eyes and decipher her emotions. Staring at her, I stood still, until she ran to hug me, thus giving me a new breath of life. Romy held me tightly and I sighed with relief, heartened by that unexpected warmth. I kissed her and thanked God I hadn't lost her forever.

Germany – Sauerthal, November 6, 1937

Romy and I travelled at night in a car bought from a guy whose name I don't even remember. He was a poor fellow that I had no difficulty persuading, since the proceeds of the sale would finally give him the means to feed his family.

To reach Romy in Germany and to cross the border, I had walked at least thirty miles, then cycled for another two hundred and fifty, avoiding all the main roads, and it had all been to no avail. But, in leaving the country I had her by my side and everything was more complicated. Despite that, getting out was easier than getting in. Thanks to Annunzi and Orsini's informants, I knew the location of the main checkpoints and learnt that we would have to evade at least three before reaching Sauerthal. I remembered that Romy could drive, but not that she was that bad at it, nevertheless I needed her to be at the wheel because I couldn't risk being spotted by the soldiers. About half a mile before every police checkpoint, I would get off while she went ahead and let the officers search the car and check her documents. The agreement was to meet again half a mile beyond. Everything went smoothly for the first two inspections, but we had troubles with the third. I had found a sheltered spot on the side of the road to wait for her, but after more than thirty minutes I still couldn't see her coming. I had Karl's handgun and its magazines with me. I began walking towards the checkpoint and prepared for the worst, when I finally saw the lights of a car approaching: it was her. Amused, she explained that the engine had stopped and that she hadn't been able to start it again, so she had got the police to help her.

We had to run away from Berlin before her colleagues reported her disappearance to the authorities or before someone found Karl's corpse. Romy's false German identity had also fooled the last roadblock without any inconvenience. I didn't have many alternatives, so I thought we could go to Thomas and Agathe's to set the SS on the wrong track: they would be looking for a couple fleeing towards the border in the following days. I told Romy all about the Krügers and my affection for them. While I was driving, I pictured Agathe washing the dishes and Thomas sunk in the armchair, reading yet another book on the history of oenology and Roman viticulture systems. I knew he was willing to buy a new plot of land to cultivate red grapes without giving up the beloved Riesling, which made his fortune. He had repeated it at least ten times when I was his guest and I wondered if he had finally convinced Agathe, who, on the other hand, considered the ripening of their grapes too demanding already.

Romy listened to all my stories with interest, commenting from time to time with an exclamation of amazement or a sigh. I didn't tell her just about Thomas and Agathe, I decided to confess every moment I had lived away from her, including the worst ones. After all, what could ever be worse than seeing me kill like a coldblooded sniper?

When we reached the Krügers' vineyard, it was pitch dark and I couldn't say what time it was. I was tired because of the emotions of those days and because I hadn't slept more than two hours per night for at least a week. Although I had turned off the lights of the car from afar, Liebe, Thomas's bitch began to bark and woke everyone up.

It was quite cold. Romy hugged me and almost instinctively we both looked up at the starry sky. Neither of us was in the mood for romance, but our melancholy was somewhat relieved by that immensity.

In the house the lights lit up and, suddenly, the front door was thrown wide open. I caught a glimpse of my good friend, shotgun in hand, wearing a pair of shorts that would have bemused even the most rustic woman.

«I'll tell you what's with that bitch: she saw the fox, that's what's with her!» I heard him yelling at his wife. «Or maybe she's barking because she heard you rant and rave at dinner!»

Agathe came out of the house like a fury. «Shut up, you old goat! Of course, she saw the fox! That beast is a curse. It already tried to kill the chickens twice, this week. Shoot anything that moves and get it over with for good» she yelled.

Despite the bright moonlight, they didn't notice us.

I slowly walked away from the car while Thomas was still bellowing. «Don't worry, woman, you'll have a nice fur collar sewn to your coat for Christmas» and was loading the rifle, when suddenly Liebe became silent. She was by me and I was stroking her. The bitch started jumping around and yelping of joy.

I heard Agathe's moving exclamation: «Thomas, it's him, it's Alexander. He's back!»

I ran to hug them fondly and felt an immense emotion for seeing them again. I had really missed those two crazy ones! It was like hugging my parents again.

«Such a joy seeing you again, son!» Thomas exclaimed, emotion colouring his deep voice with a streak of uncertainty. Just a glance and I knew that his disease was wearing him out. His joviality was still there, but his face looked marked by a suffering that was stronger, in that it was unspoken. «You escaped Haase then» he told me.

«Yes, but not the Ahnenerbe» I replied, forewarning him.

«Are you in danger?» Agathe asked me, scared to death. «Let's hide the car in the barn and come on in the house. You'll be safe here.»

«I'm not alone» I replied, motioning towards Romy. «I didn't know where to go. You're the only ones I can trust.»

Thomas looked at his wife and saw she was happy. «Would you let your girlfriend freeze out here, or will you come in and introduce her to us?»

«I'll unload the car: I packed the boot with food and two cases of good red wine. I hope you like Trollinger!»

«Ah, you are the son I never had!» he exclaimed playfully. «See, wife, he's on my side, too! Ah, why do I keep trying to explain, you cannot understand me!»

Agathe ignored him because she was engrossed in welcoming Romy with her customary kindness. In the meantime, I unburdened myself to Thomas, who seemed to live my vicissitudes as if they were his own.

«And so Haase was killed by a woman. But now tell me, about this girl who has you on a string, Hauptmann Wagner!»

«I'm no longer Alexander Wagner.»

«Who gave you a new identity?»

«The two Italians who were with me in Egypt. Thanks to them, we will sail from Genoa once the dust has settled, with the pope's best wishes, nonetheless, and his thanks for my help with both the capture of dangerous criminals and the recovery of venerable Saint Bernard's cloth.»

«Hence, I have a hero in my house!» he rejoiced inviting me to toast.

«Hell, no hero! I'm now a common teacher named Gabriele Ferrari. Purebred Italian, of course, to my mother's delight.»

«A suitable name for a ladykiller like you. If you think your new job sounds dull, you can always play the pilot card or that of the undercover Nazi spy. But tell me, do you really mean to publish your story, and broadcast that some infamous priests would have granted ancient knowledge to Egyptians, Romans, Jews, and even a certain Mr. Wagner, but not to the Führer?»

«I don't know yet. As of now, I have to think about Romy's safety and mine, too, if I can. Then we'll see if it's appropriate to spread such news.»

«That guy you told me about, the Egyptian... was he the head of those priests?»

I smirked complacently and handed him Abdel Ahad's envelope and letter. «Follow the instructions written on this sheet of paper and remove salt from your diet» I ordered with a wink.

Thomas looked at the paper bag with a frown. It contained a strange yellowish powder that released a nondescript smell and, to be honest, was not reassuring at all. «What is this stuff? It will give me the final blow, won't it?»

«Trust me, the Egyptian who gave it to me is a doctor with a century-long experience under his belt!» I explained to him as I walked towards my room. Then I turned to announce him that we would be on our way in a couple of days, if that was ok with him and Agathe.

«Don't be hasty and don't rush things. Two weeks from now, I'll be loading the tanks for wine fermentation onto the truck. They're made of steel and large enough for you to hide in. Meanwhile, if you help me, we'll build a false bottom. One hundred and fifty miles separate you from the French border.»

I smiled and nodded at his proposal. «Thereafter I'll manage to get by on my own… how could I ever pay you back?»

«You already have by returning to visit us: I hadn't seen Agathe so happy for months and I know that her smile will fade when you'll cross that threshold again. Poor elders like us, are easily pleased and a letter, from wherever you are headed, could be better for us than any medicine.»

«I won't forget you. You're the only family I have left.»

«Let's go to bed now. Busy days are ahead. Tell me, have you ever gone hunting?»

«I'm always on the hunt!» I replied with a mischievous grin that won me a smile.

«Then you'll show me your skills tomorrow, hunting boars.»

«Not the kind of game I was referring to» I said, amused, «but we'll still have fun, right? And then… it's time for me to settle down.»

Italy – Genoa, November 24, 1937

Professor Gabriele Ferrari and his travelling companion, Mrs. Elena Mariani, had been registered on boarding the ocean liner Rex that would take them from Italy to New York. Right, those were our identities now, and I was finding it very difficult to familiarise myself with the new names. Orsini and Annunzi were at the dock with us, surrounded by a thousand other people preparing to greet their loved ones.

Although it felt surreal, Lorenza shed some tears when saying her goodbyes. «I don't think I'm going to miss your stupid jokes» she declared after regaining her composure, but a moment later, she hugged me and wished me luck. «I fear your file has been miscatalogued. In all likelihood, the archives won't regurgitate your documents before some seventy years, and then that'll make the fur fly!» she said with a streak of sadness.

«Seventy years... um, longevity is only for the gods» I answered her. «And then, it's better to live a short and intense life, than a long and apathetic one.» It was then that Romy squeezed my hand tightly, shook her head and, without speaking, made me understand that she hoped the exact opposite would happen.

Annunzi exchanged a conspiratorial look with the marshal. «Ah, I almost forgot our farewell gift» she said, taking my Walther out of her purse: yes, it was really my own. They recovered it when Abdel's men freed the *omphalos* from the sand. «So you'll remember me, Gianni and the Shemsu Hor forever.»

«That would have happened even if my gun was still buried in the desert» I answered and thanked them before getting ready to board.

I couldn't have asked for more than they had already done: they had provided us with new identities, two tickets to the States, and enough cash to pay for decent housing. Annunzi explained that those were the thanks from the Prelature of the Mysteries of God, for having personally contributed to the recovery of the linen and for my commitment to stem Ahnenerbe's greed. In her words, I had practically acknowledged my tacit affiliation to the Arcana Dei. In short, I had gone from black to white and, in that regard, I recalled with pleasure one of Abdel Ahad's sentences: *"Water and fire, good and evil, both coexist in each of us; it's up to you to find the balance between the two drives. Only then will you be able to say you have achieved Harmony, and It will reward you with the Wisdom of the greats"*.

Ironically enough, I, Gabriele Ferrari, would have boarded the fascist pride and joy of those years: the ocean liner that had beaten its German opponents to the draw. By moving away from the magnificent Ligurian coast, the ship would leave Alexander Wagner's past ashore, while carrying Gabriele Ferrari's future with it. In those hours I think I checked my passport at least a hundred times to read my name. Romy liked our new identities well, but mine was still too tight a suit for me.

The Rex provided its passengers with all kinds of entertainment. The high-ranking ladies from the first class, wrapped in cumbersome fur stoles, got lost in chatting about the furnishings of their cabins, or about the occupations of their husbands, who were more intent on getting rid of them than on negotiating business. I soon ended up detesting all that buzzing, which was becoming somewhat soporific. So, I took the lift up to the cabin floor and stopped at the barber's, some talkative "figaro" named Ernesto.

In spite of myself, I had to play a part in his speeches, but I kept on the safe side. I knew my linguistic limitations, so I avoided too complex sentences. For the first few minutes, I felt proud of how I faced up to the situation but, unfortunately, I had to change my mind when the barber asked me about my origins.

«Professor, you have a rather unusual accent I can't put my finger on» he told me with an inquisitive look.

I kept quiet when I realised what serious fault there was in my new identity: I had a name, a city and a date of birth but, ironically, I, of all people, didn't have a past behind me. To set it right, I said that my job had forced me to a wandering life throughout Italy and that was the reason for my uncommon accent. After making sure none of the customers knew the area of Todi, in Umbria, I stated that I had spent the last two years in a village of about twenty houses, called Borgo San Terenziano. That was the only name that came to my mind: the hamlet where my grandparents had spent part of their life. Everyone at the barber's fell for my comedy and they all were as satisfied with my nonsense as I was with having them fooled.

I left the shop with a new look, well groomed just the way I liked it. Ernesto was a professional and, after all, his talkativeness had been innocuous and, very often, enjoyable. By then, my face, tanned from the days in

Egypt, and my pitch-dark and well-outlined beard could only confirm my new identity. I had the silly impression that I was a new man and, all things considered, a radical change was just what I needed.

That November evening was not particularly cold, perhaps because we were still sailing through the Mediterranean basin. I rested my elbows on the balcony railing and stared out at the sea: a black expanse without beginning or end. Uncharacteristically, I had no thoughts, my mind was finally able to take a vacation after a long time of conspiracies. Like a curious child, I leaned out to look at the side of the ship: it was huge and carried two thousand souls to the new continent. Instinctively, I wondered if there were others on board who, like me, were hoping to start over, to have another chance, perhaps a new name. I peered into the distance and plunged my hands into my pockets. In that small neglected oblivion sat the soapstone scarab that Angelika had given me. Her again, as if she hadn't completely abandoned me in that Cairo alley. But I wanted to leave her, though, and rebuild a new life, so I made to throw that jewel into the sea and then Romy showed up on the doorstep. She was wearing a gorgeous blue evening gown, that caught my full attention.

«I was sparing this dress for a special occasion and I thought this was the right one» she said, her voice betraying some embarrassment.

«You're a feast for the eyes» I whispered, shuddering at the sight of her alabaster skin. The thin fabric softly caressed her hips, the plunging neckline girdled the fullness of her beautiful breasts, and the shoulders were left naked at the back. Every detail was impossible to ignore.

«Well? Shall we?»

«Of course» I replied helping her into her coat.

«What's the matter, Alexander?»

«Forget that name» I answered reluctantly.

«You know I can't and you also know I don't want to.»

«Alexander Wagner made so many mistakes in his life. He killed so many people and forced you to leave Germany. You should hate him for that.»

She smiled at me with the infinite sweetness that was so distinctive of her. «That's never going to happen. He was my best friend. I hope Gabriele Ferrari will be worthy of him.»

A shiver ran down my spine. «I really hope not. Only the ignorant perseveres in his error.»

«Well, now you won't be forced to work for the Luftwaffe or the Ahnenerbe anymore.»

«I meant something else» I whispered taking off her coat and feeling a certain trepidation for what I had decided to confess to her. «How is it possible to silence the feelings for the woman you've been dreaming of for eight and a half years?» I asked, all in one breath.

«Ah» she hesitated bewildered, «just a fool wouldn't tell her.»

«You're right, just a fool, or someone who wouldn't want to lose love and friendship both outright.»

Romy looked at me with an expression that I'll never forget. I don't know if she was happy or stunned, rather, maybe just seraphic as it suited her. «No, I definitely vote for the fool» she replied smiling.

I had found my serenity, I was sure of it, because in the moments I shared with her, I felt like I had finally conquered my Harmony and balanced the light and the darkness that had always been vying with each other for my ego.

Gibraltar – November 25, 1937

That morning I was awakened by a faint ray of sunlight seeping through the draping curtains, but I lay still so as not to wake Romy, who occasionally rested a hand on my chest, probably to make sure I was still beside her. Romy, my sweet Romy, had been able to cope with my inner turmoil by appeasing the ferocity without weakening my daring. I gently pulled the sheets aside to look at her and saw her shiver, so I left the bed and covered her up again.

«Will I see you again in two years?» she asked, opening her eyes and smiling at me.

«Be optimistic, I'm just going to get you breakfast» I replied grinning at her joke.

When I went back into our cabin with tea and pastries, I found her pacing the room with some papers in her hand. I decided to stay still and watch her, until one of the teaspoons clinked on the silver tray.

«I couldn't resist the urge» she explained, handing me the sheets of paper.

«Neither could I, last night» I answered instinctively. I never imagined she would look uncomfortable as a teen, but I found her magnificent when she blushed over what I had said.

«I didn't mean... well, you know. I was talking about this manuscript» she replied, covering her crimson cheeks with her hands.

I stared at those yellowed pages with bitterness, and some contempt. «I'm keeping no more secrets from you. Read on, if you want to.»

When Romy finished reading, she turned to me hesitatingly. «That's almost unbelievable. Are you going to make it public?»

«Ridiculing the Ahnenerbe's research and disclose the circumstances behind the expedition in Egypt would make even Gabriele Ferrari's life a living hell, in the end. And now I can't allow myself to make mistakes anymore: I'm no longer on my own.» I confessed with a lump in my throat.

I went out on the balcony of our suite and stared at the ocean, finally feeling free. When Romy put her arms around my waist, and rested her face on my chest, all residual doubts suddenly vanished. So, I threw all my pages into the sea and watched them floating on the waves. Thus, while the result of so many sacrifices was drifting away carried by the icy Atlantic waters, I could eventually plan my future in the new continent with the enthusiasm of someone who is reborn to a new life, pervaded by a feeling of hopeful expectation. I understood that the memory of my past would watch over my actions, so that I would never repeat the same mistakes. In that moment I could claim I had finally found my very own *Uat Hor* and that life was, at long last, becoming complaisant.

The Rex managed to astound Romy and me in all respects. On the one hand, I believed that the Italians had tried to amaze mainly American passengers, judging by the furnishings, so rich in historical references, on the other, I, myself, wasn't immune to the appeal of that magnificent ocean liner. While heading to one of the dining rooms, we let ourselves be beguiled by the elegance of the tapestry, the flawless efficiency of the crew and the scents distinctive of the different areas of the ship. From the smell of tobacco we easily guessed that we were approaching one of the smoking parlours, just as we realised we were just a few steps from the restaurant when a delicious smell of broth whetted our appetite.

Romy couldn't believe her eyes when she saw the huge amount of food available to the guests of the ship: five different cold buffets, appetisers, soups, all kinds of fish and meat and tropical fruits. She confessed to feeling a little out of place, but I assuaged her discomfort paying her a compliment.

The waiter kindly escorted us to our table, which we shared with a couple of quite talkative Americans. We had already agreed on the details about our private life, so I wasn't afraid of running into some contradiction. Although we were prepared, all the same we tried to avoid the chit chat. But when one of the two took his leave and returned to the cabin, the other had to make up for the lack of an interlocutor by pouring all his chatter on to us.

We soon discovered that our dinner companion, an elegant young man who liked to flaunt his liberalism, worked as a correspondent for the Columbia Broadcasting System. Romy was fluent in English, while she was careful not to converse in Italian because she didn't know the language enough. In fact, we had resolved we would help each other to gain credibility. On that occasion, however, the American made more effort than us and talked mainly in the official language on board; he told us about the article he was writing on the fascist regime in Italy, about his travels and he bragged that he had connections in Washington, no less, where he was often a guest at the White House. Through his verbal incontinence, he was able to convey many positive emotions to us and it wasn't difficult to understand that, despite being a man of culture, he felt a certain reverence for Italian scholarship. I tried, as long as I could, to keep a low profile, but when he started talking about jazz and that phenomenal Armstrong he was supposed to meet on the radio upon his return, I thought I could venture a bit further. My memories had already been in disarray for a while by then, but that fusion of rhythm and melody was still alive in my ears. Those unmistakable sounds and timbres tasted like freedom and love for life to me. It was as if jazz also reflected my aspirations. When the American took his leave, he gave us his business card inviting us for a drink in the Big Apple. After all, it had been a pleasant chance for conversation and that Mr. J. F. Smith, as witty as he was affable, had led us to hope that our future fellow countrymen could be as friendly as he was.

New Jersey – Bayonne, September 11, 1938

Lorenza Annunzi had given us a new identity and also the hope of a future, as she recommended me for an assistant position at the Union Theological Seminary in New York. Despite her zeal, after a few months, Romy and I reckoned it would be a good idea for us to cut that "umbilical cord" still connecting us to the past and build us a life of our own.

At first it wasn't easy to start all over again. In New Jersey, Bayonne more precisely, I managed to track down a lad, a certain Alfonso, known to the law for his dealings with illegal immigrants. Over a span of a week, that pointy faced man with deep-set eyes, similar to slits, had given us a new identity: the third within a year. After spending a good part of my wages to pay off the debt with Alfonso, we rented a room with the rest of the money. Romy was confident and the odds finally seemed to be in our favour when, a few weeks after the move, I started teaching in a small suburban school. My pupils were ten to twelve-year-olds, nearly all of Italian origin and poorly educated, but full of life and enthusiasm. I taught them history as if it were a great adventure and soon I could enjoy the positive results of my "storytelling" method, which, in some ways, reminded me of Abdel Ahad's tales. I finally felt fulfilled. The wage was as poor as my students, but it didn't matter;

Romy also earned some money from occasional translations or embroidering wealthy people's clothes.

We would live on little, but it meant a lot to us: everything indeed. By then, we were looking at the beautiful New York only from afar. To tell the truth, we feared it as we feared Berlin, and yet it still allured us, especially at night, when its lights reflected on the river separating us from the city. So, Romy and I would sit along the embankment on the left side of the Bayonne Bridge and spend a few minutes there, contemplating the skyline of the city and that iron colossus that, at least in our thoughts, managed to get us closer to Staten Island.

I remember going back to New York only once since last spring, because I was looking for a book I could only find in Manhattan. As I walked briskly through the city streets, I scrupulously avoided meeting the gaze of passers-by. I went past the Church of Saint Paul and Saint Andrew and then, at the corner with 86th Street, a skinny kid slammed a flyer into my chest, and just like many other passers-by, I ended up holding the German American Bund application form in my hands.

The Bund proudly wrote: "Combative spirits and anyone seeking the truth are welcome in our ranks." I smiled patronisingly and threw it in the first litter bin, then, after a few steps, I felt a fit of that rage I thought had died out, burning inside of me. What could an American know about the Führer's aspirations? None of them could imagine what lurked within the walls of Wewelsburg, nor what Himmler was really looking for. Not even a German would understand its meaning, if he wasn't part of it. It was a world infinitely distant from anyone, and that desire to emulate the Nazis seemed to me more pathetic than ever, especially in a welcoming land such as the United

States.

During those months, I often wondered if someone had investigated our disappearance, but I shunned the thought every time, because I had learned not to dredge up the past. I was trying to look ahead. Romy had taught me that.

One night, we decided to go to the theater. Calling theater that sort of oratory was more than flattering, but Romy liked that kind of entertainment, especially because, in public places, people sat next to us uninterested in asking who we were. That night I wasn't feeling in good shape, she, on the other hand, looked radiant and beautiful. She had cut and styled her hair in the current fashion and had put on a carmine lipstick that was repeatedly drawing my eye.

The shadows on the walls seemed to awaken those remnants of darkness that I had managed to stifle until that moment. Lately, I would often feel followed, spied on. I had become paranoid and was aware that my previous life had marked my psyche more than I wanted to admit. Romy, on the contrary, seemed to have found that balance, that harmony that I was losing again. She didn't know it, but I would always bring my gun with me; I was used even to take it to school and would only part from it when I was at home, where I took up the habit of hiding the weapon on top of the wardrobe when she couldn't see me.

When we left the theater, it was about to rain and the sky was definitely menacing, as if it was warning us against the seemingly innocuity of that rainfall. I took off my hat to offer it to her, since she didn't want to get her hair wet. I laughed at her and we reminisced about the German winters and our teen days, spent playing in the snow and then drying in front of the wood stoves. Hardly could I imagine that our every smile would fade away a few moments later. I didn't notice anything. All I know is I heard a hissing and when I turned to look at her, she was no longer at my side but lying on the ground. I grabbed and dragged her towards the darkest side of the street. I could feel the hostility of the steps of the man who had fired. He was close, very close, but I didn't think of defending myself, for I had to take care of Romy. I tried to figure out where he had shot her. I guessed in the shoulder, because I felt the warmth and dampness of the blood on the arm I was holding her by, but I was wrong. She wouldn't move and it was so dark that I couldn't see anything. But my fingers felt wet, sticky, and I caught a smell that I sadly knew all too well. Suddenly, I started trembling like a leaf and the cold set upon me, freezing my arms up to my chest. The pain took my breath away and I cried desperately in silence, as I realised she had been shot right in the chest. I stayed next to Romy and held her hoping for a miracle, but the killer soon discovered our hiding place; he fired another shot, but he missed me. Then, reluctantly, I decided to move. I had nothing left to lose, nothing, and revenge was the only strength that still allowed me to breathe and think. I pulled out my Walther and charged the shot at the same time as he fired, to prevent the noise from revealing my new location. I saw a medium-height silhouette in front of me. He was staring at the body of my Romy, his arm outstretched and his weapon loaded. I waited for the right moment and, with noiseless agility, I stole behind him and pointed my handgun at the back of his head. I didn't kill that monster cold-bloodedly just because I wanted answers, but the desire to tear him apart was burning in me with irrepressible vehemence. My right hand had won back all its strength as I was yet again dominated by Alexander Wagner's worst side. I heard him swallowing, then he raised his hands, dropped his gun to the ground, and turned to look at me in the face.

«Why?» I shouted with all the voice in my lungs. Otto Heyder didn't answer right away, so I grabbed him by the neck and dragged him to the light of a lamp-post. «Why did you kill her?»

«She wasn't my target» he replied. «I'm sorry, the hat misled me.»

«So much for taking her here to save her life! Damn you! Oh my God!» I shouted I don't know how many times the name of that God, who had abandoned me again.

«I had no choice. The Ahnenerbe wanted me to make a clean sweep: none of those who took part in the mission in Egypt had to survive. That's why they broke me out of the prison: to run after you and retrieve the material you brought with you. Abdel Ahad died before you and it's now open war between the Ahnenerbe and the Keepers of Horus. We cannot risk having anyone who can read between the lines of our "business". Your mistrust has been fatal to you this time. That chap... Alfonso, he would even sell his mother for a few dollars.»

I looked at him with repugnance, although I was still trying to convince myself that it was a dreamlike vision, just another of those nightmares ravaging my American nights. Overwhelmed by a blind rage rising from my gut, I hurled myself at him and began to strike with unprecedented ferocity. While throwing all the frustrations of my life to that vermin, I replayed the scenes of the people trying to escape from my bombs; Angelika, shot to death in the alleys of Cairo; my sweet Romy lying onto the ground.

Heyder, in his desperate effort to defend himself, drew a dagger. I don't know how, but I managed to snatch it from him and, with an accurate and violent blow, I severed his femoral artery. I stood up and walked a few steps away. He understood the seriousness of the cut and all his resolve vanished in an instant. He begged me to save him, to help him stop the bleeding, but I impassively looked upon that man as he was sitting on the ground, trying to press on the leg with his hands. I waited for him to regain some of his dignity before stepping back to kill him with the same coldbloodedness of that day in Guernica.

Romy had been the only person capable of seeing in me the man I wished to be. But I had sunk again into darkness. I stared at her until I realised that my Walther could be the only solution to my torment. I got ready to load it for the last time; suddenly its cold metal became comforting like a sincere friend, and it was then that I thought of Thomas, just when I should have had nothing else on my mind but the desire to put an end to my life. *"It takes more guts to live with remorse than to die with a clear conscience!"* he had said when telling me about the Lusitania. *"Who leaves no shadows behind him closes his eyes with a smile, but people like us, Alexander, must resign themselves to live, in order to pay for every committed sin, to the very last. A long life is our punishment."*

Washington DC, October 20, 1938

For the first time in my life, I understood the true meaning of "hope". At dawn, on September 12, I left Romy in the care of the Bayonne Medical Center doctors, who saved her life by pulling the bullet out of her chest. I was sure I had lost her forever. But she had kept breathing, albeit imperceptibly and, after I raced to the hospital, I discovered that a rib had diverted the trajectory of the shot and that, although she had bleeded copiously, no vital organ had been damaged. After making sure she was not in danger anymore, I provided the nurse with some wrong personal details, telling her that I had found Romy next to the dead bodies of two men. Then, heartbroken, I disappeared forever from her life.

In the days that followed, I wandered outside Bayonne and devoted myself to writing the document I'm holding even now, neglecting to eat and sleep. I knew that the rancour, while depriving me of my sleep, would also help me remember in detail every moment I lived since that August 24 of last year. I wrote for days, until one morning I decided to contact my friend from the CBS. A colleague of his answered and kindly offered to provide me with his new address in Washington, where he had moved not many months earlier. Smith was happy to hear from me. I hesitated a few moments before asking him for a meeting in the capital. I explained that I needed his help and that I would have a lot to confess, but didn't add anything else on the telephone, except that I would carry a present for him.

I'm now aboard a train that will reach Washington station in about twenty minutes. I have all the chronicle of the last year of my life with me, along with a package containing the documents, which certify my previous identity as a Luftwaffe officer. I know for sure that Smith will believe me and that, due to his unconditional love for his country, he will hand this writing over to a man who will be guided by the *Maât* more than I had been. Or so I hope. As for me, I'll drop out of sight, after trading my testimony for the assurance from the US government that they will protect Romy, to whom they will testify to my death.

Until 1938, the US government had adopted a neutral stance on Nazi politics; the Congress had committed to pass a series of laws to protect the relationship with Germany. In the fall of that year, a young J. F. Smith, a reporter working for the Columbia Broadcasting System, secretly handed over to a member of President Roosevelt's staff a memoir from a German officer, revealing the darkest side of the Reich to the White House. The President, who had already clearly expressed his concerns about the Führer's policy, found in that paperwork the perfect grounds for his distrust.

On November 10, the Nazi fury struck the German Jewish community: thousands of shops were destroyed, thirty thousand Jews abused or killed and sixty synagogues throughout Germany set on fire. At that point, the American government took the event as the last straw to officially declare its position against the Nazi regime, and condemn the episode that would go down in history as the "Night of Broken Glass".

In 1939, Roosevelt himself, who had been aware for several months of the existence of the Ahnenerbe foundation and its studies, issued an arrest warrant for everyone the House Committee on Un-American Activities deemed to be potential Nazi spies. The existence of a dossier on Luftwaffe officer Alexander Wagner was never confirmed nor denied. However, some statements by J.F. Smith led to believe that the Dies Committee investigations had been partially devoted to tracking down the author of the report, who revealed to the House the role of the SS Ahnenerbe, as well as the studies that guided the foundation to the Guardians of Horus and their legendary cellular regeneration.

Obersturmbannführer (Paramilitary rank: Senior Storm Unit Leader)

Hauptmann (Captain)

Feldwebel (Sergeant First Class)

Leutnant (Lieutenant Second Class)

Reichsführer (National Leader)

Generalmajor (Major General)

Standartenführer (Paramilitary rank: Standard Leader)

Hauptsturmführer (Paramilitary rank: Head Storm Leader)

Special thanks go to my husband, Paolo, for his support and advice.

This novel is a work of fiction, although some real historical events and characters are described in the plot. The introduction of some derogatory expressions, in spite of not being shared by the author, became nonetheless necessary in order to make the narrative plausible.

Printed in Great Britain
by Amazon